REMEMBER, REMEMBER

By

William S. Grant

Contents

Dedication

I shout an immense thank you to the READER, to you… yes you, whom without, I may starve to death.

To my wonderful wife, I thank Yvonne for her encouragement to finish writing Remember, Remember, for her nuggets of wisdom and for enduring my constant chatter and questions about the book, the book, the book.

To my eldest son Grant, who read my initial completed manuscript, edited and pointed out areas for improvement, deletion of far too much unnecessary information, and errors.

To my youngest son Scott, who, with his wizardry, created the initial book cover and helped with countless revisions, and for his ideas for the website, social media connections and videos.

To Kym, far away in the UK, who read my manuscript, even though she's not a fan of thrillers. Her comments, suggestions and grammar corrections kept me on my toes for sure.

To Margo, who is enthusiastic and encouraging every time I see her.

To Leo Badger, just for being himself and always so happy to listen to me, and with whom I share everything.

Acknowledgments

To Ann, a dear friend and powerhouse who I hope will be my guiding light in every book I publish.

To Julia and Marc at Edit 911.

The Publishing Team for an amazing and unexpected kinship on the journey of getting Remember, Remember in shape to print. Their editing, advice, comments, and encouragement helped produce the finished article. From the cover to the content, they, mainly Mike, never lost patience and maintained sincerity and positive suggestions throughout. Thank you.

About the Author

William, the youngest of seven children, was born in London, England, to working-class parents. His deep fascination and love for the arts blossomed during his formative years when he discovered his passion for the guitar in his early teens.

His musical prowess caught the attention of a leading rock band, catapulting him into a career as a professional guitarist. For years, he toured and relished living in France and Spain, sharing stages alongside renowned guitarists such as Eric Clapton and John Sykes, enriching his journey with diverse experiences.

After leading his somewhat nomadic life, William made the decision to return to school, obtaining his Diploma in Psychology and Degree in Electrical Engineering. While immensely grateful for this experience, his gregarious and spirited nature led him to venture into entrepreneurship and set up his own business.

As a successful entrepreneur, he was invited to explore business opportunities in the USA, where he ultimately settled with his family and obtained citizenship. He held a Secret Clearance in the USA for several years. Driven by an unyielding curiosity, he then pursued and earned his Criminal Justice Degree.

William's passion and broad appreciation of life, culture, and the arts span from Dickens to Dostoevsky and from Rembrandt to Dali. And his fascination with the human psyche has now propelled him to venture into writing psychological thrillers.

"Remember Remember," is his first novel.

Prologue

Deanne Jackson was born and raised in San Diego, California. She looked forward to marriage and believed in building a life with someone she loved, just not anytime soon. Her focus is on her career, and she enjoys being single.

Attractive, confident, kind, and caring, she radiates warmth from her heart and is admired by both men and women.

Work required her to travel domestically and overseas, which she thoroughly enjoyed. Nevertheless, Deanne always looked forward to returning home to San Diego, where she declared she would live forever.

Just 12 miles from her downtown office in San Diego and 15 miles from her apartment, Deanne loved to unwind and jog on La Jolla beach, enjoying the fresh air and the sound of the waves, and occasionally seeing sea lions temporarily leaving the water to rest on its shores, cliffs, and bluffs.

From the outside, it looked like she had it all. As an only child, Deanne was used to her own company. However, her favorite times were with her dad. Since she had been a small child, they would take the short one-hour drive to Pine Creek Trailhead. Their adventures of camping, climbing, riding and the stories her dad would share made him her hero, and she learned to trust herself and her instincts. The repeated exposure to situations that elicited fear and required action, led her to have more courage than her peers, with a more suburban upbringing.

Little did she know that these past experiences forged her future and would save her life and, perhaps, her sanity.

Deanne had not found school easy; her jet-black hair had a natural sheen, and her golden-brown eyes appeared to reflect the sun. With the addition of being tall with long limbs made her a target for jealousy, like bees to honey. She would be taunted or worse, ignored. Very few wanted to hang out with such competition as Deanne represented.

Born and raised in London, Matt Wallace is also single and has rarely thought about marriage. At six feet tall with natural curls in his black hair and blue eyes, dating was not difficult. His easy-going nature and hard work ethic kept him busy. As he ran his own small electronic engineering business, his employees referred to him as one of the good guys.

He believed that a love resulting in a wedding would come along at some time, contrary to a couple of his married friends who had declared, "I fell in love right away and knew she was the one." Matt knew and stated, "Impossible, there's lust at first sight, not love," and would shake his head from side to side.

Over 5,500 miles separated them, and neither knew the other existed.

Through a normal business event and despite the awkward introduction, Matt's persistence paid off and they still got together.

Shocks come in three forms: Good, acceptable, and bad. Horrific is rarely one of them.

Chapter One

It was 7 p.m., Monday, November 1st, a typical English winter evening with frost on the branches of leafless trees and frozen grass that crunched when walked on.

This quiet area on the outskirts of the city of London had preserved numerous elements from the nineteenth-century village era.

Everything outside of the home looked gray, in fact, monochrome; the color contrasted like a '40s movie. However, their home was bright all year round, reflecting the personalities of the inhabitants, Matt and Deanne Wallace.

Tonight, the activity in the Wallace household mirrored any other weekday. Having just completed dinner, the warmth from the fire harmonized with the subdued glow of the wall lamps and two strategically placed candles on the table.

Matt lifted the bottle of 2018 Chateau Laffitte Laujac, a Bordeaux merlot, from the table. "Shall we finish this off? There's not much left."

Deanne looked at Matt, "*Wine* not?" She laughed.

"It never gets old, sweetheart." Smiling and raising his eyebrows, he poured the remains evenly into the glasses.

"We're so lucky. Look at what we've done to this place over the years." Deanne said as she turned in her chair.

"It's what you did, not me."

"I love our home. I never dreamed of a house like this. In the US, almost everything is modern. A home like this never came into my mind." Deanne rose from her chair, kissed his cheek, and started to clear the table.

"So, you had a long time on calls to the States today," Matt said.

"Yes, presentations to HQ. How did you know?"

"You said 'pharmacy.'"

"What?"

"When you called, you said you were going to the pharmacy, not the chemist." Matt chuckled.

"I try. But with Wesley being American and my boss and HQ conference calls, I spend a lot of time talking in US English. Anyway, you mess up, too. You say 'gas' instead of 'petrol' most of the time and 'panties' instead of the crazy word 'k-knickers.'"

Both burst into laughter.

From the dining room, Matt could see into the living room where Smarts, their German Shepherd mix, had placed himself near the warmth of the log fire fronted by a mesh screen protecting the dog and carpet. Smarts, large, rough, and ready, was full of mischief but loving, obedient, and devoted to his master and mistress.

Matt got up from his chair, signaling to Smarts that it was time for his walk.

"Come on, boy. Time to go out."

Smarts was up by Matt's side in a second, tail wagging at full speed in excitement. His eyes were focused on his master's every move.

"I'll come too. I need to blow the cobwebs away."

"Great," Matt said as he clipped the leash on, and Deanne retrieved their overcoats from the row of hooks near the front door.

"Come on. Out the door, Smarts," Deanne said with a smile.

The weather outside was cold but pleasant. They walked arm-in-arm as Smarts pulled on his leash toward the nearby woods.

Once away from traffic, the leash came off, and he ran in and out of the foliage, sniffing and exploring. Occasionally, a bark pierced the air as Smarts encountered woodland residents, with badgers being the most frequent, emerging soon after sunset.

"They're building the bonfire for Guy Fawkes Night," Deanne said. "What was the story again? I remember that Guy Fawkes tried to blow up the House of Lords, but I forget the rest."

"Well, that's pretty much it," Matt said. "I just know that Guido Fawkes or Guy Fawkes as he's called, tried to blow up the Parliament Building here in London, and that was in 1605.

"He and some colleagues buried a few tons of gunpowder under the building with the intent of blowing up King James I and including anyone else at the House of Lords. Guy was quite famous in England at that time; he got caught in the cellar with the fuses and kindling in his pockets."

"Really?"

"He did. He was so famous that exactly one year later, on the 5th of November, an effigy of him was burned all over England; hence, Guy Fawkes Night is a uniquely English story and celebration. He failed, as you can gather. He and his co-Catholic accomplices were executed for treason.

"So, these days, November 5th is a great excuse for the English to build bonfires with an effigy of Guy Fawkes on top."

Matt broke into verse:

Remember, remember the fifth of November,

Gunpowder, treason, and plot.

I see no reason why gunpowder treason.

Should ever be forgot.

"Well done," Deanne said as she nudged him. "Only four more days, and we'll see the bonfire."

Matt called for Smarts to return. He ran back, tail wagging with forest floor remnants of small twigs and dead leaves attached to his fur.

"Look at him. We're going to have to wash and brush him. Now, that's something he's not too happy with."

Deanne and Matt chuckled as they walked back to their house.

"I'll take the dog round to the boot room," Matt said.

Deanne watched as Smarts, tail between his legs, followed her husband. She smiled to herself as she opened the front door.

Matt succeeded in washing Smarts and endured the shake-off. Smarts, towel dried, waited for his owner to take him to the main house. Once in, he knew he would go by the fireside and lie on a blanket Deanne had already placed for him.

Matt discarded his clothes and walked to the bottom of the stairs, naked, just in time to see Deanne at the top of the stairs after her shower.

"Now there's a sight," said Deanne, laughing.

"Oh, come on. I look great." Matt, hands on his hips, did a twirl. "Take a good look. Many women would pay to see me like this."

Deanne, dressed in a black mid-length skirt and pale blue top, strolled down the stairs; Matt maintained his stance as she passed by, tapping his rear.

"You smell of dog," she said, holding her nose.

"And you smell wonderful," Matt said as he went upstairs, shortly returning showered and fully clothed to the living room.

The couple cuddled up on the sofa with Smarts dry at their feet.

"So, is it time to start a family, or do you just want to keep practicing?" she asked.

"I love to practice, but you're right. I'm ready for an addition to our family if you are. Financially, we're doing good, and I reckon we'll stay together for a while yet; don't you?"

Deanne grabbed him by the neck. "Well, let's get started." She guided him upstairs to their bedroom.

Saturday, November 5th, 8:15 a.m.

"Why are you always awake so early?"

"Sorry, sorry. You just curl up and go to sleep. I'll wake you in an hour."

Matt was an early riser, very rarely needing to set an alarm. Once awake, his head filled with thoughts. Quietly slipping out of the bedroom, he descended to the kitchen, where Smarts awaited, well aware of the morning routine: a brief outdoor break followed by a treat before breakfast.

After that, Matt brewed a cup of tea, checked his phone for emails and messages, and then tuned in to local TV. At the right time, he made tea for Deanne: letting the black tea bag steep for five minutes, adding a single sweetener and a dash of almond milk.

"Hello, darling," he said with a smile. "There, it's an hour."

Deanne looked up, and he bent over and kissed her forehead gently.

"Shall we go into the city tonight and see the fireworks display at the docks?"

"Not now. Let me wake up first and enjoy my tea. OK?"

"OK. Later, dude," he said, laying on the American accent, kissed her forehead again, and left the room. Matt never fully understood why anyone would need *time* to wake up, not unless they were unwell or drunk.

He asked about going to the city to see the fireworks again about an hour later when Deanne was fully awake, showered, and casually dressed.

"Sure. Should we take in dinner before we go too?"

"OK. What about Jorge's Seafood?'

"Great! See if you can book a table. Anywhere will do."

"We'll leave around 7–7:30, eat, and then watch the display at 10."

Matt knew he could get a table at Jorge's, especially as he had booked it six weeks ago.

The day passed with various chores: car washing and yard work for Matt, food shopping, and nails and hair for Deanne.

At five, Deanne took a bath while thinking about what to wear. Matt walked into the bedroom and saw her standing in her underwear.

"What are you looking at?" She frowned at him. "Don't even think it. I'm trying to get ready, but I'm still unsure what to wear."

He smiled. "OK, OK. But you shouldn't walk around like that, tempting me and then refusing my advances." He crinkled his eyes and huffed.

"Later, darling." Deanne walked by, kissing his cheek on the way. "I'll wear the skirt and top I wore on Monday. I think it's in the laundry. Do you know what you're wearing?"

"The black shirt, I think. Do you know where it is?"

"It needs ironing. I'll do it when I'm downstairs."

Deanne retrieved the clothes, returned to the bedroom, and got dressed.

"Smarts is whining," she said.

"I'll take Smarts out before we leave," Matt said.

"No. You take your shower and do whatever you have to. I'll be ready in a few minutes."

"Are you sure?"

"Sweetheart, I'll only be twenty minutes," she said, putting on her dog-walking sneakers.

Deanne put a leather topcoat over her outfit and left the house with Smarts trying to pull her along. She noted the time was 7 p.m., precisely. She knew the festivities started around six as the adults brought their children from nearby houses. The occasional rocket zoomed through the air and burst into an umbrella of color and light as a forerunner to the main event. The bonfire would burn on a pyramid-shaped wooden lattice filled with branches and trimmings. The final touch would be the effigy of Guy Fawkes on top.

It took her eight minutes to reach the woods. She took Smarts off the leash, and he ran into the undergrowth.

Oh, no. He's going to get covered in dirt again. Deanne's thought processes stopped as she heard Smarts barking, growling, and snapping in a way she had not heard before.

"Come on, Smarts. Come here."

Smarts kept barking.

"Smarts, come here!"

The barking stopped, replaced by small, sickly yelps.

God, what has he done now?

In the distance, she could hear the crackle of a bonfire, accompanied by the noise of fireworks emanating from the park just beyond the woods.

Deanne called Smarts again with no response; her heart was beating faster. Checking her pockets, she retrieved her phone, intending to call Matt, but ultimately decided against it. She stood still, looking into the dark mass before her, thinking that Smarts must be nearby. She also thought of her father and the wilderness treks. *There's nothing to be scared of,* she told herself.

She moved into the wood in the direction she had heard Smarts last, calling for the dog and hearing the crunch of the leaves under her feet and the smell of the bonfire smoke mixed with barbequing food. She stopped for a second or two as she thought she had heard other leaves being crushed underfoot.

"Get a grip, Deanne," she muttered.

Deanne could see the streetlights and car lights. She was not too far from the sidewalk, and the light was enough for her to avoid bumping into trees. Scanning the surroundings, she noticed no sign of Smarts. A rocket burst above; casting borrowed light that allowed her to see a little further. Her heart skipped a beat as she saw a crumpled heap about ten feet in front of her.

As she ran to him, she could see blood across the dog's face. He was on his back, head to one side, his front paws at right angles to his body, straight out on either side; they had been broken.

Smarts was dead. Deanne could not believe it. She knelt and cradled his head in her lap, crying in shock.

Deanne took her cell phone out of her pocket for the second time. She heard the rustle of leaves behind her; she began to turn her head.

"I've been waiting for you," a male voice said. "You dirty bitch. You dirty fucking bitch."

As the last word finished, she felt a hard blow to the side of her neck and then another on the side of her head. She caught a faint glimpse of the attacker's face as she fell backward, almost unconscious. Her brain could not react fast enough to the messages being transmitted from her body; her senses were in total confusion.

The man punched her in the face and knocked her to the ground. "Lay still, you tart. I'm going to give you just what you want."

Tearing her top from her neck to her waist, then hoisting up her skirt, he removed her panties and pushed her legs apart.

Deanne was murmuring as she tried to fight the man off, "Stop! Get off me."

Her words were halted by another hard slap to her face, followed by a punch to her stomach.

After a few brutal thrusts, he climaxed and withdrew from her body. Standing up, he put the used condom in his pocket, adjusted his clothing, and, motionless, he looked at her almost naked body.

"Fucking bitch," he muttered. "Where the fuck does she get off, walking in the woods at night? She wanted fucking; that's why she did it. That's why she walked in here; that's what she gets for fucking up my life."

He took a few steps away from his victim, then turned back and grabbed the branch he had hit her with. It was about three feet long and three inches in diameter. He used it to prod her neck and head. Deanne's body reacted to the force and direction of the branch. She looked like a rag doll. He squatted between her legs staring at her vagina.

After staying in this position for a minute or so, he shoved the branch in between her legs, inside her body. An unconscious moan came from her lips as her body squirmed in reaction to the violent invasion.

"See what you get for leaving me and stealing everything I had! Fuck you!" he shouted.

He stood up and kicked Deanne in the side of the head and then again in the face; the impact caused blood to spray from her nose and mouth.

Convinced she was dead, he walked off whistling, feeling good that he had expelled his rage and resentment. "Fuck you!" He laughed.

Walking into the woods and toward the fireworks, he climbed over the four-foot railing and joined the happy children and parents standing around the bonfire.

It was now 7:31 p.m.; just seventeen minutes after the ordeal had begun.

Chapter Two

att waited a little impatiently. "Deanne, where are you?" He picked up his phone and dialed her cell. No response. "She probably left it in the car," he thought.

Another five minutes go by. Matt walks out the front door and looks in the direction Deanne would be returning. He sees no sign of her. He shouts into the darkness, "Deanne! Deanne, are you there?"

Met with silence, he begins to feel a rising fear.

He looks in her car for her cell phone, then runs upstairs to see if she left it in the bedroom. He redials her number, believing he would hear it if it were turned on in the house.

Running from the house, Matt begins calling again, "Deanne! Deanne!"

Within a few minutes, he is parallel to the woods where they would typically release Smarts.

"Smarts! Deanne! Smarts, come on, boy!"

Matt's head fills with scenarios about where she may be, what could have happened, and where she had gone. He redials her cell phone. This time, he hears a faint, distinctive tone Deanne uses for Matt's calls.

Delirious with worry, he follows the sound. He cannot run in that direction as the sound of his steps on the leaves drowns out the phone.

As the sound grows louder, his steps gather speed. He almost steps on the motionless bodies of Deanne and Smarts. He stumbles backward, falling onto the ground near where they lay. His horror stills him, and for what seems an age, he is frozen.

In shock, confusion, and denial, he dials 999, the emergency service.

"Hello, hello, my wife has been attacked. She is lying in the woods. I need an ambulance quick; for God's sake, quick!"

"Sir, what is your name? Where exactly are you?"

Matt gives the information as effectively as he can to keep from wasting time, but he still stumbles over his words. He tries to move the reality of what he's seeing and somehow wakes up from a nightmare, "This is not real, it, it…."

Matt cuddles Deanne's seemingly lifeless body. Rocking back and forth, he cries and asks, "Why didn't I take the dog for a walk? I could have done it easily; why, why?

He cradles her and gently coaxes her, "Come on, Deanne. Please, for God's sake, please." He remains in the same position for what feels like an eternity. The sound of the police and ambulance sirens breaks up his self-recrimination.

He looks at his phone to see only five minutes have passed. Picking up Deanne's phone, he turns on the flashlight and places it by her so that he can see exactly where to return. He carefully sets her down on the ground.

Matt runs to the road, waving. He can see lights flashing in the distance from two vehicles. As they approach, he sees a police car with an ambulance not far behind. When the police car pulls up, two police officers get out.

Officer Jacob Strong is thirty-seven years old, five-foot-eight inches, 175 pounds, and clean-shaven with short black hair: he's been in the force for twelve years. His nature is calm, though if anyone mistook his calm for weakness or tried to take advantage, his expression would completely change, and his look defuse a potentially combative situation.

Alison Peers is five-foot-six inches tall, 130 pounds, and twenty-nine years old, with fair bobbed hair and blue eyes. She's been with the force for eight years and a partner with Jacob for four of those years. They have a strong work connection but little in common in their personal lives, nulling interest beyond an occasional drink or quick meal after a workday.

Matt is already shouting and pointing, "Here, follow me. She's there where you can see the light from her phone."

Strong introduces himself and his partner, then adds, "My colleague will stay with you here while I follow the paramedics."

Matt retorts, angry and breathless, "No! No! I'm going with you! I must see if—"

Peers takes Matt's arm and says, "Mr. Wallace? Matt? I know you want to help your wife. The paramedics are attending to her right now. Why not come and sit with me in my car? I'd like to ask a few questions. Your answers would help us, please."

As she is talking, she guides Matt to the passenger side of the police car and opens the door. Matt, in a daze," sits in the seat and slumps forward, immediately vomiting on the floor of the car. He begins to sob, trying to apologize through his retching.

"Take deep breaths, Mr. Wallace," she said. "It's OK. It's OK."

Peers watches as two paramedics carry Deanne on a stretcher toward the ambulance; right behind them, Strong spots her and puts his thumb up. "She's alive," he mouthed.

"Matt, your wife is alive, and we'll be on her way to the hospital soon. Would you like to ride with her?"

He looks up. "Yes! Yes, of course. Thank you, God. Thank you, thank you."

"Wait here for a few minutes while your wife comfortably settles in the ambulance. I'll be right back." She walks a hundred feet to meet Strong as he returns from the ambulance, ensuring they are out of Matt's earshot.

Strong said, "Well, this is a first for me. She's a mess. It's a wonder she's still alive. Call it in, and let's secure the area and cordon it off. We need forensics here to gather evidence."

"What happened?"

As Jacob describes the scene, Alison pales, biting her lip, and waits for him to finish. Despite her anger and disgust, she contains herself and takes a deep breath before saying, "We'll scan the scene, so we need to call the photography unit to take pictures."

Jacob nods. "Did you get any statement?"

"Nope, it wasn't the time, and I think it's more in line for Brian White. What do you think?"

Jacob nods again. "Yeah, come on. Let's get this started. It's going to be a long night. Would you ask the paramedic which hospital they have been directed to? His name is Jack, by the way; his tech is Vince."

As he starts to walk away, he asks, "That is vomit I can smell, right?"

Alison nods, grimacing. She walks over to the open, red-striped rear doors of the ambulance, where she sees Deanne lying unconscious, equipment already attached and monitoring her condition.

She looks at the paramedic sitting by Deanne and sees the name *Jack* sewn above one of the pockets on his shirt.

"Hi, Jack? What is your designated hospital?"

"St Thomas,' directly across the Thames from Westminster."

"I know it. Thank you. Are you ready for me to bring her husband, Matt?

"Yes, we're good to go."

Matt is in the same position she had left him with the same expression of bewilderment and fear. "Come on, Matt. We're ready to go." She opens the car door, offers her arm, and walks him to the ambulance.

"Don't worry, sir. We're making good time, and we'll get to the hospital as soon as we can," Jack said.

Alison looks at him questioningly. The slight tilt of Jack's head indicates that Deanne's survival was in doubt.

Jack nods, and she closes the rear doors of the ambulance.

Alison watches as it pulls away, staring at the blue lights until they disappear around a curve a quarter mile away. She notices how pretty the rebound of the blue lights is on the frost-laden branches of the trees the ambulance passed and its contrast to the ugliness of the victim inside the ambulance.

Matt sits in the ambulance with Deanne, holding her hand, his glassy eyes gazing at her, his body intermittently shaking while he pleads silently to God.

Jack calls the hospital and provides a rundown of Deanne's condition when they found her, the treatment given, and the effects of the treatment he has administered. He is careful in describing the object still embedded in her body, though not visible, as she is delicately covered with a blanket.

The streets of London are not forgiving of the demands of the constant traffic, even less so in Westminster.

Jack called to Vince, "How's the traffic?"

"Could be worse. We'll be there shortly."

The ambulance comes to the entrance to the hospital A&E and is received by a team on arrival. The severity of Deanne's condition enacted a rapid intake, bypassing the regular, what some would call mayhem in the Hospital Emergency Department. Matt would not be so fortunate.

Vince alights the ambulance to help Jack. The handover to the nurses and clinicians is swift, and they immediately begin to wheel Deanne toward the ICU.

Expecting to accompany his wife, Matt follows the clinical staff. He is halted when the clinical lead holds up her hand, saying, "You'll need to go through security before you go to the registration area. Try not to worry. We'll take it from here, and we'll take good care of her."

"No way, no fucking way," Matt said. "I'm coming with you."

Jack said, "Sir, the doctors will take over now, and we don't want to delay any procedures, do we? Come on, let's get you though.

As they approached the A&E doors, he could see queues in front of each receptionist, "Fuck this, this is fucking stupid…"

Jack firmly puts his hand on Matt's shoulder, "You are going to have to listen to me; there's no short cut. Your wife is being cared for; those," pointing to the people inside, "are waiting and all in need of attention. It's Bonfire Night, and like every year, you have the dumb shits jokers with burns, plus the regular number of emergencies. Receptionists are overworked and underpaid, and cranky, and no doubt ruder and more patronizing than normal, especially as most of these assholes have been drinking and thought throwing a firework at their mates would be fun."

Matt is silent, and tries to quell his desperation. He starts to respond, "But…." Jack cuts him off.

"There are no buts; you either calm yourself down, have a reasonable manner and accept that you will need to wait, complete forms, answer questions, and be patient, as it could be a couple of hours or more. Everyone in there has, to them, an emergency. You don't, and if you create a fuss, they could ask you to leave, and those big security guards would be happy to carry you out. Got it?"

Matt draws a deep breath, "Sorry. I got it." His words do not disguise the anger on his face.

After two hours, the initial procedures and paperwork are complete. I'll get you a cup of tea, coffee, or something." Jack holds Matt's elbow, guiding him toward Vince, who is sitting by the vending machines. He deposits coins in a machine. "Coffee's better than tea from these things. Here you go a nice cup of coffee, sugar?"

"No, no thanks."

Matt takes the plastic cup; his hands shake, and the contents spill over the edge. Matt places the cup on a side table, puts his hands in his face, and sobs, full of what ifs, and recriminations, and how things could and should have been different, as *if onlys* flood his brain.

Now, what's your name?"

"Matthew, Matt Wallace. My wife's name is Deanne."

"Do you live near here?"

"No, I live a few minutes from where I found my wife, just up the road from the woods."

The bustling of movement by patients, hospital staff, and visitors remains silent to him. He is in a fog about the new reality as if the events he has seen were part of a newscast or movie. He has no idea how long he has been sitting there; half an hour, two hours, he really does not know.

"Mr. Wallace, Mr. Wallace?" someone is asking. Matt looks up to see a man dressed like a surgeon.

"Yes, I'm Matt Wallace."

"Hi, I'm Dr. Paul Proctor. I've just finished surgery on your wife."

"How is she? What's happening?" Matt is on his feet in seconds. He looks pleadingly at Dr. Proctor, his heart beating fast.

"She's stabilizing, so we're through the worst. She has a concussion and needs some stitches on her face and neck, though any scarring will be very minimal.

We had a great deal of difficulty in the lower region of her body. We had to go in through the stomach to remove the object and ensure we removed any foreign particles. You understand what I'm saying, Mr. Wallace. Matt?"

"Yes, yes, I do. Is she going to be OK? When can I see her? What do you mean to go in through the stomach? What for?" Matt lets out a huge breath, and his eyes go up looking heavenward.

The doctor explains to Matt what surgery he has performed and why. This new revelation takes Matt to the edge of passing out. The mixture of fear, anger, and sorrow for Deanne is overwhelming. With his heart racing and tears falling, he tries to speak, tries to ask questions, but he sits down in silence. He knows the surgeon is speaking but does not hear any words.

When Matt does manage to speak, he quietly asked if he can see Deanne.

"You can take a quick look with me now if you wish, for just a minute. Then I suggest you let her rest. Come back in the morning, say, around 9 a.m., when we'll know more about her overall condition. Let nature take its course and let her rest, OK?"

Matt slowly nods. He and Paul walk together in silence; Paul opens one of the doors to let Matt walk through.

Matt looks and holds Deanne's hand; tears start to flow down his face.

Deanne looks peaceful and much better than the last time Matt had seen her. One side of her face is bandaged.

The sound of monitors intermittently breaks the quiet,

Matt spends time speaking to Deanne, though he knows she cannot know what he was saying.

"You really must go now, Matt. She has to rest," the doctor says.

"I love you so much, Deanne. I'll be back in the morning, darling.'

"Let's get you a taxi," Paul says, putting his arm on Matt's shoulder to guide him through the door to the corridor. Matt nods, says thank you, and begins walking to the bank of elevators, subconsciously entering the first available descending carriage. The suffocating reaction of dread when he thought Deanne would die coupled with the relief and overwhelming joy of knowing she was alive, has put him in a state of shock. He returns home, still not believing what has happened. As usual, he expects to walk through the door and see Deanne and Smarts waiting for him.

He doesn't bathe, eat, or drink; he just sits, hour after hour, praying and recriminating about how the whole event could have been avoided. The words "if only" are his constant unwanted companion.

He sits on the living room sofa, his eyes finally closing, waking sporadically before drifting back into slumber. At 8 a.m., he is sharply awakened by the sound of the doorbell. Snatching his dressing gown from the floor, he rushes downstairs and glimpses the shadows of two people through the frosted glass around the door frame. He swings the door open to see two men, whom he correctly assumes to be police.

"Good morning, Mr. Wallace. I'm sorry to call on you this early. I'm sure you feel our coming here to ask questions is inappropriate, especially considering what you must be going through. Still, the sooner we gather information, the sooner we'll be in a position to catch the person who attacked your wife."

"Yes, I understand. Come in."

Matt looks disheveled and distraught as he walks them to the family room. He sits in one of the leather armchairs, gesturing for the visitors to sit across from him on an accompanying sofa. The two remove their hats and sit down on the sofa.

Matt watches as they produce pens and notepads. On their two badges, he reads *Metropolitan Police Officer*. One with *Constable*, followed by their name, Peter Bailey, the other with just the surname of Wilson, no given name. He absently wonders why.

Peter breaks the silence. "I'm terribly sorry about these circumstances, Mr. Wallace, truly. I do understand the trauma you must be going through, but we're duty-bound to ask questions, some of which you may find offensive, but it is necessary, including reading your rights. OK?"

"OK," replies Matt, though he was thinking, *you don't understand what I'm going through.*

Peter reads Matt his rights. Matt agrees he understands.

"Thank you. We'll get started. Tell me what happened last night. Take your time; try not to miss any detail."

Matt recites the events leading up to Deanne's taking the dog for a walk, what he did while waiting for her to return and how and when he found Deanne.

Peter delicately interjects with questions to clarify and expand Matt's recollections.

"How is your relationship with your wife?" asked Geoff.

"It's great. No problems."

"Do you know anyone, or have you seen anyone you think we should speak with?"

"I've no idea."

More questions are asked, and more answers are given. Peter and Geoff clearly feel that they should eliminate Matt as a suspect.

"Sir," said Peter.

"Call me Matt."

"OK, Matt, we can give you a ride to the hospital if you wish. We need to check in and speak to the doctors and possibly your wife."

"Thanks, yes. That would be good."

Peter smiles at him. "Do you think a shave, shower, and change maybe? You don't want your wife to see you not looking your best, now, do you?"

"You're right, yes. I'll do just that. I wasn't really thinking." Matt walks out of the room and upstairs to his bedroom.

"Poor bastard," said Geoff. "He's out of it completely."

Peter shakes his head. "What about his wife? God, I can't even begin to think how she felt. And that sick fucker shoved a branch right inside her; fuck me. What a sick, sick bastard."

"They find anything at the site yet?"

"Not much yet, plenty of blood from the dead dog. We won't know until Forensics has gone through everything. The leaves were dry and covered the ground, so there were no footprints. The guys are there today, so if there is anything, they'll find it."

Matt returns, cleaner and better clothed, though still haunted in expression. The trip to the hospital is mostly silent, barring the police radio, relaxed comments, and chit-chat between the police officers. Once at the hospital, Matt and the police officers separate. Matt is ushered to the surgeon's office and the police to administration.

Matt knocks on Dr. Proctor's door.

"Come in."

Matt walks into the bright, spacious office, a window taking up most of the rear wall overlooking the Revolving Torsion Fountain at the front of the hospital. The décor of a modern white U-shape desk, five comfortably padded chairs interspersed with end tables, and uniform wall artwork give little sign of a medical environment.

Doctor Paul Proctor stands up from his desk and walks toward Matt with an outstretched hand, ready to greet him. He is dressed in black slacks and a light blue shirt with a dark blue tie overlapped by an open white lab coat. His smiling face radiates empathy and kindness. Though he is only in his early forties, his gray mop of hair and John Lennon-style glasses make him look older. His coworkers liken him to Father Christmas, minus a beard and a hundred or so pounds.

"Hello, Matt. Come and sit down. Can I get you anything, coffee or tea?"

"No thanks."

"What I'm going to share with you is a mix, some good, some less so. It's the best we have at the moment."

"How is my wife?"

"She had a good night and is out of danger, but we have concerns."

"What do you mean, 'concerns'?"

"Deanne will recover physically, though unfortunately, she will not be able to have children. My biggest concern is her brain activity. She's in a coma, and there are blood clots, which means additional surgery." Paul sees Matt's expression change. "Matt, it's nothing we have not seen before and resolved."

Matt looks up, biting his top lip. "When will you perform surgery?"

"There's bruising around her head; this regrettably clouds the scan results and means that we will have to wait a few days before we operate." Paul draws a deep breath before continuing. "At this stage, we are not sure of the full extent of the damage or when she will come out of the coma."

Matt's heart and spirit sink. He sits silent for a minute, stands up, and says, "Doctor Deanne will recover, that I can promise you. She's strong, stubborn, and has too much willpower to let go. So, please, do what you need to, when you need to, and mark my words; she will recover."

"I'm sure Deanne is all you say, and I'll trust your judgment." Paul smiles, stands up, and walks Matt toward Deanne's room.

"Come on. Let's go visit your wife."

Deanne looks much better than yesterday. The swelling around her face has reduced, and some color has returned.

"I'll leave you two alone. Take your time."

Matt kisses Deanne, pulls up a chair close to the bed, sits down, takes her hand in his, and starts to pray. The only sounds he hears are those of the monitoring equipment and the sound of voices as people pass by the room.

A nurse knocks and opens the door. "Good morning, Mr. Wallace. I'm Nancy."

Matt turns his head to look at Nancy, mid-twenties, with auburn hair, smiling, high-spirited, and with what Matt determines to be a sweet, caring face. She walks up to the bed, checks the charts and monitors, and fusses around Deanne to ensure everything is in place.

"Call me Matt."

"Don't you worry. I can tell your wife is going to be OK. You get a feel for these things, and I can see that she's tussling inside. You know, the body and brain have a great thing going, and they work well together." Nancy walks around to where Matt is sitting, pulls up another chair beside him, and touches his hand.

"If the body needs to be healed, then your brain needs to rest in proportion to the body's damage. That way, all the energy can be focused on the repairs. When that job's done, it'll work on itself. See? Easy. So, ease up on the worry and start taking care of what Deanne would expect you to be doing." Nancy says this so sincerely and kindly that he feels more hopeful.

"Thank you for that. Is there any way I can stay here, I mean, overnight?"

"Well, you don't have any hour restrictions, so it's up to you, sweetie. Do you intend on doing that?"

"Yes, I'd sure like to. I'd like to talk her through and help where I can."

"Good for you. Now, let me see what I can do for you." With that, she gets up from the chair. "Must be off. I'll be back later. Bye for now."

"Bye, Nancy."

Matt soon learns what Nancy means about seeing what she could do. A hospital orderly comes through the doors, pulling a hospital bed behind him.

"Hello. I understand you may need this. I'll set it up here, shall I?"

"Great, thank you very much," Matt responds in surprise.

Matt remains by Deanne's side until late evening, praying and talking to her all day, reciting various stories and experiences they had shared in their years together.

It is now Sunday evening, so much has happened, and Matt is still numb from the terror of the experience. His thoughts are only with Deanne and her well-being, coupled with gratitude for her continued survival.

Matt leaves the hospital and takes a taxi home. Again, for a split second, he half-expects Deanne and Smarts to be there. Once inside the house, he knows he has to focus on practical aspects, such as notifying relatives, friends, and Deanne's office—his office too.

He knows he has to begin to function coherently, not so much for his sake but for Deanne's and the people he would be engaging with to inform them of what had happened.

He leaves messages at both offices, merely stating that Deanne has had an accident and was in the hospital and that he would call and update them once he'd settled down. Matt decides to shower, get something to eat, and gather his thoughts. This he does, though his meal is meager. It is all he can manage.

He sees the answering machine has two messages. He listens; one was from a friend, the other from Peter Bailey, the police officer, who left his cell and home number after asking Matt to return his call.

Matt takes a deep breath and makes several calls, the first being to Deanne's parents, who naturally are overcome with the bad news, saying they would catch the next flight to London. That is the most difficult call to make. He continues notifying other relatives, his own, and then friends.

The questions, comments, and condolences are all similar. They are all shocked, and many are overcome with emotion. The genuine sympathy and offers of help touch Matt.

Matt has to be strong, focused, and put careful thought behind his words. The questions he is asked include, "Who was it? Has he been caught? You must want to kill him." These and other brief, pointed questions begin to weigh heavily on his mind and he feels a rising sense of vengeance.

He phones another number. "Hello, Peter. This is Matt Wallace. You called."

"Hi, Matt. Thanks for calling."

"Peter, can you tell me what's happening, what you're doing to find this guy?"

"The good news is we've got blood samples. It appears your dog bit him; there was blood on the ground and blood on the dog's teeth, so we'll be able to obtain good DNA samples, though this doesn't help much until we get a suspect who matches. When your wife is in a position to speak with us, we'll have more information to go on."

"So, this bastard is still roaming the streets, and he could do it again to anyone at any time?"

"Once we have the DNA results, we'll see if we have a match in the databases. We're doing all we can with what we have at the moment: profiling and checking released felons in the area with a history of sexual or violent offenses. We've also been going door-to-door in the area and tracking down people who may have seen anyone or anything suspicious at the fireworks display."

Peter's voice softens. "Matt, I need to come around and take a sample for DNA purposes. We just need to eliminate as many people as possible."

"Sure, come around now if you wish," replies Matt.

"Thank you. We'll be with you in an hour or so." Hanging up the phone, Peter wonders if Matt Wallace was too calm, as victims' relatives and friends typically got indignant at the veiled accusation of this request. He muttered to himself, "Mm, we'll see."

Two unmarked police cars arrive an hour later, around 10:15 p.m. Peter and another person, older and in plain clothes, come to the door.

"This is Detective Brian White," Peter said.

"Come on in."

Brian speaks first. "I can't tell you how sorry I am, and I want you to know that we're pulling out all the stops to get this guy, OK?"

Matt nods.

"Right, if I can take a swab from your mouth, I'll be off. I'll leave you with Brian here, alright?" Said Peter.

"Go ahead, fine."

Peter uses two cotton swabs to take saliva samples from Matt's mouth and puts them in a sealed tube. "OK, that's it. I'm off. I'll be in touch, of course." He gently pats Matt on the back and leaves.

Brian has been wandering around the house, sucking on an unlit pipe and picking up photographs and other items as he did so.

Once Peter had left, Brian faced Matt with a gentle smile. "I'm so sorry. There are no words of comfort I can say at this moment that would make you feel any different from how you do right now. However, when I say how sorry I am, I truly am. Do you have any immediate questions for me, or would you prefer me to share a little history and information about myself to get an idea of who you are dealing with?"

Matt has plenty of questions, but he knows that asking now would not yield the answers he was looking for. "No questions right now."

"Can I light this thing up?" Brian taps his pipe.

"Do you mind if we sit out on the porch?

"No problem."

They both go through the kitchen and to the porch, where Brian lights his pipe.

Sitting down, he says, "Ah, that's better."

Brian hesitates, looks at Matt, and then relaxes in his chair.

"I've been a detective for decades; I'm going to retire in a year or two and to be honest, I've been taking it easy and spending most of my time in the office. Well, there's not much use for an old fart like me hanging around. I'm of the old school before cell phones, computers, and who knows what else. I can tell you; it gets too much for me to get to grips with at times."

"What made you come out of the office to see me?"

"Well, I'd like to offer you some help in coping in these initial days; hopefully, with words you'll remember when you start to lose control of your thoughts and feelings. Regrettably, I've seen partners of rape victims many times; it's not that the partners are all the same; they aren't, but they are similar in the way that most of them react. It follows a pattern. First, the victim's spouse is numb, then is enraged at the villain and filled with vengeance, which is an expected emotion. Unfortunately, the point of no return is when questions spill over to the spouse, such as 'Did you scream? Did you try to fight him?' What you are really saying is, 'I can't get over what happened; you've been violated, and I hate it.'"

Matt opens his mouth to speak, but Brian continues.

"Do you not think your wife would have done all she could to protect herself? Do you intend to ask her for all the details? Are you going to tell her how you're going to get this guy and kill him or something along those lines?"

Matt doesn't answer, and both know the answers are highly likely yes. Brian sucks on his pipe and leans forward.

"The problem is the spouse of the victim - how the spouse feels, emotions that pass on to the victim about how they feel. Are you getting the picture?"

Matt does not respond.

"Let me tell you this. We may have zoomed into the twenty-first century and used advanced gizmos and gadgets, but emotions and human reactions remain the same.

"Your wife has gone through enough, and believe me; she does not want to have the burden of carrying you, fearing for you, or spending time feeling even more guilty about what happened. She will feel bad enough without all that, and you, Matt, must help her.

"She needs you to be the epitome of calm, understanding, patience and forgiveness."

Matt knows Brian was right.

"Nothing you do now or in the future will change what happened. Your wife is alive, and I'm sure that's everything in the world you want. If you doubt me, reflect on how you felt when you thought she might be deceased.

"What I'm saying is, every time you feel like expressing your anger or talking about getting even, getting revenge, or just asking questions about what happened to her, just think about that initial feeling you had when you thought she was gone."

Matt nods. "Yes, I see what you mean. I do see what you mean. You asked if I had questions. Well, I do, and that's how the hell can I begin to stop everything that's going on in my head? It won't stop; it's the same rage, questions, loathing, regret, guilt, and everything." Matt sits back and draws breath. "I love Deanne even more if that's possible, but this, this obscene tragedy, is not like real life. I mean, it makes everything you thought was important seem pointless."

"You can choose to keep this horrible event alive, day-in day-out, year-in year-out, or you can slowly begin to move on, one step at a time, and through habits of better thoughts and determination, you will move on.

"We choose our own values; make our own choices, which obviously includes what comes out of our mouth, our facial expressions, and demeanor. Our senses do not know the difference between success and failure or happiness and misery. It's up to us to choose whatever we wish to focus upon, and in turn, whatever we focus on will become our reality. So, think happy, think move on, and that's what you'll aim for in life. Sounds simple, doesn't it? It's a work in progress."

Matt absorbs Brian's words, words that he will not forget.

Brian stands, his lifeless pipe dangling between his thumb and forefinger. He bends over to tap the remains of his pipe on the edge of the brick path and repeats, "It's a work in progress; the guy needs to be caught, and it's a process, so I will ask locals in the area to volunteer to give DNA samples. That's going to take a while, many weeks.

"You can bet your arse that the villain is in the area, so, by a process of elimination, we can reduce the suspects. We'll check the hospitals, doctors, and chemists and see if anyone has been in with a bite injury, one from your dog, with any luck, but that too will take time.

"So, for now, you need to go put effort into going about your business; sitting here feeling sorry for yourself won't do any good. Your job will suffer; your friends will disappear 'cause they won't know what to say anymore. Do you know what I mean?

"On top of that, you've got a duty to make Deanne feel comfortable. This includes your family and friends, as they will feel awkward and not know what to say around you. Don't forget that their lives have not changed like yours. They have their own domestic problems, children, pleasures, and chores. They will want to help you for sure, but your part is not to make them feel tongue-tied when they try. So, all in all, you've got a big job to do. Can you do it?

When you see your wife, even though she may or may not be awake, be upbeat when you talk to her and recite good memories. She may not hear you directly, but she'll feel what you're saying and how you're saying it.

It's like playing music in her room; would you play a nice melody or a screaming rock song?

"Fuck the rapist. He's done his worst as far as you and your wife are concerned; you need to look forward. Yesterday ended yesterday, and today is a brand-new day."

Matt is silent, pondering that he has been left alone with his ceaseless calamitous thoughts and that swimming in well-meant sympathy and condolences in every direction was drowning him. He slowly shakes his head from side to side as if dispelling a hex, looks directly at Brian, and says, "Detective Brian White, you're a great guy. I can't thank you enough." Matt stands and puts his hand on Brian's shoulder as he opens the garden door to go back inside the house.

"Hey, steady on. I'll get big-headed." Brian gave Matt his card and walked to the front door.

"Hey, call that bottom number day or night, got it?"

"Sure. I've got it and thank you again."

Matt's viewpoint has changed. He is now focused on others and what tasks lie ahead for him. He knows it will not be easy, but what choice does he have besides adding more misery to a catastrophic situation?

He returns to the hospital, under his own steam, this time. He parks his car and walks toward the entrance. Upon entering, he notices the impressive interior, with the reception area more like a hotel check-in desk, with bright-colored floors, walls, and eye-catching artwork.

He waits twenty minutes for his turn to engage with one of the receptionists, "What can I do for you? "Hi. I'm Matt Wallace. I've come to visit my wife in Ward A11, please."

"OK, Mr. Wallace. You know how to get there?"

"Yes, thank you."

Matt walks directly to his wife's bedside and sees that she looked as she had earlier. He kisses her, then lies on the spare bed that has been set up earlier, talking to Deanne until his eyes close. Fully clothed and completely exhausted, he sleeps.

He doesn't hear the visits made by the night nurses or night doctors.

He wakes up, startled at his surroundings for a second or two, at around 7 a.m. He jumps from his bed and goes over to Deanne. He holds her hand, saying, "I'd give anything to reverse time. I'm so sorry I was not there. Sorry I did not come with you. I wish." Matt stops as he remembers the main point of something Brian had said: *When you see your wife, even though she may or may not be awake, be upbeat when you talk to her.*

"Hi, sweetheart," Matt resumes. "I'm thinking we should go on a vacation as soon as you're up and about, nothing strenuous, a nice, self-indulgent, relaxing vacation." He stays another hour or more, remembering recent and distant fun events and discussions they'd had about their house, their jobs, and their plans. He leans over, kisses her goodbye, and says he will return soon. He opens the door and says, "Think about where you would like to go. We could even retrace our steps in California—you know the trip we first went on." As he says this, a natural chuckle comes out of his mouth, and he smiles a genuine smile as he remembers what Deanne said just a few weeks ago, asking:

"Do you ever think back to how we met?"

Matt replied, "How could I forget? You remind me often enough?"

Chapter Three

Matthew Wallace and Deanne Jackson met in San Diego, California, where Matt was visiting from England to attend a seminar, "Technology in the 21st Century." Deanne was one of the seminar organizers from the San Diego Economic Development Council. Due to Deanne's personality, personability, fluency in Spanish, and near-fluency in French, she is an ideal communicator. Her background in performing arts in high school and college helped as well. She is a natural on stage or one-on-one. Indeed, there was a time when she thought acting would be her future.

After college, Deanne held various positions, one of which was at the San Diego Economic Development Council. Initially, she considered it a temporary stopgap. However, her coworkers welcomed her warmly, making her feel like an integral part of a large family.

She also loved interacting with people from the US and all over the world seeking to expand their business in the San Diego region. The weeks turned into months, the months into years. As the assistant director, she was the senior representative for prospective businesses interested in expanding to the US from overseas. Her dedication, passion, and integrity grew her position to become one of the principal speakers at most of the functions.

Deanne's adaptability and language skills soon saw her travel overseas and to many other US cities. She enjoyed the freedom of being in and out of the office, the exploration, and meeting new people.

Deanne also found most of the business ideas of potential investors interesting. From hi-tech to low-tech to no-tech, her main objective was to encourage small and large businesses to expand to San Diego. Her accumulated knowledge enabled her to discuss comfortably the initial particulars that most clients would ask about, such as San Diego incentives, regulations and permitting, site selection, services, research, and marketing.

Matt is the CEO of Circuit Systems Ltd, a technology company specializing in circuit board design and data translation. Based in St. Luke's, about forty minutes from Central London, Circuit Systems expanded its services to include several US companies. Matt and the rest of the management thought exploring the possibilities of a small startup in the US would be a good idea.

Matt could still recount the day he saw Deanne at the Universal Conference Center, sitting three rows back from the front of the stage, where various male and female speakers came to welcome the sizable crowd. When the introductory speakers had finished, Deanne walked on stage to thank them and announce their activities and time schedules for the next two days. She stood five feet six inches tall, with shoulder-length black hair and a slender figure.

At that time, Deanne had no idea Matt Wallace existed. He was just one of many faces.

Matt is attracted to her as soon as she enters the stage; he looks at his program to verify her name and at the same time, he notes that she is Ms., not Mrs. Deanne Jackson.

At the end of the conference, the audience is informed that the package on their seats contains a questionnaire for completion and for participants who require a one-on-one meeting to check the box, and they will be contacted. Matt checks the box and hands it to one of the many ushers as he departs.

Back at his hotel, Matt changes clothes to more casual wear and decides to wander around the area, but just as he's closing the door, his phone rings; he sees it's a USA number and returns to his room. "Hi, this is Matt Wallace."

Mr. Wallace, I'm Curtis Wolf, coordinator with the Economic Division; we're delighted you're here. I see you checked the box and have questions; how can I help you?"

"Yes, thank you for calling. I should tell you that this is on exploratory mission; no direct plans right now."

"That's a good position to start from, and I'll do my best to point you in the right direction. I see you provide electronic services and have clients in this area. Would you share who they are?"

"Yes, we provide printed circuit board design and create electronic components' libraries for Qualcomm and ViaSat, in the UK divisions mostly, and on occasions, the US divisions, which is why I'd like to find out more about other prospective customers, potential locations for an office, costs and get a general feel."

"Sounds good, and we can certainly help. I suggest Deanne Jackson as she represents and assists our office in London from time to time, not too far from your location. She has the knowledge and resources to create a customized package of applicable programs for you. I'll ask her to call you today if that's good with you. Do you have any other questions I can assist you with now?'

"No, I'm good for now, thank you."

"Great. Deanne may call later in the day or early evening unless you have plans. Is that OK."

"Yes, I don't have any plans."

Deanne called at 6:15 pm. "Mr. Wallace, this is Deanne Jackson, San Diego EDC. Thank you for your interest in expanding your business to San Diego; we will do our best to make sure everything goes smoothly and to your satisfaction. Curtis Wolf provided the questions you have. If you have time in your agenda, I can meet you tomorrow at 8 a.m., 2, or 4 o'clock in the afternoon, or anytime the following day up to 1 p.m."

Matt was surprised; she sounded warm but clinical, like a physician's assistant, before seeing the doctor.

"Thank you. Yes, any of those times tomorrow will be good; I am free all day. I'll be flying back to the UK the following day, so tomorrow would be perfect."

"Let's make it 8 a.m. If you have a little time now, I'd like to ask some questions so I can make an itinerary."

"Yes, of course, fire away."

"Good. I understand you would like to see the area, so I'll give you a short tour. If you have a specific destination or place you would visit, just let me know. OK, all I need for now is the minimum and maximum of square footage for your office, and do you intend to be resident or temporary, your answers will help me refine potential sites for tomorrow."

"Err, 500 minimum, 1,000 maximum, and temporary."

'Will you be here with your family or partner? I ask as we'll provide options according to your family size.

"No, no family, no partner."

Deanne asked a few more questions that would help her plan the event.

Her final words being, "I'll pick you up at your hotel at 8 a.m. I look forward to meeting you, Mr. Wallace."

At 7:57 a.m., the phone rang in Matt's hotel room," Hello."

"Good morning, Sir; Deanne Jackson is in the lobby."

At the same time, 7:47 a.m., USA, local time in London, England, 3:47 p.m., a married woman is deciding on a proposal.

A male has desired her since they were introduced. Over time, by gesture and trickle-feeding compliments, he has been gauging her reactions. Today, he confessed his adoration and is making an offer. The female, the wife, has two options: one to say," I'm happily married, so no," with a firm expression and walk away, or two, to smile and say, I'm married." If she chooses the latter, the repercussions will have a devastating effect on Matt and Deanne's lives.

Either way, they did not know and never would know of Deanne or Matt's existence.

Chapter Four

att, dressed in dark slacks and open neck white shirt, puts his jacket over his arm and picks up his iPad bag. One quick glance around his hotel room confirms he has all he needs before leaving to go to the lobby. He recognizes Deanne right away.

"Mr. Wallace?" Deanne stands up, dressed in a suit jacket with a pair of dark blue jeans, and greets Matt.

"That's me." Said Matt, smiling as he walked over to shake her hand.

"Shall we sit for a few minutes to go over the agenda before we head out?

Deanne moves away from the busy hotel entrance doors and sits on an armchair on one side of a table, and Matt sits opposite her. Deanne opens her folder and recites what she has gleaned from Matt's application, the brief she received from Curtis Wolf and the conversation with Matt the night before.

"Any questions or requests, Mr. Wallace?'

"No questions yet, but I have a request. Please call me Matt," Matt looks at Deanne, he smiles."

"Fine. I suggest, Mr. Wall…., Matt, that we take a detour via the scenic coastline, including some of the highlights as we drive to the office locations; you'll have more of a feel for our city.

Matt agrees.

On the two-and-half-hour trip, Matt is impressed with her business acumen and the selection of potential offices. He has many questions and is surprised by the details, figures and numbers Deanne recites without hesitation. He sees San Diego Bay, ships, and other notable sights throughout the trip. She is courteous, very pleasant, and thoughtful. But he knows he should not behave in his flippant, somewhat flirty self; she is all business.

When Deanne pulls up at the hotel to drop him off, she says, "If you have any spare time, I'm sure you would enjoy San Diego's 59-Mile Scenic Drive or taking some of the Trolly tours. It really is very nice here, and we'd like you to be a part of it. Call if any questions come to mind before you leave or when you're back in the UK, but please try to remember the time difference. It's a pleasure to meet you, Mr... Sorry, Matt, and thank you for the opportunity to show you what we have."

When Deanne drives off, there is no wave, no looking back at him. Not that he expected her to do that. He raises a quizzical eyebrow as this experience, and what he feels is new to him, and he wonders why.

Matt returns to the UK as planned, and relays the features, benefits, costs of opening a US office to his team, and decides to hold off until Qualcomm,

ViaSat, and, or other US companies require their services to make it more feasible.

A standard email from Deanne Wallace arrives shortly after. Matt replies with his company's decision, thanks her, and states that he will be in touch when things change. General newsletters followed intermittently which he would glance at and save in his EDC folder.

Three months after his visit, he is surprised when he sees a call from EDC CA; he answers, "Hello, this is Matt Wallace."

"Mr. Wallace, Matt, this is Deanne Jackson from the EDC in San Diego?"

"Hello. Yes. This is a surprise; how are you," he stutters. "Sorry, you sound different on the phone." He looks up and rolls his head, thinking to himself, "What am I saying?"

"I didn't mean to startle you. We sent a newsletter and invitation a month ago to announce our new incentives, particularly to selected industries that have shown recent interest in the EDC. It's a small group, and I'm calling the recipients to verify their attendance. And I see you, and one other did not respond. Basically, I'll be in the UK in a few days to discuss them at a forum at our London office and wondered if the topic is of interest to you."

"I must have missed that. I don't think I..." Silence followed.

"Sorry, I didn't catch that."

"Yes, that would be of interest. Would you email me the details again, please?"

"Yes, of course. Thank you, I look forward to seeing you." The call ends.

Matt checks his inbox; the newsletter has arrived. Scrolling down, he sees the invitation and checks the boxes, presses send, and prints out the location, time and information. He is aware his only interest in attending is to see Deanne.

It is a small gathering with nine attendees, representing five companies who have shown prior interest in expanding their business to San Diego, including pharmaceuticals, A.I and three engineering companies, of which he is one. The entire rear wall of the podium is a screen, which will transform into several resizable frames according to the topics and questions. Applause greets Deanne as she walks to the lectern, a wave of her hand and smiling face is shared with mouthing thank you's, and good to see you again.

"Thank you for your welcome and for your attendance; I'm sure you'll be delighted with the contents of today's presentation. Please raise your hand if you have any questions as we move through, and my colleagues or I will step up and answer, "Deanne sweeps her hand across to where her associates lift their hands in acknowledgment.

Deanne's expertise and warm enthusiasm put everyone at ease, and questions and answers flowed. The conclusion of the presentation covers the newly available incentives, producing applause, nods of approval and frequent positive comments.

In closing, Deanne thanked everyone and addressed the groups by their individual names, indicating the EDC personnel in the room whose specialty is pharmaceutical and A.I for continued discussions or questions and that she will meet with the engineers.

Matt hangs back as his fellow engineers spend time with Deanne. When he sees she is free, he walks up to her, now feeling more confident on his home turf, "Hi Deanne that was a great presentation."

"Thank you, Matt; I'm glad you made it."

"The incentives have got me thinking, but deciding is still in the future. I do have one question though."

"Of course, how can I help?"

"I wondered if I could take you to dinner while you're here. We could discuss the incentives again," Matt smiles and looks directly into her eyes.

"Thank you for the offer, Matt, but no. My time is short here, and I have a lot to do before I leave. But thank you." Revealing a gentle smile, she walks away to join her colleagues.

Matt, disappointed, heaves a sigh and walks towards the exit door; he hears, "Mr. Wallace, Matt, just a second." Deanne walks over to him, "I'd like to ask you a favor.' Her eyes widened. "Would you be able to get tickets for Cabaret at the Playhouse, I've tried, but no success. I'd be happy to join you if you can, and we can discuss if the EDC can do more to help," her eyes flickered.

Matt, surprised, instantly said, "Yes, I'm sure I can; I have a friend who's the concierge at a hotel; he'll be able to get them,"

"Wonderful, thank you. Any evening, tonight and the following two nights. That's great, thank you."

"I'll let you know when I have them and let you know the time. Where are you staying? I can pick you up?"

"No need, I'll get a cab." Deanne opens her purse and pulls out one of her business cards, scribbles a number on the back and hands it to him," Here's my cell number; give me a call or text me, and I'll meet you there. Thank you again." Deanne touches his cuff as she walks away.

As soon as Matt is in his car, he calls his contact and secures two tickets for that evening. He texts Deanne the address and time, Kit Kat Club at the Playhouse Theatre Northumberland Avenue, 8 a.m. and asks if she would like to eat after the show, which she declines and states that she would arrive by cab at 7:30 and asks him to look out for her.

Matt arrives at the theater at 7 p.m. via Uber and positions himself near the entrance, making sure he has a view of vehicles dropping off passengers, his head going right and left for the next twenty minutes. Then, he sees Deanne as she alights from a taxi; she turns, not seeing Matt for a few seconds. As Matt walks toward her, he smiles and mutters internally, "My God, she's stunning." He feels awkward, not knowing if he should shake her hand or give a polite nod; he is awestruck by the change in persona. "Hi, Deanne, glad you could make it. Wow, you look incredible."

Deanne tilts her head to one side, "Thank you." Wearing a black tweed midi dress, gray shoes with a matching clutch bag, and a lightweight coat over her arm, she is beautiful and elegant.

"Would you like a drink before we sit down?' Matt asks as they walk towards the entrance.

"Yes, please, Chardonnay would be nice."

Noise from throngs of people at the entrance and inside prevents any further conversation. Matt takes Deanne's hand as they venture to one of the three bars inside the theater, weaving in and out of the other patrons to a less busy bar where their voices can be heard. Matt releases her hand, "Sorry for grabbing you. Most people go to the nearest bar, and others follow; this one is quieter, and you could not hear what I was saying out there."

Deanne lifts her head with an understanding smile, saying, "It's OK, Matt."

This was the first time their eyes meaningfully met, and it lingered just long enough to feel a little uncomfortable. Deanne blurts out," Shall I sit at this high-top while you get the drinks?"

"Yes. Yes, of course. I'll just be a minute."

Matt returns with two glasses of Chardonnay, sits, lifts his glass and says, "Cheers."

"This is a sold-out show, I know, I tried. I'm very grateful and excited to see it. Let me pay for the tickets, Matt; I can claim the money back as a legitimate expense."

"No need. I've just collected the tickets from Jason, the bartender, and paid nothing for the tickets. Roger, the ticket guy, is a retired engineer, a friend. He gets me tickets, and I layout printed circuit boards for the gizmos he engineers, so it's quid-pro-quo."

Their conversation is unobtrusive and more relaxed. At the sound of the gong, indicating the show is about to start, they finish their wine and proceed to their seats in the stalls. During the brief intermission, both decide to stay in their seats instead of joining the rush for the bar.

"Would you like to go for a drink or snack after the show?" Matt asks.

"Sorry, no. I need to be up early and prepare for another meeting, but thank you for asking."

After the show, Matt escorts Deanne across two streets where it is easy to get a taxi.

"You take the first one," said Matt.

"The show was wonderful; I can't thank you enough."

"My pleasure. Let me know if there's anything else you'd like to visit." Said Matt as he opened the car door for her. They smile at each other, then she's gone. He received a text message, *thank you, I really enjoyed this evening.*

There is a mutual, though unspoken, attraction between them, but both are aware of the impracticality of their situation. Nevertheless, both found their thoughts turning to each other very frequently. Matt texts the following day and invites Deanne to dinner or lunch if she has time, but she explains she is too busy. He responds by asking her to let him know when she is coming to London and asks for her personal email address so he can keep her up to date on what new shows are coming. He knew this was a weak excuse to obtain her email, but it was the best he could think of, and he was not surprised at the lack of response.

Four weeks go by, during which time business discussions regarding an office in San Diego cease to be a topic. Matt's thoughts of Deanne also become less frequent, but she quickly becomes full focus again when he sees an email from her.

Hi Matt, I'll be visiting the London office again in two weeks; we're at the closing stage of the A.I Company, and they requested I attend. You asked me to let you know.

I hope all is well.

Best Regards,

Deanne.

It's 5:15 PM Thursday in London, UK, and 9:15 AM Thursday in San Diego, CA. Without any thought, Matt calls Deanne's cell; she picks up.

"Hello, Matt?"

"Hi, Deanne, sorry. I just got your email and called as it's a nice surprise to hear from you."

"Matt, I'll call you back." The phone is dead. Ten minutes later, his cell rang.

"Hi Matt, I was in a meeting. How can I help?"

"As I said, it's nice to hear from you, and I just called to say hello, nothing to do with business, I'd like to see you again. Maybe dinner, a show. We had fun last time."

There's ten seconds silence before Deanne responds, "Matt, we went to a show; the show was fun. We spoke for all of 30 minutes, if that and I'm very grateful that you took me." There is another long pause. "Matt, I'd like to ask you a question, no bullshit, OK?

"Of course."

I'm wondering what is on your mind Matt – I'm feeling you are trying to pursue more than a business relationship with me. Is that right?"

"Deanne, I don't have any idea. All I know is that when I saw you for the first time, I was attracted to you then, when I met you, the attraction increased, and since I took you to the show, I've had a hell of a job trying *not* to think about you. I saw your email, and now I'm back to square one, only more so than I expected. I've been on two dates since we went to the theater with very beautiful women, I hasten to add, and you keep coming into my head." He draws a deep breath and sighs, "I know, it's a dumb situation. You're in the States, and I'm here, so it makes no sense at all, but

I'll never forget the jolt I felt when our eyes met outside the theatre, and forgive me for saying so; I think you felt something too."

"Damn you, Matt, why did you tell me that? Because of my job, I engage with scores of men over any given year; I've been asked out to dinner enough times to stem any famine, and I say no every time, apart from once, about five years ago. I dated a guy I met from one of the seminars, a nice guy, soft-spoken. He had his own business and had to travel quite a lot, which was OK with me as I travel too, so we only managed to meet two to three times a week at most.

"One day, at my office, a woman visited, asked for me, and told the receptionist that she was expected and had an appointment with me. When Julie, the receptionist, buzzed through and told me about the appointment, I came straight out to the front. Well, you can imagine my surprise when the woman smacked me in the face, told me I was a bitch, and accused me of trying to steal her husband.

"It gets better," Deanne continued. "After a torrent of verbal abuse, his wife walked out and left me red-faced, humiliated. Oh, and by this time, several people from my office had come to reception to see what the commotion was about. I had no idea the guy was married, not an inkling. I just stood there in shock.

"I explained the situation and asserted my innocence to my coworkers, but I knew no one believed me. What made it worse was that Mitch, the supposedly nice single guy, kept harassing me to the point that I had to get a restraining order against him, and I almost lost my job because of the whole situation.

And just so you know, I was never really scared of Mitch, the married guy who was harassing me. I probably could have taken care of myself if he tried anything. I am a gym fanatic, and at that time, I was dabbling in martial arts."

"I don't know what to say except I'm sorry that happened to you."

"I need to think; I'll call you again before I come over, but if I can exorcise you, I will do, and there will be no call. Please don't contact me again; I will contact you."

"Does that mean you feel the same?" Matt looks at his phone. The call had ended.

The following morning, Matt saw a text from Deanne. *I feel the same; let's see where it takes us. I'll be there for three nights only; I have Wednesday night free. I'll call you later.* Prior to Deanne's arrival, the calls increased in frequency, and their conversations became more natural and easier.

Matt booked Langan's Brasserie in Mayfair, London, for dinner and booked a driver to pick him up at his home, then to pick up Deanne and repeat the same at the end of their evening. He hears Deanne's words from their last call: *I'm excited to see you, but let's not rush our first dinner with any false expectations.*

On their dinner evening, Matt's driver picks him up as arranged, and they head to Deanne's hotel to collect her. On arrival, Matt gets out of the car and starts to walk up the steps and sees Deanne coming through the door of the hotel, he is mesmerized. They embrace lightly, uneasily. The driver opens the car door for Deanne, and Matts follows. Hand-holding, compliments, excitement, laughter and questions continue throughout their journey to Langan's. Dinner could not have been improved. At the end of the meal, Deanne took out her phone and asked the waiter to take pictures of the happy couple. The journey back to Deanne's hotel is a little more amorous, but only to the extent of kissing Matt gently on his lips before she says goodnight. Matt reminds her to send him a copy of the photos. They shared occasional photos via their phones; Matt had some framed and put them alongside other photos he had around his home.

Six weeks after Deanne returns to the USA, she happily agrees to another trip for a requested, in-person meeting by the UK office to discuss a future opportunity. Excitedly, she calls Matt.

"Hi, great news, I'm coming back for a short trip again next week, just a few days, and this time I'd like to meet your supposed housekeeper you keep telling me about. I'm wondering if she is as you described, and of course, I'd love to see your home, maybe have dinner?"

"Wonderful, and yes, to both questions. I'll ask Jane if she'll cook a traditional English dinner for us."

In fact, Jane Tilling, his twice weekly or, when he needed her, housekeeper, as he had described to Deanne, reminds him of one of his old schoolteachers, perpetually dressed in various midi skirts and blouses with reddish mid-length hair and eyeglasses that hung around her neck on a cord.

After finishing his call with Deanne, he calls Jane and shares the news. She's excited to meet Deanne and happy to cook a traditional meal; she suggests a cottage pie. "I'll make the place spic and span and make a nice dinner and dessert. Oh, in case she uses your bedroom bathroom, you best get the door fixed. It doesn't close, and the taps in the wash basin are hard to turn."

Matt had, in fact, wondered if she would spend the night.

Matt began his journey home after a short visit to his office the following morning. On the way, he notes the numbers of a couple of trade vehicles with Handy Man, Painting, Plumbing, and Electrical signage. He calls the first number and makes an appointment.

"This is a good omen," he said.

The expected handyman arrives as planned, writes down the details as Matt explains what he needs and emphasizes the urgency of the work.

The tradesman informs Matt he needs to get a new lock and hinges for the bathroom door and will call back within two hours with an estimate and could be back in the morning. No callback came.

Jane calls, "Hi Matt, I'm just going to the store. Is there anything you need?"

"No, I don't think so. I'm just about to call another guy to fix the door and taps, as the guy who came here earlier said he'd call back with a quote, and that was hours ago. Strange guy, but seemed OK, just not much of a conversationalist, though he did look at a photograph of Deanne and said she's a fine-looking lady and asked if she is my wife."

"Sounds nosey to me," retorted Jane.

"She is a fine-looking lady. Nothing wrong with that. Let's hope the next guy I call works out. I'll let you know. Thanks for calling."

Matt calls the number and explains his problem, adding that a new lock and hinges are needed for the door. Handyman, number two, said he could be there around eight the next morning, and he is.

"Hi, Ray Miller?" Asks Matt.

"At your service," said Ray with a smile, "Let's see what we're dealing with, shall we?"

Matt liked him right away, and was much better than the prior contractor.

After an hour, Ray walks down the stairs, "Good news, your taps are fine now. I just gave them a good clean and greased them and the door has a new lock and hinges."

Matt followed Ray back upstairs and checked the taps and door, "Perfect, thank you." Once he closes the door behind Ray, he looks around the rooms to see if anything should be done and hesitates near the sideboard. He frowns at the display of photographs; "That's odd,' he says out loud. Out of the plentiful collection, he thinks one of the pictures is missing and looks around the house, but he can't see it. With all he had to do, coupled with the anticipation of Deanne's arrival, he soon forgot about the missing photograph.

Matt's London home is an eighty-year-old three-bedroom, two-bathroom, two-story property, detached from the neighboring houses by 100 feet or so on either side. It belonged to his grandfather, who unfortunately could not maintain the house properly. Matt had readily stepped in to help, physically and financially. He had been shocked when his grandfather died and doubly shocked that he had willed his house to Matt. On a good day, a drive to the city could take thirty minutes; on a bad day, three times longer, but he loved the house, and with his fond memories of his grandfather, he felt he would never part with it.

Two days before Deanne's departure to London, and the final call before they meet, she calls: "Matt, I'm flying first class. I upgraded my ticket with air miles, which means I get a free limo ride to and from the airports, so . . . I could bypass the hotel and come directly to your place, assuming the flight is on time, I'd be there at about one o'clock in the afternoon, and you take me back to my hotel later Sunday. What do you think?"

Matt is elated. The conversation lasted only another five minutes as Deanne needed to triple-check that she had everything in order before leaving for the airport. Matt goes to bed at midnight, not falling to sleep until 2 a.m. He wakes at 7:45 a.m. and lies in bed, gazing at the ceiling and thinking how lucky he is. Dom Perignon is in the refrigerator, and there is plenty of food in the house. It's going to be a great night. Yes, superb, it will be superb.

The morning is cold, but the sun is trying to force light and warmth through the clouds. By noon, Matt is peering through the window sheers, looking, and listening to every vehicle going by.

At 1:30, a car pulls up outside Matt's home. His heart is racing. The car door opens, and the first vision he has of Deanne is her legs swinging out the door, standing up and thanking the driver. Then she turns to face the closed front door. Matt quickly steps back from the window, feeling as if he'd been caught in wrongdoing by peeping out.

Why would I not be looking out?

Deanne looks back at the driver and begins to walk to the car's rear. She looks magnificent, dressed in a mid-length black dress, black heels, and a gray leather topcoat loosely tied with a matching leather belt. Matt has been longing for this moment. He feels nervous excitement and has mentally played out the reunion. He was not prepared to be overcome by the sight of Deanne.

"You look amazing."

Matt tips the driver and helps place the suitcases inside the foyer.

"Champagne?" Matt asked.

"Please."

The champagne poured and sipped; Matt began the tour through the house, first the first floor, then the second floor.

"This house is soooo old. Does it have ghosts? Do you need to put pots everywhere when it's raining? This door squeaks when you open it; it really squeaks, listen. It's wonderful."

"You must be tired. Would you like to rest for a while? The ghosts promised not to come out when you're here,"

"I'm good, I slept, and I sleep on a plane just fine, though I would like to freshen up before I meet Jane if that's OK."

"She'll be here at five to start dinner, so you have plenty of time."

Deanne walks to the foyer and picks up a small case, "Everything I need is in here."

Matt picks up the case and walks Deanne to the master bedroom, and points, "Right through that door." They look at one another; Deanne says with a smile, "It's good to see you again," and closes the bedroom door.

Matt patiently waits in the living room, where he can view the staircase. Hearing the bedroom door open, he looks up to see Deanne closing the door. He can see a pair of sequin slip-on muffin sneakers and her tanned calves in his line of sight. With the support of the handrail, she slowly descends, increasing Matt's view of her ensemble with each step, finally revealing her in a pink sleeveless mid-length dress tied with a thin black belt and her radiantly smiling face.

"Wow, look at you! You look sensational."

Though Deanne had visited London many times, they were business trips, with an occasional theater performance. She is fascinated with Matt's house, going from room to room, touching the walls, the fireplace and objects of interest to her.

At 5 p.m. the doorbell rings, "Come in Jane, the door's unlocked." Jane opens the door, looks at Matt and smiles, then walks toward Deanne, "Well, there's a wonderful sight if ever I saw one; no wonder Matt's head over heels about you." Matt shakes his head and blushes a little.

"Can I give you a hug, dear? I've heard so much about you," Her arms are outstretched, and Deanne's the same, "I have heard so much about you too, Jane. I'm happy to meet you."

They hit it off right away, Deanne spending much of her time with Jane in the kitchen, sharing stories, discussing food and pastimes. Matt laid the table, and Jane served the dinner, after which she said, "There's apple crumble in the oven for dessert. The ovens off, but it will keep it warm. OK, I'll be off now and leave you two alone."

Deanne thanks and hugs Jane saying, "I hope to see you again soon.'

"Will you be staying over tonight?"

"No, I have work in the morning and need to get back to my hotel."

"Have a lovely night, and if I'm needed, you know where I am." Jane says, closing the door as she leaves.

At the same time, 8:47 p.m., the married woman is meeting the male who has made several proposals. He is successful in his amorous pursuit, and this time, the woman smiles, saying, "I'm not happily married." This sets in motion a disruption that will affect and shatter the lives of Deanne and Matt.

Chapter Five

Deanne and Matt sit opposite each other at the dining room table, a simple setting, the only adornments are a small floral centerpiece and faux candles in two matte black pillar candle holders.

"She is all you said she is, including the look, and I think she's great.'

Yep, she's hard-working, trustworthy, flexible and reliable, plus she's happy to cook for me when I ask, like tonight, and it's more money in her pocket when she does, so she's happy."

Deanne tastes the cottage pie, "This is delicious." she says, with wide eyes of enjoyment.

Matt smiles, "I told you it would be good." His tone changes as he asks, "Why a return trip so soon? You never told me. I could not be happier that they asked, but that's not usual, is it?"

"No, it isn't. You remember the A.I representative?" Matt nodded. "Well, it seems like it could be a big deal, and the next two days will be mostly at their company so they can demonstrate artificial intelligence in daily life and industries and I guess, quiz us to death. They really want to dive into the opportunities and support we can offer. Wesley, my boss, will be there too, maybe others. This trip is going to be all work."

"So, will I see you in the evening?"

"I don't know. I do know we're out to dinner one of the nights with the same client. I'll let you know after tomorrow."

"You could do as Jane suggested and stay tonight, and I can take you to your office in the morning. You would have your own bedroom."

Deanne looks into the middle distance, puts her elbows on the table and rests her head in her hands, shakes her head slowly and says, "No," She sits back in her chair and looks at Matt, "The more we dig, the deeper we go, and if you keep digging, you may never get out, so be careful. My Dad told me that when I was a kid. I'll be leaving after dinner, in an Uber, alone Matt. I need to slow down." She smiles an awkward smile, picks up her glass of wine, saying, "Cheers." Matt's glass chinks with Deanne's, his forehead creasing, saying, "Are you OK?"

"Yep," expressing a cautious look. "I told you about Mitch, the guy who turned out to be married, but not all of it. The relationship was good, his work took him away as mine did, and he always picked up the phone, or if I left a message, he'd call back as soon as he could. He was thoughtful and fun to be with, and there were no signs of another relationship. He had an apartment downtown, his wallet and phone would be on the coffee table, a couple of photos of us, clothes in the closet, I mean, all normal. How could I know he had two phones, two wallets, a house with a wife and kids?"

Deanne gets up from the table, walks around to Matt and kisses him on the cheek, raises her finger and says, "Now, here's the good part." She returns to her seat opposite Matt, who is fully engaged.

"He took advantage of me, I gave him my trust, and he betrayed me, used me and humiliated me; he'd planned it and taken me for a ride. I was, to him, an easy mark, and I won't, I can't let that happen to me again. I am fond of you, Matt. I know you're not married, and I've checked you out as much as I could. I just need time, more chat time to get to know each other better than we do now."

The evening closed with an affectionate kiss, more sweetness than sexual attraction.

Deanne did not have an opportunity to see Matt during the remainder of her visit, but they talked on the phone frequently, their relationship growing with each call.

The meeting with the A.I group was a big success. Wesley, Deanne, and the team of the London EDC excelled, the most persuasive influence being Deanne, which did not go unnoticed by Wesley, "Deanne, you did great; we may not have pulled this off without you."

"You can repay me by getting me a three-month stay here; you still have gaps I can fill with the potential companies you're pursuing."

On one Wednesday night, at 7 p.m., Matt's phone rang.

"*I have a surprise,*" Deanne said in a calm but volatile voice.

"What surprise?"

Deanne screams, almost bursting Matt's eardrum, "I'm coming over to England for three whole months! I'll be back in a few weeks! What do you think? I've been working on this for an age!"

"I can't believe it; how did you manage that, and why didn't you tell me?"

"I wasn't sure if Wesley could pull it off and I've just found out myself."

"This is wonderful, Deanne! Wonderful. Will you stay here, at my house, I mean? I have three bedrooms."

"The EDC provides accommodation, but we'll see."

Deanne and Matt make contact almost every day through regular calls, video calls, and emails; ultimately, the calls become more intimate as their affection grows.

On the day of Deanne's arrival in London, Matt feels less apprehensive than he thought; in fact, both feel the same due to the bonding and familiarity they have shared over the past weeks.

Deanne is quickly through arrivals and in Matt's arms, where they hug with passion. After collecting Deanne's luggage, they are soon in Matt's car, excited and both trying to talk at once.

Once they arrive at Matt's home, they sit on the sofa, consuming champagne, sharing stories, and laughing. Soon, the champagne is finished; the humor has turned into sincere gestures and words of affection. The gestures become embraces; the embraces become more intimate. Soon, clothes are discarded, and they make love on the sofa and again upstairs in the main bedroom. Exhausted and a little tipsy, they both drift off to sleep.

Deanne had a couple of free days before reporting to the office, enabling them to become more relaxed in each other's company. Deanne called

Wesley to let her know she had arrived and to tell him she did not need EDC accommodation; she would be staying with Matt.

Apart from walking to the nearby woods and passing a row of equally old houses, they spent the day at home. Deanne had never been happier, and Matt was never so grateful.

Tuesday, they ventured out. Matt drove Deanne to different parts of London that she had not seen before, at least not with a tour guide. Matt took her from Westminster to Soho and Tower Bridge to Portobello Market, interspersed with breakfast, lunch, and dinner.

Deanne began working in the EDC office Wednesday as planned. It was an easy start as her prior visit was recent, and the success she had achieved at that time was still in process.

Wesley Snipps, head of the division, a fellow American, and Deanne's boss, had been in the London office for six years. He had helped Deanne secure the posting to England for the three-month period, but not as a favor. He knew her character and capabilities and was delighted to have her working with him. He respected her, not just for her passion and drive or how she would get to know the customer and their product. It was more that she always had the customer's best interests in mind; she would heed their questions and concerns. These attributes, coupled with her patience and natural friendliness, were her winning combination, as Wesley thought, *She just shines.*

Wesley was practical, intuitive, and meticulous in his routines and processes. He said it was his form of therapy and kept him sane. He stood six feet tall and was marginally overweight. He was a smart dresser, wearing a suit and tie every day at the office.

Matt and Wesley had not met in person; however, they were familiar with each other through Deanne and had spoken on the phone briefly. Deanne made a point of inviting Matt to her office to meet him, where the two of them, as Deanne said, hit it off right away, and whenever Matt went to meet Deanne for lunch, he would say hello to Wesley.

On one occasion, Wesley asked Matt if he planned to set up a business in the US, and Matt said not at the moment. But he said that one of his own customers had remarked that they had looked at Florida to expand their UK business. Immediately, Wesley reacted, stood up, and, with a mock-serious tone, stated, "Deanne, you need to step in and stop the fools Matt's talking about and steer them away from Florida! It's no place for them. San Diego is where they must go; they just don't know it yet."

Deanne and Matt laughed.

Wesley said, "Matt, how big are they, and what do they do?"

"They are high-tech. The company name is MiraTech; we design their printed circuit boards for medical equipment. Hospitals are their main customers. Some are in the UK, some in the EU, and some in the US. Their revenue is about 400 million sterling annually." Matt smiled, adding, "And a net of around 30% over the past two years."

Wesley's' voice turned serious and pleading. "Seriously, would you let us have a shot at them? Nothing formal, just an introduction. No heavy-handed stuff, just an introduction."

"I'm happy to call. They can only say no."

Matt called later the same day and spoke with CEO Lewis Miller, who keenly agreed to meet Wesley, stating that it was always good to look at options.

Matt called Wesley with the good news right away.

"Hi Wesley, it's your lucky day. Lewis Miller, the CEO, is happy to visit your office in the morning. Is 10 a.m. good for you?"

"Yes, of course. I'll offload anything on my calendar. Thank you, Matt. I really appreciate the opportunity."

"It's a pleasure. Good luck."

Lewis went to the EDC London office, where he was greeted by Wesley and taken into the conference room. Wesley pitched what San Diego could offer, displaying various potential locations on a large screen as he voiced the list of benefits.

Wesley would have asked Deanne to accompany him in the presentation, but both he and Matt thought it would be unethical and might cause awkwardness in the business relationship between Matt and Lewis.

Lewis did have the courtesy to call Wesley to thank him for the introduction, saying that he was impressed and might have considered San

Diego. However, his company had already invested in Florida, and the time and money spent looking at an alternative location would have been a waste.

Wesley informed Deanne. Both were disappointed but not surprised. Deanne wondered if she would have made any difference if she had attended the presentation. She decided to perform her own due diligence on the company, MiraTech. Additionally, she would look into incentives and inducements that may help. Neither Matt nor Wesley knew of her intentions and had no idea of a plan she was concocting. She remembered a friend from college; he was a year ahead of Deanne and moved back to his family's home in Florida after graduation. They kept in touch as he took a position with the EDC in Florida, and their paths would cross through programs and updates from the National Economic Development Administration. On occasion, they would meet up at class reunions, where Rick made a point to connect with Deanne as they both worked for their regional EDC, and they would invariably offer each other passes for respective events and theme parks if 'they were ever in the area.'

Four years ago, Deanne and her friend, Lisa, took Rick up on his offer for Disney passes when they vacationed in Orlando. Rick was introduced to Lisa at the ticket handoff, where he, as he put it, was smitten with her. He called Deanne every day, pleading to get a date with Lisa, "Rick, she has a boyfriend, and sorry, she has no interest."

After a call two days before they were returning to San Diego, Deanne tried again with Lisa; "Why not just go for a quick dinner, or lunch, or whatever? He did get us the tickets."

"OK, OK,' said Lisa, raising her eyes and huffing.

Their date resulted in a temporary, long-distance relationship, with Lisa moving to Florida and marriage two years later.

Rick stated repeatedly to Deanne how grateful he was and, *if ever she needed anything, anything at all, she just had to ask.* Today was the day she did so.

Deanne walks into her office, closes the door, and looks at her watch, "Good, it's 3 p.m. in Florida', she says to no one and punches in a number, "Rick, is that you?"

"Deanne?"

"How did you know?"

"You came up on the phone. I haven't spoken with you for a while; you always call Lisa and never have time for me," he laughed.

"Well, I am now, and I need a favor, a big favor, privately."

"Of course."

"OK, this is a big favor, I know, but I'm in a similar situation you were in four years ago with Lisa, and basically, to make it work, I need to be transferred to the UK, London office, which is where I'm calling from."

"What, you're going to stay in England?'

"Let me explain."

Deanne relayed her story about Matt and explained the situation concerning MiraTech.

"I don't see how I can help Deanne; we're waiting on their decision. I know we made a great offer."

"Yeah, well, that's what I need to know… please." Deanne gritted her teeth.

"No, there's no way. I'm sorry, Deanne, but no."

"All right, it was worth a shot."

"Anything else would probably be a yes, and I am sorry.'

"It's OK, I understand. Thanks anyway." The line went dead.

Deanne didn't give up; she called Lisa and told her the whole story.

"That's a tall order, Deanne."

"OK. Let's ask another way. I don't need to know any figures, and if I send you a list, you could say, mark it with a 1 for higher, a 2 for lower and 3 for lowest. Would that work…? I mean, you are married now, and I'm still single."

Lisa laughed, "Oh, come on, Deanne, that's low even for you, and in any case, you've never been short of offers for heaven's sake."

"I know, I know. I'm just desperate, and I can't think of any other way, and you are my very best friend, at least until you moved to Florida and left me all alone." This time, they both laughed.

"Send the damn list, and I'll see what I can do. I love you."

"I love you too.'

Two days later, Deanne received a cryptic text, one word and a list of numbers. She replied with a smiley face text.

From what Matt had said about Lewis, he seemed like an approachable person. He was a family man and had two teenage children, so she gauged he would be in his late forties. A day went by, and Deanne didn't have a plan as such and was trying to find a subtle way of meeting Lewis. She couldn't, so she met the situation head-on and spoke to Lewis Miller herself.

Deanne had spoken with Cindy, Lewis's assistant, when she had called the house phone to speak with Matt, and Deanne had picked it up. The first time was a brief instruction between them, and subsequent times grew more personal before Deanne passed the call over to Matt.

Deanne had an idea. She checked the house phone to find Cindy's number. She takes the plunge and calls.

"Good morning. This is Cindy."

"Hi, Cindy. This is Deanne. I'm calling to ask a favor. Matt does not know I'm calling."

"Is everything OK, Deanne? Is anything wrong?"

Deanne quickly responds, "No. Nothing is wrong. I just want to come in and speak with Lewis for five minutes, probably less." She explains that neither Matt nor her office knows anything about her intended visit and fills Cindy in on her plan.

"It's San Diego, right?"

"Yes."

"Sounds good to me. I've been to Florida with Lewis twice. It's nice, but, my God, the heat. It's not that hot in San Diego, is it?"

"No, it has a wonderful temperature all year round, does not rain often, and we don't have hurricanes."

"I'm in. Can you be here in an hour? I know he's not leaving for another two hours."

"Yes, of course."

"Good luck. Oh, remember we did not have this conversation. I know nothing about it, OK?"

"Thank you. Thank you. Thank you!" She gets off the phone and shouts to Wesley that she will return in two hours.

"Where are you going?"

"I'll tell you when I get back!"

Wesley sits in his chair, shaking his head.

Deanne arrives at MiraTech in less than an hour. She asks reception for directions to Mr. Millers' office, where she is told to take the elevator to the second floor. As the door starts to close, she thinks she sees a figure outside the entrance of the office looking through the glass directly looking at her and frowning, though not clear due to the reflection on the glass.

The figure is a man, an angry man she would encounter in the future.

The doors open on the second floor, where Deanne sees a sign, Mira Tech; she walks up to a woman, whom she assumes is Cindy.

She smiles, saying, "I'm here to see Mr. Miller, please. I have an appointment."

Cindy looks at her and winks. "What is your name, please?"

Deanne smiles. "Deanne Jackson."

Cindy calls through to Lewis, "Deanne Jackson is here for your appointment. I'll show her in." She puts the phone down.

"What appointment? Diane who?" comes through the intercom.

His door opens. Cindy ushers Deanne through the door, closing it after she stepped through. Deanne takes two steps into the office and waits for Lewis to raise his gaze from the papers on his desk.

Lewis looks up, then stands up. "Please, sit down and forgive me, Ms. Diane Jackson. I seem to have forgotten why the appointment was made. Cindy may have forgotten to tell me. Anyway, how can I help you?" Lewis smiles and sits back down in his chair.

Deanne ignores the misinterpretation of her given name. She does not care what he calls her right now. "I only need five minutes of your time, Mr. Miller. I'm Matt Wallace's fiancé. Neither he nor Wesley knows I've come to your office. I'm here in England temporarily from the San Diego office."

Lewis is more confused than angry, which renders him temporarily speechless. All he can say is, "Ah, so you're American." He inwardly cringes at his own words.

"Yes, I'm here for three months, then I return. I'm sorry to visit you without making an appointment, but I'll be completely honest, then I'll get out of your hair." She explains why she had been omitted from the initial meeting with Wesley, also sharing that she has been looking into his company profile.

"I won't bore you with a sales pitch and a long list of reasons why I feel your business would benefit from considering San Diego. I want to share with you that I believe you could be missing out on an opportunity to make an informed comparison when choosing your expansion to the US.

"San Diego and the surrounding cities' best-known asset is its highly skilled workforce, especially in technology and A.I. The weather is consistently pleasant, not humid, not too hot, no hurricanes. Our education system is world-leading, and we have many more key relationships with mega-corporations, not just in San Diego but all over CA. And I'd like to offer you the opportunity to visit. We'll pick up the tab for flights to San Diego for you and your team, put you up in a hotel, and provide you with a list of contacts of major hospitals, scientists, and other healthcare professional companies whom you can call and visit at your leisure."

Silence fills the room. Lewis widened his eyes, smiled, and said, "Wow, so you're Matt's fiancé."

Deanne nods and smiles.

Lewis stands up, looks out of his office window, and turns back to face Deanne. "I admire you for coming in and for getting to the point, but, as I said to Wesley, we've covered a lot of ground in Florida, and we came to a good arrangement regarding tax benefits and incentives, going through the hassle of that again isn't appealing. So, I have to say sorry, no."

Deanne didn't miss a beat. "The major benefit if you select Dan Diego is that we will meet the same incentives, plus no lease payment on your offices for the two years, and I understand that your requirement is 20,000 square feet or 1,858 square meters. First-level office and development, second-level engineering, freight elevator, and passenger elevator."

Lewis now has a broad grin on his face. "I'll talk with the principals to see if they would entertain convening another Board meeting. I'll let you know. Where can I reach you?" Deanne provided her card, stood up, and shook his hand vigorously.

"Thank you, Mr. Miller."

Lewis walks from the other side of his desk and opens the door, saying, "I'll see if we can meet and make a decision before the end of this week, Diane." Cindy looks up and gives Deanne a quick smile.

The days went by, and Deanne was nervously waiting for the call and finding it difficult to focus on anything else. A multitude of calls came in, but none from Lewis, not until 11:15 a.m. on Friday.

"Good morning, Deanne," Lewis said. *"I see on your card I mispronounced your name. I apologize, but I have good news to make up for that. The board decided that we should take you up on your offer. Are you able to set it up for six weeks from today? There will be four of us. Separate rooms, please? Also, we would prefer you to be there if that's possible."*

Deanne leans her torso back, punches the air with her free hand, mouths, and inwardly shouts a loud, elongated *yes!* Then, as calmly as she can, she replies, "Thank you, yes, of course, and no problem with my name or with accompanying you and your team. It will be a pleasure. I'll send the flight and hotel details for your approval this afternoon. Thank you again for the opportunity. I'm confident you will not be disappointed." She hangs up.

Unleashing a long outward breath, clasping her hands, head down, and looking at her shoes, she stands still, mumbling, "My God, this is wonderful. Now, gather yourself and casually pop in to tell Wesley with your sad face on."

Deanne goes over to Wesley's office. "Are you busy?"

"No. What's up? Is there a problem?"

Deanne goes in and closes the door behind her. Still wearing the sad face, she looks directly at him, then grins the largest grin possible while shrugging her shoulders upward as high as possible, stating, "I'm going back to San Diego in six weeks. I won over MiraTech, and they are flying to San Diego in six weeks. And they asked if I would be there. I said yes."

She smiles as she explains everything. Wesley is overjoyed.

"Hell, we can foot the bill for a 400 million revenue company. If you bring this in, I'll make a damn good case for getting you here full-time if you want."

"Really? You think you could pull that off?"

"I don't see why not. It'll be a great coup. But we need to close the deal first."

Deanne did close the deal. Wesley made a good case for why HQ would benefit if Deanne were based in the UK, and his suggestion met no resistance. They were sad they would lose Deanne in the US, but they knew she would return to San Diego frequently, so it was just goodbye for now.

The most natural development for Matt and Deanne was marriage. This occurred one year after Deanne's arrival, first in England, where relatives and friends visited from the USA, then again in San Diego, where friends and relatives from England visited the USA. This double wedding appeased all parties concerned on both sides of the ocean.

During their first year of marriage, they acquired a dog from an animal shelter and named him Smarts.

Deanne had in mind a small dog, but she could not help noticing a Labrador-Australian Shepherd mix, standing two feet tall and weighing about seventy-five pounds, whose eyes followed her wherever she moved. She tried to ignore this but could not. When she looked in the dog's direction, his tail wagged. She feigned reluctance, looked, and said, "Oh, come on, then. You're the one."

Matt said, "That's a smart dog." Hence, his name.

They adore Smarts. He has a friendly temperament, is loyal, and is a lifelong ally, coupled with high energy and a guarding instinct. The three of them are a perfect match.

Chapter Six

Now, a full four years on from their marriage, life had delivered a savage blow neither could have conceived. Two months had passed since Deanne's attack. She was still in the hospital in a coma. Parents, friends, and relatives visited her many times. Thankfully, Jane, the housekeeper, had stepped up and offered to help more frequently, which Matt accepted with gratitude. She ensured the pantry and refrigerator were always stocked up and the house was kept in good order, enabling Matt to come and go comfortably without any undue concern.

Matt visited local animal shelters in search of a replacement for Smarts, and eventually, he spotted a puppy, a mongrel with a black coat. The pup was shivering in a corner. Matt noticed that the dog had one ear lower than the other. He picked him up, and the pup started to lick his face.

"Hey, steady Loppy," Matt said, and with that, Matt took ownership of him.

Loppy soon became acclimated to his new surroundings, though not without a few puddles on the floor or the occasional tearing at anything that looked like fun. Work and home life had returned to a facsimile of normality or as nearly normal as one would ever achieve under the circumstances.

The police had been diligent in their efforts to identify any suspects. DNA samples had been collected from volunteers, and house-to-house calls had been made, yet nothing had turned up so far. Even their hope of a dog bite report was fading. With several thousand people choosing not to provide DNA samples, they had hit a wall, especially as those who had not come forward were under no legal obligation to do so.

When Matt visited the hospital, he would always read to Deanne, tell her stories, play music, and pass on comments about current television programs. One weekday evening, before visiting Deanne, Matt came across their wedding videos. He decided to take it to the hospital to play it for Deanne. Armed with the video on his phone, he drove to the hospital.

Entering Deanne's room, he gazed at her. She looked beautiful. Traces of the attack had gone except for a few almost unnoticeable scars. Recent brain scans were all normal, and her abdomen only showed a slight line of scarring from the prior surgery. Matt kissed her, as he always did, and began to have his one-sided conversations.

Matt reached over and held Deanne's hands in his.

"I am so much in love with you, and I feel in love with you every minute, every day. The zing, whatever it is that I felt when I got near you the first time, has never diminished.

"I watched our wedding video last night and brought it in for you; some parts still make me laugh. The ceremony audio was overpowered by the sound of the massive pipe organ, and when we came out and stood at the church entrance for photos, a wind gust blew the bridesmaids' dresses up in the air, and you got the heel of your shoe caught in your dress. It was a fun wedding."

Matt kisses Deanne's forehead: sitting beside her, he holds his phone and starts playing it.

He also provides a commentary as the video is playing. The first part of the video concludes as Matt and Deanne leave the church for the reception, the last scene being of them waving from a white Rolls-Royce.

The second part of the movie, duly titled *The Reception*, opens with them welcoming their guests, followed by the obligatory speeches by the father of the bride, best man, and groom. Dinner is served, champagne flows, and the whole atmosphere is beautiful. After dinner, it was time for the bride and groom to start dancing. Matt and Deanne had chosen "Three Times a Lady" by the Commodores.

Thanks for the times that you've cared for me.

The memories are all in my mind.

And now that we've come to the end of our rainbow.

There's something I must say out loud.

You're once, twice, three times a lady.

And I love you.

Matt hears a sudden gasp, then a scream. Deanne sits bolt upright, waving her arms and pulling at the inserted tubes, which set off high-pitched alarms. Matt has Deanne in his arms in a split second.

"It's alright, darling. It's me, Matt. I'm here, sweetheart. Everything is OK."

Deanne opens her eyes, looks at Matt, and has collapsed back onto the bed by the time the nurses come into the room. They re-insert the tubes and settle her down. Deanne is coming out of her coma, still clearly dazed, weak, and disoriented, but she is coming out of it.

The nurses provided words of comfort, making sure that she felt comfortable and secure, but Deanne just stared, eyes wide open but no sound from her lips. Matt was asked to leave, just for a while, as the doctor was on their way. Though upset, he could not stay. He knew he would be in the way. He went to the waiting room filled with a particular elation he had never experienced before.

For what seemed an endless time, Matt watched doctors and nurses scurrying back and forth. Soon, Deanne is wheeled away for a CAT scan and wheeled back, still semiconscious. Matt only receives direct communication from the head nurse, who informs him that Deanne will come around gradually. She also tells him that Deanne will be very confused, probably agitated, and certainly very scared. The nurse rambles on, stating that the cerebral cortex, the part of the brain responsible for thought, perception, and behavior, is damaged and that it's too soon to determine her cognition. Matt does not really absorb what he was being told.

Over the next week, Deanne showed signs of improvement. The doctors conducted a positron emission tomography using the imaging agent fluorodeoxyglucose. Additionally, a functional MRI, monitoring real-time brain activity, indicated some level of consciousness. The physical therapists also reported that Deanne had shown signs of resistance, muscle strength, and some self-stability over the same period.

The next few days were a blur of emotion, disbelief, and prayer as family and friends visited and questioned when they could see Deanne. *How is she? Can she talk? Does she remember anything?*

Deanne was in an isolation ward with round-the-clock attendance by nursing staff, frequent doctor visits, and therapists every four hours. Matt was almost a resident visitor and encouraged to talk to her since he had been told that it would help Dianne's transition to consciousness as they were slowly weaning her off medication.

Apart from unavoidable obligations, Matt visited daily and slept at the hospital as often as possible, reciting the day's news and events. He actually had full-blown conversations and would respond to his imagined answers from Deanne. Some would say he was crazy.

He always answered, "It's the only thing that keeps me sane."

Three more days passed before Matt was allowed to get close to her; each day, he would talk to her as if she could hear him. He thought he saw Deanne try to respond. Her eyes would open, and her lips would part, only to close again after a few seconds. He was at her side every day. On the eighth visit, Matt sat in his usual place next to Deanne and greeted her with the same announcement, "Hi, Deanne. It's me again, your favorite husband."

He was shocked when she opened her glazy eyes and said in a slurry voice, "Hello, Matt. Where have you been?"

With the biggest smile, Matt says, "Right here, darling. Right here." Tears were streaming down his face, and he was sobbing uncontrollably.

"Don't cry," she said.

"I missed you, that's all," he replied.

Deanne responded, "You're silly. Now, come and lay by me. Let's go to sleep." Still dazed and sedated, she closed her eyes and went back to sleep, this time with a smile and the warmth of her husband's touch.

Chapter Seven

Leaving the hospital, Deanne receives heartfelt goodbyes, hugs, tears, and well-wishes from what seemed like all the hospital staff. Deanne was tearful and full of gratitude. Due to her life-long regimen of exercising, she healed physically faster than expected, enabling her to return home one week after awakening. However, physical and emotional therapy were still a priority every week.

Matt came along to give her unneeded encouragement for physical therapy. The emotional therapy was for Deanne alone.

Matt had told Deanne about Loppy, and he'd taken photos to show her. He said how Jane had been helping and was at the house, making it *"Spick-and-span before the lady of the house comes home."*

In the car, Matt told her, "I've been dreaming of this day every minute."

"Me too," Deanne replied.

Matt saw the smile on her face but did not feel it. Deanne tried to ease the underlying tension. She reaches over for Matt's hand, squeezes it, and with a heartfelt smile says, "I love you, and thank you so very, very much. You are my everything, and I'm so lucky to have you. Everything will be all right, darling. You don't have to worry. I just need to get used to everything: new dog, going back to work and, well, you know what I mean." She lets his hand go and says, "Look at that. We're home."

Matt pulls the car into the garage, swiftly comes around to open the passenger door, and holds his hand out to help Deanne. "I'm not an invalid, Matt," she says with a smile. "You get the bags, and I'll go inside."

As Deanne approaches the door, it opens. Loppy runs out, gives a muffled bark, sits down, looks up at Deanne with curiosity, decides she is OK, and runs up to her with his tail wagging.

Deanne becomes aware of the noise each of her steps makes while walking on the gravel of the driveway. She thinks each one is too loud and wonders why she has never noticed before. She sees Jane at the door, thinking she looks just the same. Now at the door, she could smell something, she thought, *A pie, cookies? Everything is the same. Everything except me.*

Jane remains by the door. They greet each other with a smile and a hug.

"Welcome home, dear. I've made a nice pot of tea and a Victoria sponge cake, just in case you feel a bit peckish."

Deanne touches Janes' hand. "Thank you. Thank you for taking care of Matt. I don't know what he would have done without you."

"I'll leave you two love birds alone. If you need me for anything at all, remember I'm just up the road, and I'm happy to come back for whatever you need whenever you need me." Jane kisses Deanne on the cheek and leaves.

Matt had followed Deanne through the door and deposited the suitcase at the foot of the stairs, and then he immediately came to Deanne's side.

Deanne walks into the living room, sits on the sofa, and rubs her hand along the arm several times; casting glances at all she could see from her position: the window, floor, chairs, carpet pattern, and books.

"What can I get you, my lady? What would you like to do? Go out? Stay in?" Matt asks.

She looks up at Matt, who was standing close as if waiting for a command. She thinks he looks like a waiter in a restaurant. At that moment, she begrudges everything she sees.

She looks up at Matt, then looks away; she can feel her resentment rising. At that glance, she thought Matt to be a pitiful excuse for a man. He is almost bending over in servitude. *You weak specimen, you're of no use.*

"Nothing at the moment, just to sit and—"

Matt's phone rang. "It's the detective, Brian White," Matt said.

"Not today, Matt. Not today. I don't know if there will be a day." Deanne's expression was fixed and resolute; Matt let it ring until it went to voice mail.

Deanne took a breath and smiled inwardly, fully aware that Matt was the opposite of what had flown through her head. She just wanted to vent against everything inwardly and irrationally. She also knew she would not want to manage without him and that she loved him very much.

Deanne sat in the corner of their three-person sofa. Matt moves to sit next to her. There, they sat in silence for what seemed a long time. The only sound was panting from Loppy, who had walked over and sat by their feet. Matt broke the silence.

"Brian's a nice guy. He's been in the police force most of his life. He's unassuming and not too interrogative, which I know contradicts his profession. He's been focusing on the case since day one." While Matt was talking, Deanne looked expressionless, occasionally leaning forward to stroke the dog. Matt continued without a break, updating Deanne with every detail Brian had shared regarding the investigation.

Deanne sits up and looks at Matt very deliberately and calmly. "So, really, there's nothing. What is it they say about the first forty-eight hours or something? If they don't have a lead, a suspect, or an arrest within forty-eight hours, the chances of solving the case are cut in half. And here we are, over forty-eight days later." Deanne pauses. "Matt, I need to say something, and I want you to understand that I do not need any answers, questions, or suggestions, and most of all, I'd much prefer you did not bring up what happened to me. I love you very much, probably more than before, if that's possible.

"While I was, let's say, sleeping, you were in a living hell, afraid that I might never wake up. Yet you never wavered, reading to me, showing me photographs, telling me stories. I want to ask you to be just as patient while I share with you now." Deanne smiles, raises her hand, and squeezes his cheeks.

"Time has passed for you," Deanne continues. "Not so for me. I remember everything, absolutely everything, as if it were yesterday, as in my mind, it pretty much is. I need my time now, my awake time to think. Right now, my brain is playing havoc with me. My thoughts are jumbled and nonsensical. I will call Barry White."

"Brian," Matt said. "It's Brian."

"What?" asked Deanne, cocking her head and frowning.

"You said 'Barry White.' It's Brian White." Matt grinned.

At this point, they both laughed, cuddled up together, and continued to laugh until tears ran from their eyes. Slowly, the laughter subsided, and both wept tears of sorrow and joy, releasing all the tension of their homecoming together. Questions about what to do and what to say rushed through their heads like ants in an invaded nest.

The interlude of something close to normality had diluted Matt's awkwardness, and he could see it had also reduced Deanne's strain, and her expression showed this. "I'm giving thought to what I'm saying, and for now, these will be the guidelines until I process more. OK?"

Matt nods his head in agreement.

"I will call and speak with Brian. I will also go to therapy, where I'm hoping to unburden myself, listen, learn, and do all I can to move on from where I and we have been and where we are. I want nothing more than to get to where we left off."

Deanne kisses Matt on the lips, "I love you with all my heart." They gaze into each other's eyes and simply smile. Matt says nothing.

"I will also go to physical therapy, of course. However, that is the only function where I would ask you to join me. Any time I spend with the detective and emotional therapist, I will be on my own. If I choose to discuss it with you, I will do so, and if I do not, please don't ask."

Matt said, "I won't. If that's where your thinking is, I'm 100 percent behind you."

At this, Deanne stands up, smiles broadly, and says, "OK, now. Let's check the pot of tea, and the Victoria Sponge Cake Jane made for me. Not for you, Matt, for me," she teases.

Later, they take Loppy for a walk, Deanne deliberately turning left as they exit their house, walking hand-in-hand with easier conversations. After an hour, they were back home. Deanne was more exhausted than she thought she would be and decided to go upstairs to rest. Matt caught up with office calls and responded to the many personal calls about Deanne's' return home.

As evening started to close in, and after her nap, they walked through the house at Deanne's request.

"Chinese order in, please," Deanne said.

"Sure thing. Your usual?"

"Absolutely."

As the first day came to a close, they slept in the same bed. Their feet touched, their hands touched, both of them relieved and comforted to be back together with the nightmare of the attack and the coma, temporarily not overwhelming their thoughts. It would last at least for this one night, at least for now.

The following morning, Deanne insisted Matt go to the office as normal and that she would be fine and prefer it if he did. Matt was not comfortable with her request but did not make a fuss because she seemed enthusiastic to be at home on her own. An hour later, while driving to his office, he called Deanne several times to ensure she sounded and felt okay. Deanne assured him that she was fine and told him she would let him know if she needed him, which she said with a smile.

Deanne thought she should call Brian White and get that out of the way. Picking up the card Matt had left by the phone, she entered the number.

"White here. How can I help you?"

"This is Deanne. Deanne Wallace. Matt said to call you."

"I'm so pleased you called. How are you feeling today, Deanne? It must be nice to be home?"

"I'm feeling OK and well-rested after being asleep for months."

"I've wondered if there's a convenient time for us to chat. No rush, nothing too formal. Just a chat." White was quizzing himself as she was not the normal mold of a victim, especially of such a heinous crime.

"Do I need to come to you, or will you come to the house?" she asked.

"Oh, I'll come to you, no problem at all. When is good for you?"

"Any time, as long as it's before Matt comes home. I need you to be gone before he arrives."

"No problem. I can be there in about an hour."

Brian sat in his office chair, leaned back, and tapped his forehead lightly with a pencil. *So, she does not want her husband there, but why? He knows all the details of her attack, so why not have him there?* He got up, informed his office where he was going, got into his car, and drove to meet Deanne, all the time wondering what kind of reception he would get from her.

When Deanne had finished the call, her hands started to shake. She felt sick, anxious, and nervous.

"Get a grip," she said aloud as she got up and paced around. Loppy was following her from room to room, thinking he might be going out. "The worst is over," she murmured. Her brain was starting to engage the horrific events and bring them to the surface. She realized this and started to channel her anxiety into anger.

"Who the fuck is the guy?" she screams out loud, opening her arms with palms up and her face looking upward. "You son of a fucking bitch! You raped me and then tried to kill me!

"Calm down, Deanne," she says to herself. "So, the so-called detective knows nothing, and the guy, the rapist, murdering bastard, is left to roam the streets."

She thought taking Loppy out for a walk would help her calm down. Loppy was delighted. She put on a long coat, as it was cold outside. She put an eight-inch kitchen knife in the right-hand side of her coat pocket. They walked out the front door, with her making sure it was locked.

Deanne walked up the drive and turned left, staying on the saffron, rust, and crimson leaf-laden path. She wondered at how beautiful it looked and if she would ever really appreciate the scenic views as she once did. She was temporarily distracted by Loppy as he was scuffing up and wallowing in the fallen leaves, looking at Deanne for approval of his behavior.

"Are you having fun, Loppy? I know you are. You're such a treasure."

Cars and an occasional truck would pass, both wafting up leaves in proportion to their size, providing more entertainment for Loppy.

After fifteen minutes, Deanne turned around, saying to Loppy, "Best get back; the detective will be here soon. He sounded pleasant on the phone, so let's find out if he is."

Changing her focus from Loppy's eyes and back to the path, she sees a figure in the distance walking in her direction; her heart jumps, and instinctively, she wraps her hand around the handle of the knife in her pocket and crosses to the other side of the road, continuing in the direction of her home. "Fuck, this is new," she says out loud, her voice on the verge of quivering. In her head, Deanne is becoming more aware of situations she had not readily thought of before.

As her fellow walker came nearer, she saw it was a man. When he was opposite, he nodded at her, smiling, "Lovely day for a walk," and carried on.

Deanne breathed a sigh of relief, and crossed the road, and at this moment, she realized that stuff she couldn't t control would happen or not, no matter what she did. She looked at Loppy and said, "Why can't people be like dogs, like you, like Smarts? You give unconditional love and are so faithful; all you want is to be near us. I love you, Loppy." Loppy looked up and wagged its tail, and continued investigating the leaves.

Back inside, coat off, Deanne soon heard the noise of car tires on the gravel drive, waited for it to stop, and then opened the door.

"Detective White?"

"Yes, ma'am," he said with a smile. He was at the door and showed his credentials.

Though Matt had described White, Deanne looked quizzically for a few seconds. She thought he looked old and disheveled but had a nice, kind face, not as officious as she expected.

"Come in, Detective."

"Do you mind if I take my coat off?'

"No, that's fine. They sit in the living room in the comfort of a wood-burning fire. Brian sat in one of the armchairs opposite the sofa where Deanne had placed herself.

Deanne sat back and initiated the discussion.

"Matt brought me up to date with your investigation and the police efforts, which have resulted in zero leads so far."

Brian moves as if he were going to speak.

Deanne continues, "I appreciate you not bringing out a notepad or recorder and for not opening up a conversation by stating how you will catch the attacker or any other clichéd statements.

"In the States, we see constant murders, mayhem, and misery on just about every news channel, basically whatever it takes to draw in viewers. Of course, you must have seen and heard just about everything in your line of work, along with interviewing countless villains and victims, and trying to ease a victim's pain must also be an important aspect."

Deanne stares into the middle distance and Brian waits until she begins again.

"There are no words to describe what happened to me, and I realize I'm one of a multitude of victims who feel as I do today and there will be the same number tomorrow. I'm finding it hard not to crack. I go from disgust and shame of what happened to me and feelings of guilt, no matter how unfounded. Then, I get hit with the realization that this will never really be behind me. The damage is done, and my life will be forever changed. I'll never be the person I was before the attack."

Deanne draws breath. "How will I ever confront the constant triggers? Everything is a trigger: Matt, where I live, where I go, what I do. Will I ever have sex again? My head is saying no, never. Will I ever feel free to walk alone at night on a simple mission of, of, of, of taking my dog for a walk? No. No. No!" Deanne's voice grew louder. "So, what is the way out? You tell me. What is the way out? The only way I see it is to take my own life."

"Deanne—"

"No, please listen, Detective. I'm not saying what I will do. I'm telling you what is racing through my mind every second." She sat back with her posture now less rigid. "You have to remember that my reactions and emotions are new and raw. Time does not heal all wounds; it leaves a scar as a reminder. I hope time will—what can I say—ease and formalize my wounds into being manageable.

"All I ask from you is quite simple: the truth, that's all. No embellishment, no false hope, just the truth. If I feel I have that, it may help me going forward. Now, I'll be quiet and listen to all you have to say." Deanne sat back; her posture relaxed but with intensity in her eyes.

"Do you mind if I stand up? I like to walk and talk."

Deanne nodded.

"Let me say, first off," Brian said as he started to slowly pace, "that even with my lifelong experience in all manner of crime, I've learned that there is no magic wand, neither is there justice for all, and karma is not there for everyone. You ask me to be completely truthful. My suggestion would be that you let me, us, do our job, and you dispense—"

"What can be grimmer than knowing the truth? Do you genuinely think that I would be worse off? I want to know the reality from the get-go."

Deanne's voice had risen to a crescendo with this statement. She looked up at him.

"OK. You're right when you said we've gone nowhere in your case yet, and that's not usual in a crime such as this. We have his DNA, but nothing has come up in any database, including Interpol. What would help us now is a description of anything about him: his voice, characteristics, accent, and his behavior. Anything at all, no matter how small or insignificant you may feel it is.

"I know today has been a big step," he continued. "And I'm grateful. I suggest we leave off now, and if you feel up to it in a couple of days, I'll have a female police officer visit. She can write it down, record it on her phone, whatever is better for you."

"I'd prefer to write it down," replied Deanne. "And I agree; I think that's enough for one day. I'll give you a call when I've written all I can remember. Is that good with you?"

Brian agrees. They both walk to the front door. Brian thanks Deanne again, and just as he opens his car door, he looks back and says, "You have my number. Call me anytime about anything. I have a big shoulder." He smiles and drives off.

Deanne goes to the kitchen to make a BLT sandwich. She calls Matt to let him know she had a conversation with Detective White, and it went as well as it could. She also tells him that she's having lunch and would probably just relax for the rest of the afternoon. She has a little uplift in her voice, just a little, but better.

She takes out her laptop and a legal pad and wrings her hands as a pianist would. In a detached manner, she types the headers *Victims of Attempted Murder, Rape Victims,* and *Psychological Therapy.* She reads phrases and summaries of what one experiences with PTSD, including guilt, check, fear, check, changing moods, feeling dissociation—check, check, check. She concludes she must have minor PTSD but is confident that she will improve over time on her own.

Deanne continues her research for the next five hours, only breaking off to let Loppy out into the yard and to pick up the phone when Matt calls; assuring him she is doing OK and has been busy. After consolidating her notes, she feels she has made good progress today and has improved. She decides to call her therapist, Charlotte Morgan, and postpone the session for one week. She also leaves a voicemail for Detective Brian White, saying she will get her recollections to him after seeing her.

Over the next week, Deanne certainly appeared much improved. The first evening when Matt came home, she had showered and suggested they go out for dinner. Through the coming days, they had friends visit for snacks and to play Scrabble and cards. Everything seemed to be going well, and Deanne seemed to be getting much stronger physically and mentally.

Tuesday came, and all was as it had been during the prior seven days. Matt had gone to work. Deanne had taken Loppy for his morning walk, knife always in her coat pocket. She had done more reading on victims, PTSD, and cognitive behavioral therapy. She had looked up profiling, thinking it would help with the report she had promised Brian. Reading the material did not appear to impact her; she had emotionally distanced herself from the implications as to why she was reading it.

One morning, Deanne sat on the kitchen stool, opened her computer, and poised herself to begin. She asked aloud, "Where do I start? I guess from the beginning and going out the front door with Smarts would be the best place."

She started to type:

It was after dinner, 7, 7:30 p.m. Monday, November the 5th. I left the house with our dog Smarts and turned right at the end of the driveway toward the wooded area; I don't remember seeing anyone, just a car or two passing. There were a lot of fireworks. Smarts was... Deanne stopped abruptly.

For the first time, her thoughts deliberately focused on the evening of the fifth of November and a place she had been ardently avoiding. The image of their mutilated dog flashed into her mind. Recollections came flooding in like a tsunami. She started to shake a little at first, but within a few seconds, her whole body was contorting, sweat dripped from every pore, and her head felt like an electric whisk had been forced into her brain. She had no control and tried to reach up for air as if she were drowning. Her arms flayed as she tried to stand up, then she fell to the ground as everything went dark.

Chapter Eight

s usual, Matt called around noon and thought nothing when Deanne didn't pick up. At 12:15 p.m., when her phone went to voicemail again, he was concerned, and by 12:30 p.m. he was racing home. He found Deanne in a heap, looking like a wet rag doll. She was breathing, but he could not rouse her. He called 999, and an ambulance arrived within twenty minutes, though it felt like an hour to Matt. He felt, and was, helpless.

Deanne was once again in the hospital, in stable condition but sedated.

Matt was pacing up and down and wringing his hands in torment, waiting for news from inside the emergency unit. He saw Doctor Proctor opening the door and asked, "How is she? Has she relapsed into a coma?"

"No," Paul said, "It's not a coma. Deanne suffered a severe anxiety attack from post-traumatic stress. We'll keep her moderately sedated until we feel her vitals have stabilized, probably just for a few hours."

Everyone, especially Matt, was caught off guard by Deanne's sudden change, except Charlotte Morgan. A renowned psychiatric therapist who worked at the hospital, Charlotte, was concerned after Deanne's call the week before. She understood what could happen to victims after an attack.

Charlotte knew she could not force action on Deanne, which might add to her distress.

She picked up the phone and called the nurses' station, asking if they would inform her an hour or so before Deanne was discharged.

Three hours later, she received the call. Charlotte canceled her appointments for the afternoon, got up from her chair, and started walking to Deanne's location. She opened the door to Deanne's room just as a nurse was leaving.

"Hi, Wendy. How's our patient today?" Wendy smiled at Deanne and gave a knowing nod, then looked and answered Charlotte, still holding the smile.

"I'm just leaving. She's better now she knows she's being discharged."

When Wendy had left and closed the door, Charlotte pulled up a chair by the bed and said.

"Hi, Deanne. My name is Charlotte Morgan. We've met before, though you would not remember as you were still in a coma. I'm the dreaded therapist." She gives a cheeky grin and wiggles her hands on either side of her head in a childlike gesture. "Good to see you and good to see you awake." She pulls up a chair, sits down, and clasps one of Deanne's hands between hers.

Deanne tried to smile.

"I think I remember," she said. "The nurses told me that you had visited. Were you giving me therapy when I was in a coma?"

Charlotte laughed. "No. I would come in when I knew your husband was not here and share women's talk, from shopping to cooking, TV, movies, and gossip, of course."

"Why?"

Charlotte shrugged, smiled, and said, "Well, you never disagreed with my opinions."

"Did you hold my hand like you are now?"

"Yes."

Deanne opened her eyes wider and said, "I somehow think I kind of remember. I know that sounds silly." Deanne's expression changed, and her eyes tore up. "I don't know what to say. I'm so ashamed."

Charlotte looks steadily into Deanne's eyes. "You don't need to say anything."

They sit in silence for a minute or two. Charlotte could see that Deanne was trying to piece together her thoughts.

"He took my worth away. Why me? Then I guess everyone asks that." There is another pause. "Can you help me, Charlotte? What do you—how do you make it all go away? How do I get on with my life? I'm strong, but this? This has crushed me."

Deanne hesitates, already feeling she had said too much to this stranger. She stares at Charlotte's face, then directly into her eyes, not knowing which conflicting emotions to let out the door. She turns her head away, saying in a pathetic voice, "I don't know you. What use could you be to me? You think talking about my feelings, my emotional state, is going to help?"

Deanne now starts to feel resentment, her voice rising. She gently takes her hand away from Charlottes, turns her head to look at her, and then says in deliberate, well-spaced words, "You can fuck off. You're about as much use to me as giving a blind man a pair of glasses."

Charlotte watches Deanne's head turn away from her. She waits for a short time and, in a supportive tone, says, "I recognize the difficulty, and you don't know me. I am here for you, and if you allow me, I will support you in any way that I can and maybe over time, give you the confidence to trust me."

Deanne lets out a big sigh and turns her head to speak. "I'm scared. I have no control over my mind, but I've tried to have control over my speech and my behavior, and I've managed most of the time. But it's killing me. Inside, I want to shout, scream, punch, and kick. So, no, I'm not fucking OK. Can't you see I'm fucking damaged? Damaged and fucking worthless. A lot of time, I feel like smashing everything I can get my hands on."

She was out of breath, then took a deep breath, relaxed a little, and said with pleading eyes and shaking her head, "Don't you see? No one can help me. Really, what in hell or heaven do you think you could do for me? Please answer that question: what the hell could you do for me?'

"I can be your release valve," said Charlotte, looking at her with a warm, knowing smile.

"Yes, I guess you could, and thank you for letting me, ah, express myself?"

"Deanne, I'm nonjudgmental, I'll listen, and I'll help you find the strength and courage to confront and make sense of your difficult experiences and emotions so that you can learn and thrive. You've already made a good start."

"A good start?"

"As you just said, and as you demonstrated with me today, it seems you do have a lot of control. I can help by guiding you through this crisis. I can provide you with the necessary skills to live a better life and make positive decisions to prevent another relapse."

"It's like… it's like my life didn't exist before the rape; that person is gone, and now every conversation, every choice, every action revolves around it. I will forever be defined by it. We planned to start a family, but now I can't conceive. How will you help me get through all this?"

"Very, very gently and at your own pace."

That was the beginning of a relationship that transcended therapist and patient. Over the next few months, they developed a friendship, an unspoken bond. Charlotte stayed by Deanne's hospital bed for two hours, mostly listening to Deanne, revealing how she felt about herself, how she could not reconcile logic and emotion, and felt hopelessly depressed.

Deanne slowly started to accept that the reactions she experienced were normal. The list was long, starting with her first determination when she came out of the hospital, trying to entomb what happened as much as possible, return to her normal life prior to the assault, having the willpower to be the person she was before, and see herself as a survivor, not a victim."

On one occasion, Charlotte suggested that Deanne join the group sessions. Charlotte offered to go through the benefits of group therapy, though she did point out that it wasn't for everyone. Deanne's response was swift and adamant.

"Charlotte, I don't know if I'm right, and I'm sure not excluding anything to help me. I've had tragedies in my life, nothing like this one, and I don't know how I will turn out, but I do know that pain teaches us who we are, and I'll either come out of the ashes or burn up.

I'll talk and share with you, but not with a group."

Before Deanne's release from the hospital for the second time, Charlotte decides to call Matt; she has a question for him.

"Hi, Matt. This is Charlotte Morgan. I have a quick question,"

"I need your help. I recommend Deanne have a neutral/mutual acquaintance around the house, a trusted female she knows, and someone who will not share a pity party or be inquisitive. Do you have any suggestions?"

"Yes. Jane, our housekeeper. She would be my choice, and I know that Deanne trusts her completely."

"Perfect, Matt. Thank you. Can you pop in to see me before Deanne is discharged?"

Matt had read through the contents of *A Guide for Partners of Survivors of Sexual Assault* that Charlotte had given to him, including a list of contacts for additional help containing sexual assault referral centers and independent sexual violence advisors. He was encouraged when reading how victims can and do get through this trauma and felt better when he read; *There is no right way or wrong way to be after rape. You behave how you need to in order to get through, and you need to do what feels right for you.*

Charlotte met with Matt and reiterated the display of emotions to expect from Deanne and how remembering them would help her and help him react, which included self-blame, depression, suicidal thoughts, feeling alienated, and being ashamed. He looked up and said, "Will she feel them all? I mean, it will be awful for her."

"Yes, Matt, it's highly likely. It'll be rocky for a while, but it will improve."

Matt shared with Jane what to expect before accepting the role of caregiver, along with her current position as a housekeeper.

Jane proved to be perfect. Her ability to seemingly anticipate action, reaction, emotion, and need that would help Deanne was uncanny. She was a natural-born therapist, companion, and friend.

"I don't know what I would do without you!" exclaimed Deanne after the first week.

"I remember a certain MP telling me the same," she said.

"A member of parliament?"

"No, Mary Poppins herself, if you please," replied Jane as she left the kitchen, filling the room with laughter.

As Jane spent more time at the Wallace house than her own home, Matt suggested she move in for a few weeks, as it would save her traveling every morning and night. Plus, it would be good for Deanne. The weeks became months and months to years, and eventually, Jane became a fixture in the Wallace household.

Deanne and Charlotte generally met twice a week for therapy sessions. One of the days when Deanne was out meeting Charlotte, and when Jane had gone out shopping, Matt took the opportunity to call Detective Brian White to bring him up to date about Deanne; he also needed someone other than Charlotte to share it with.

He picked up his cell phone and dialed White's number. It went to voice mail. "Err, Brian, Detective White, this is Matt Wallace. Would you call me back, please?"

Before Matt had time to move from his position, his phone rang. He saw it was White calling.

"Hello, Detective White?"

"Hi, Matt. I was just finishing up a call when you rang. How can I help?"

"I just want to make sure you know what happened to Deanne and that she is back home."

"Yes, I am aware. I was sorry to hear the news. I hear Deanne is seeing Charlotte Morgan frequently, which is a good sign, I think? Confidentiality rules, so I can only assume."

"Jane, our housekeeper, is here full time, that helps, and I feel that Deanne's visits with Charlotte are helping."

"I blame myself for Deanne's relapse. I feel helpless. I don't know—"

Brian interrupts. "Matt. I need to stop you there. You said I in three seconds. So, this is about you now. Not your wife, Deanne. The victim?"

"No, I mean. Of course not, I just—"

"This is where you step up, Matt. Think about what Deanne is going through. Your job is to support her and keep telling her how much you love her."

Brian gave his condolences to Matt and said to call him if he needed to talk or needed any help.

He gets off the phone and decides to contact Charlotte for informal information before approaching Deanne or Matt in the future.

Chapter Nine

November 5 came and went. Fireworks burst across the country with bonfires and children with their effigies of Guy Fawkes in the street shouting, "Penny for the Guy." The television was showing fireworks displays on the Thames and around Central London. Pyrotechnics were at their best.

Thankfully, Deanne had recovered enough to keep her emotions tucked, though the bangs and booms did give her a jolt.

There were times, at night, if she woke or when watching something on TV that suddenly showed sexual assault as part of the plot, she would begin feeling the trauma of that night. It took every ounce of strength not to allow herself to become overwhelmed.

Matt, for the most part, was unaware when this happened. When he saw and felt a change in her and did not know why or what had happened, he knew from Charlotte's "do and don't" list not to ask prying questions.

Deanne was conscious of the times Matt suspected she had an episode and was grateful when he was unaware or pretended he wasn't. When she had a flashback, she tried to ground herself and remember she was safe and in the present, not the past.

Nightmares would wake her with a blow. Her breath would quicken, and her skin would become moist with the onset of sweat. At these times, she would turn her head to look at a framed photograph that was visible by a soft hue from a night light. It was of her and Matt on their honeymoon, a happy distraction.

Her most impactful reminder, which she loathed and feared most, was the rare occasion when she had a total interlude of peace, and her attention, was completely absorbed with joy and gratitude.

All of this happened in seconds, taking Deanne back to the worst place possible. Without a word, she changed. This was the most challenging of times for Deanne to control. But she did, at least from those she loved and cared about. She would move, do something, anything for a distraction.

These were the periods Matt noticed most and calmly asked, "Are you OK?" or, "What's up?" he would ask.

Deanne would force a smile and say, "Oh, nothing."

During one of the passive appointments with Deanne, Charlotte reminded her of the one thing she had not addressed over the past year. "I know I've mentioned this before, but when you can, bring yourself to tell me what happened the night of the attack, and with your permission, of course, I would like to give the results to Brian White and see if it gives him any clues."

Deanne didn't react beyond repeating what she had said before, "Yes, one day, maybe; what is the point? Too much time has passed, and nothing has happened, so reliving that night is not something I'd leap at."

"That's OK. When you're ready." Charlotte replied.

On her drive back home, Deanne thought of the attack and wondered if she would, or could ever, relive the details. She took a sharp breath and said aloud, "No." She pondered a few seconds more, then selected her favorite current pop station on the radio, turned the volume up, and sang along, hoping the high level would dampen the unpleasant noises in her head.

Deanne was aware that her conflicting internal dialog to share or not share details was day by day. She asked herself questions on her lone drives: *If I don't disclose everything to Charlotte, how can she properly support me? But what if I have another relapse?*

The only decision she made after six days was to research for help online five days before her next therapy meeting.

In the quiet of the master bedroom, seated by the dresser with a view of the serene rear garden, Deanne opened her laptop and typed, "What should I discuss with my therapist about my rape?" Her search yielded a multitude of sites and articles. After twenty minutes of browsing, she closed her computer.

She read, "You can tell your therapist anything, and they hope you do. *Therapy just doesn't work if you can't trust your therapist. It's a good idea to share as much as possible because that's the only way they can help you.* She had seen enough to make her decision.

Deanne went to her next therapy session. She sat down and said, "Charlotte, I'm going to tell you about the night I was attacked. I feel I can do it by changing the story to a third person, so I'm not saying 'I.' I'll say 'she.' Is that OK with you?"

Charlotte agreed. "I'll record it and write a transcript, let you read it and approve, then give it to Detective White if you agree," she said.

Deanne responded placidly, "That works for me, but I don't want to read the transcript. Just give it to Brian with the caveat that he does not come back and ask questions. OK? I ask that you make that clear to him."

"No problem. Would you like me to give you something to calm you?"

"No, I'm good."

"OK. I suggest I dim the lights a little, and you lay down, but don't fall asleep." Charlotte smiled to ease the situation.

Deanne, as if she were detached, started her account of that night in the third person and began, "She left her house with her dog, Smarts." There were silent periods where breathing was the only sound; Deanne would pause, seemingly thinking before she continued. Her voice was not strained. She did not cry. She was strong and deliberate. Deanne finished her story by saying, "Then she woke up in the hospital."

It was good that the light had been turned down and that Charlotte was not where Deanne could see her. Charlotte had a lot of experience, many years of victims, and had heard many heart-wrenching stories. This one was the most painful she had experienced, and she was quietly in tears.

More telling was how Deanne recounted the events, correcting herself on occasion, almost as if she were reading a story. Charlotte wanted to rush over and hug Deanne, comfort her, and do anything she could to ease her pain, but she knew she could not remove it. The calm of her reciting the event's details moved Charlotte, particularly when she said, "She didn't feel any pain anymore. It was like she was out of her body. She could hear the sounds of the thuds when she was kicked but not feel them."

This was when Charlotte, unnoticed by Deanne, broke down herself.

Deanne described a smell "like paint and oil." She also noted. "At some points, he screamed, emphasizing particular words, and he wasn't just angry. It was like he was in a jealous rage. She also thought there was something on his face, a wet leaf, probably."

When Deanne finished, she just said, "That's it," closed her eyes, and remained still. She seemed serene.

Charlotte was grateful as this interlude gave her time to regain her composure and professional poise before resuming the session. Ten minutes later, Deanne sat up. They both drank coffee and talked. The content of that day was never brought up again in conversation. The therapy sessions continued step by step.

Brian White received the transcript. It moved him too, but there was nothing that would point him in any direction that would potentially help identify a possible assailant. When he'd asked Denne and Matt if they could provide any possible suspects, the only person that came to Deanne's mind was Mitch, the unknowingly married man she had an affair with. Though he thought it unlikely, he still checked out Mitch and his wife to no avail.

He tried countless avenues and constantly checked records for any related crimes, but nothing new turned up to improve the stalemate position he and the police department were in.

Chapter Ten

Deanne was ready to resume work in London for the San Diego Economic Development Council. Wesley had kept in touch with Deanne during her recovery. Deanne had been anxious to get back to work and was grateful for Wesley's going out of his way to bring her up to speed and assuring her that her work was covered for as long as needed.

When Deanne felt strong enough to return to the office, she informed Wesley she would return to work in four weeks. This allowed him to prepare staff accordingly,

Deanne decided to use Uber for work on the first day. She felt returning to work was a positive step and accepted the nerves and anticipation as a welcome change.

The first day was awkward for all involved, but one by one, the staff welcomed Deanne back, and the tension eased. As Wesley walked Deanne to her office, he said, "It's great to have you back."

"It's great to be back," she smiled and replied.

Deanne, however, isn't as she seems. Inside her head, there's a mix of anger and loathing, mostly aimed at her attacker, the rest aimed at everyone in the office and even the Uber driver this morning.

This day is the first time she is fully engaging in normal, and *she* feels like screaming at them. She sits in her office and looks out at her *normal* colleagues in the main office, wanting to say, "Do you fucking know what it's like to wonder if the man you see is the one, you know, the one that tried to kill me. Was it you? Did you do this to me? Was it you and forever looking over your shoulder?" Rage pulsed through her veins, but she made no outward signs.

When anyone gave a smile or waved or gave a thumbs up as they passed her office, her mouth curved into a smile, sometimes with a nod accompanied by an inaudible statement, one of them being, "Do you know that in the elevator today, I was scared when a fucking man got in; he looked as if he was smirking, as if he knew that I'd been raped."

She is startled back to her surroundings by a knock on her door, followed by Wesley walking in, "You jumped; are you deep in thought?"

"Yes, just getting my head engaged and catching up. Feels good." She lied, shaking her shoulders in gesture.

"Let me know if you need anything."

"Will do," Deanne said.

As she became involved in work, she thought, "He could be anywhere and probably nowhere near here." He was, in fact, closer than she could imagine.

The San Diego Economic Development Council was delighted when Deanne returned to work in London. Potential clients considering an expansion to California were more at ease to hear a familiar American accent. It also helped that Deanne took the time to read up on their respective business before she engaged with them. She also knew the London streets well by now and was happy to visit clients, many of whom were unfamiliar with the area.

She made various business trips in and around the city. One of her trips landed her in Hammersmith, an area where one of the potential clients had his business. She stopped at the traffic lights on King Street, near the HSBC Bank, and parked. To her left, the occupant was getting out of a white van, his purpose to cash a check he had just received after completing a window replacement in the area. The large lettering on the van stated:

Renovation—Roofing, Plumbing, Painting, Emergency Callouts

Mike Walker Services, Ltd.

No Job Too Small!

Deanne did not notice the van; it was just one of many vehicles on the road. Even if she had looked, she would have only seen the back of the occupant as he opened the door to the bank. If she had arrived at the lights three minutes earlier or eleven minutes later, she would have seen the occupant and may have recognized him. It would not be the last time she encountered the van.

In addition to her professional demands, Deanne had other pursuits, as Jane had taken over many household responsibilities.

Matt's plan to replace the old wooden garages with a three-car block-built garage and annex was nearing completion. The annex idea was initially to accommodate Deanne's family and guests when they visited from overseas. The plan changed, and they offered the annex to Jane, which she eagerly accepted.

The new structure was joined to the house by a ten-foot covered walkway. From the rear of the garage, Jane could walk directly through to her laundry room, and from there, she could enter her compact two-bed/two-bath annex. The kitchen was open to the living room. The windows and glass patio doors provided a pleasant view of the rear garden. This was her favorite area: peaceful, picturesque, and where she would often sit and read.

Jane had come up with the idea of renting her house, the advantage being that it was not too far from the Wallace household and nicely situated with the rear garden backing onto the local park. Her home had been built almost ninety years ago, a two-story, back-to-back terrace house with a cellar. Three bedrooms with a bathroom and kitchen overlooking the family room. The basement, which had originally been used to house a furnace and store coal, was a damp unused space.

Deanne suggested that Jane rent her property as a holiday home.

"Good idea. Supplemental income. How would it work?" Jane asked enthusiastically.

"Our office in the US normally uses hotels and I guess that my office alone would use three or so months a year. You would need to charge less than hotels, and with hotel prices in London, you will still make really good money." Deanne rubbed her thumb and forefingers together.

Jane beamed and raised her eyes. "Sounds great. You're right; I wouldn't want my house to be rented out all year. I mean, it's still my house, and I might like to go there sometimes. We could use Airbnb."

"We could, but I'd suggest not. Our office tried it, and for us, it didn't work. Changing dates caused us a headache. In the US, I know some people who use Airbnb. Most liked it, but they had problems if they had disputes.

"No, let's do it on our own first and see how it goes," Jane said.

Making this happen occupied Deanne and Jane over the next few weeks, creating a website and social media links, including local tourist information centers. Both found this an exciting labor of love. Deanne said she would take care of California's postings and establish appropriate rentals.

It did not take long for bookings to materialize. The first occupants were on business from the San Diego office for five days. Other potential visitors who inquired through Jane's site were checked out by Deanne, who would automatically run background checks before deciding whether to accept the clients.

Charlotte had told Deanne that the symptoms she had can sometimes get in the way of everyday life, and to help manage her tension and anxiety, Deanne should find distractions from her memories. Overseeing Jane's Holiday Home Bookings is now one of them, and when she reads an article in a magazine, she finds another: "*You have a 96% better chance of avoiding a heart attack if you can perform forty consecutive pushups.*" Though fitness and strength training had been part of her routine before the attack, she had found it harder than she thought to get back into a regime. She had been running on the treadmill and using a few low weights, but not like she used to do. The article was the catalyst to a new start, more so as she found, to her dismay, that six pushups were all she could manage. Deanne decided to enroll at the local gym and find a no-nonsense trainer. When she inquired who the best trainer was, the receptionist enthusiastically recommended Tommy. Deanne approached him and asked if she could book training sessions with him.

"I'm probably not the best person for you. I mostly train athletes, but I can recommend one of the others," responded Tommy dismissively. Deanne, indignant, looked him in the eyes, then at his nametag.

"I've trained hard before in school and college. Cheerleading to martial arts, and don't scoff at cheerleading. It's physically demanding, and training is just as hard as any other athlete. I know. I did both."

Tommy stared at her and sighed. Deanne guessed he was about to rebut her.

"Listen, Tommy; they said you train people hard, and that's what I want to do. Will you train me?" Deanne asked angrily.

"I'm sorry, ma'am. I wasn't being rude. It's just that I've had complaints about the way I push people. At my last gym, I was canned after I lost my patience and told this lady she was wasting her time and mine. I get people coming in with great expectations and targets they want to reach. Most of them don't want to do the work to get there."

"You're just what I need. I don't care what shit you give me. I want to get strong, fit, and learn kickboxing; I want something to take,"—" Deanne faltered.

"Something you can take your pent-up anger out on?" Tommy suggested, shrugging his shoulders. "Why did you do martial arts for cheerleading?"

"It wasn't for cheerleading, but it sure helped. I could see the karate classes when I went to my workouts and basic fitness classes, and one day, I thought I'd try it. I liked it, and that's all I did. It was a great full-body workout. I also did taekwondo a few years later for about three years. I reached the red belt and competed in the San Diego taekwondo tournaments. I did pretty well." Deanne gave a wry smile. "Please?"

"OK, let's make a schedule. But if you limp out or wimp out, don't put the blame on me. I can't afford to lose another job."

Tommy was not big, not tall, but every inch of his body was toned. He was all work, not one for idle chit-chat, and was true to his word. He kept Deanne on her toes. He didn't try to break her down or ask her to do exercises he did not think she could do. Over time, he methodically increased her workload to her maximum capacity.

At first, he had Deanne use weight machines after six weeks; Tommy changed her routine to include free weights and the stair climber. Later, he introduced the jump rope and the kickboxing bag.

When Deanne came to the gym, it was all work, with or without Tommy. As soon as her session was over, she left right away, drenched in sweat and red-faced. She was sometimes sore and just threw a quick "Thank you, Tommy" on her way out the door. Deanne never made any friends at the gym; she would nod to acquaintances she recognized, but that was all. She was there almost daily, but she was on a mission.

The final phase that Tommy immersed Deanne in remained much the same, but he added increased weight to keep her working hard. The key addition was that Tommy functioned as an opponent in kickboxing rather than t the bag. He took it slowly and cautiously at first; however, he quickly adapted to Deanne's strength, speed, and power. How she channeled her anger when she kicked or punched impressed Tommy. On one occasion, she leaped and gave him a forward kick in the stomach for which he was not prepared. It took his breath away and knocked him to the floor. Deanne apologized.

He held up his hand, caught his breath, and puffed, saying, "No. No. Good job."

From that moment, she always fought aggressively, and he had to be on guard and on top of his game every time. Sometimes, people would stop to watch them; it was furious, fast, and powerful. The bouts would last until one of them put their hand up. Both would be exhausted and breathing heavily, and both normally sustained a few bruises or bumps to take home.

Deanne had physically changed and was in the best shape she had ever been. *Toned and tight*, she would say to herself. She was also much more confident. Deanne soon reached the stage where she did not need Tommy as frequently, though Tommy would come up with a smile and ask, "Wanna fight?" Deanne always said yes.

This was off the clock, with no payment time. They never became friends as such. Tommy never asked any questions of Deanne or she of him. Most communication was about health and fitness. Deanne also exceeded the forty-pushup goal. She would do a hundred in perfect form as a warm-up every day.

One recurring question that persisted in Deanne's mind was *why* she was attacked. It was a question she had initially asked the police, Detective White, Charlotte, and physicians. The Detective was the only one with a questioning rationale, and he'd said, "I've asked myself the same question countless times, and I come up with the same answer: you were targeted. If you had been followed, it's likely that you would have seen, or at least heard, something, someone, or even seen a vehicle. For the attacker to be in the woods, at night, alone and waiting for you, means that he knew you and where you walked with your dog."

Detective White was right.

Deanne wondered if she had been in the great shape she was now in on that night; she might have been able to fight off her attacker.

Chapter Eleven

eanne took the opportunity to reconnect with her family and friends in the US, even attending a school reunion where, thankfully, the attack remained unspoken. Most were unaware of what had occurred.

Deanne was forewarned by her old classmates from performing arts that they would give rebirth to an old school musical, *Ragtime*, which they had performed in her college years, and for Deanne to prepare; initially, she declined, though later accepted as she felt it would be a good deviation from regular life.

Whenever Matt and Deanne were with others who knew about Deanne's past trauma, they sensed how they were noticeably still uncomfortable, picking their words with care. Of course, this was understandable. Reaching the same harmony and natural quality as before Deanna's' attack would take time.

Thankfully, this awkwardness with others subsided in proportion to the frequency of visits. It was as if each event created a thin layer of effortlessness toward the next meeting.

Matt and Deanne would comment. "If they could just relax a little, it would be so much better."

Matt and Deanne watched TV more regularly, and their jokes became more natural; laughter was not forced; bedtimes and being naked were as they had been before. Conversely, their conversations regarding intimacy were stilted for quite a while. They were at ease kissing and cuddling on the sofa and in bed, but any move by Matt that remotely indicated that physical intimacy was the next step was firmly halted.

As the tenseness reduced, a physical closeness began to return.

One evening, no different from recent evenings, Deanne came through the front door. Similar welcomes and questions about her were as usual. Deanne went upstairs to the bedroom to shower. But tonight, she paused to look back at Matt.

Matt looked at Deanne. "You OK, sweetheart? Anything I can do for you?"

"No, I was just looking. I just want you to know that I love you so very, very much."

"I love you very, very much too." Matt smiled at her.

"I know," Deanne said warmly as she ascended the rest of the stairs with tears in her eyes. She felt guilty and sorry that she had not really thought of how he was coping or what he'd been through. She thought he'd always be there, helping, supporting, understanding, and loving. In the shower, her tears met with the water spray. *I need to open up to Matt,* she said to herself.

After dressing and brushing her hair, she walked downstairs to the living room, where Matt was seated on the sofa.

Deanne joined him, sitting close, and held his hand, saying,

"You make me feel good, and I'm flattered that you still find me desirable." She held her hand up as she could see Matt's mouth open to speak. "Men will never understand women. We do preen, and if an ensemble is complete and you are feeling beautiful, well, a chipped fingernail can ruin that feeling in a heartbeat. So, with that in mind, you can probably guess what I feel like about myself physically." The hand went up again. "I'm grateful that my loving husband finds me appealing," She smiled. "I'm not immune. I do see that some guys will look at me, and I'm both pleased and disgusted at the same time, and that's something only I can deal with. It's the memory of what happened and the chipped nail thing; I don't feel sexy or beautiful.

I love you, and there've been times when I thought you might be repulsed by me and that making love to me would be the last thing you would want to do. Yet I also know in my heart that you don't feel like that. It's hard for me to explain."

There was not much more conversation that evening. Yet, Matt's loving and reassuring presence eased Deanne's apprehension, making her feel more relaxed. They found solace in the unshakeable strength of their bond, finding comfort in its enduring stability.

Navigating this journey, they mutually escalated their physical intimacy, and eventually, they reconsummated their marriage. It was never the same as it had been, as circumstances and their life had changed. Sex was enjoyable for both, and the activities were no different from what they had been before the attack. It did not bother them; neither did they speak of it, mainly as there was nothing to say. It was intangible. If either had known how to vocalize it, they would have, but thankfully, nothing carried any weight.

Matt maintained contact with Brian White and was forever hopeful that some development had taken place in Deanna's case. It had not, but Brian had not given up. They would meet at a pub, local to Brian or Matt, but never at the police station, as there was no need for formality since they had become comrades. Deanne would join them on rare occasions, always with the understanding that her case would not be brought up in conversation. They had agreed that only when a suspect had been identified would anyone approach Deanne and that Matt would be the first to hear.

This was why Brian was caught off-guard when Deanne called his cell phone and asked if they could meet up unofficially and without Matt.

Brian agreed and asked, "Shall we make it a dinner date then?"

Deanne snickered, "OK, a date it is, and you pay the check."

It was now June, nineteen months after Deanna's attack.

Brian got to the restaurant early. It was nothing too upscale, just his local casual dining choice where he could choose peace and quiet in the dining room or probable conversation in the bar area, on bar stools, or in the booths, with a good atmosphere throughout.

It was a place he visited quite often, so when he asked for a booth away from "ears," they knew exactly what he meant.

Deanne arrived on time. She turned a few heads, more so when she sat in the booth and was greeted by Brian, a much older man.

"This is a nice place, Brian; I've not been here before," she said.

"Nice to see you too. You look great. Does Matt know you're on a date?" He chuckled.

"God forbid, he might get jealous," she fired back.

They settled down. A waitress approached them with menus and placed a wine list on the table. "May I get you something to start your evening off?"

"Hi, Sally," said Brian. "Are you doing well?"

"Never better. Good to see you again."

Brian asked Deanne if she liked red wine and suggested a cabernet sauvignon.

"Good for me," she answered.

The waitress asked Brian, "2015 Hall Napa Valley Cabernet Sauvignon?"

"Yes, that's the one." He smiled.

Deanne smirked. "Well, I can tell you don't come here often."

"I'm old. I need comfort, and I don't like change."

Deanne ordered rosemary braised lamb shanks, and Brian chose a filet mignon. He said it went well with the wine. The one bottle lasted through dinner, and neither had room for dessert. The table was cleared, and they sat, wine glass in hand.

Brian intentionally waited until the end of the meal before asking Deanne why she asked to meet. He did not expect Deanne's casual directness when he asked, "Deanne, I know I'm a catch for any young lady, but I'm guessing you've asked me out for a reason other than my good looks." He raised his eyebrows.

"What does Matt say about me to you? I mean, how does he say I am?"

"I don't follow you. What are you asking?"

"I know Matt's kept in contact with you since the beginning. I know you're pals, and I know you meet up. Other than generic talk, he does not tell me anything. He would, but I asked him not to. I know you know all of this. I also know that you care about me, that you're disappointed that you have no results, and from what I detect the more you've gotten to know Matt and me, the more you feel that you've let me down.

"You're one of life's nice people, Brian. Very tough when you need to be, but you have a natural compassion, and that's the way you're made.

"I love Matt beyond anything. He truly is the love of my life, and that's a constant. I also know and feel that Matt loves me too. What I'm asking is, how does Matt think I am? What does he say about me, good and bad? I'm fine with both. For example, does he think he needs to always protect me? Does he think I'm weak and vulnerable? And most importantly, is Matt himself with me, or is he forever on eggshells? I want to know how Matt is. I'd like to feel that he and I are moving along the same path."

Brian sat back, removed his pipe from his inner jacket pocket, and said, "I wish I could light this thing." He sniffed the bowl and promptly put it back.

He said, "Deanne, you and he are interchangeable. What you feel about each other, your love, caring, and path, as you put it, is the same. He goes out of his way to be himself, and from what I gather, he takes more risks than I would. I'm all for a peaceful life. He cares about getting you to feel good about yourself. Of course, he would love to meet the guy who caused the pain, and he does express himself very well with what he would do to him if he did, though that topic has tailed off. Matt has continually told me he's the luckiest guy in the world having you as his wife. What was it he said? Something like, 'Deanne's the part of my life that was missing, and if I had not found her, my life would have been empty?' Something like that."

Then Brian laughed. "Vulnerable? Matt calls you Wonder Wife, and he's said a few times how he admires you, how mentally and physically strong you are, determined, resilient, and, at the same time, caring and thoughtful. In fact, he's said that he'd like half the qualities you have."

Deanne exhaled and, smiling, said, "That's so Matt. So dammed nice. Now, what about you, Brian? Do you feel you've let me down? You haven't, you know."

Deanne did not get an expected answer to her question. Brian sipped his wine and said, "Yes and no. Or I don't know. That's hard for me to answer. The point is, Matt is right to call you Wonder Wife as, truthfully, you're an anomaly. I've been on the force for what seems like a hundred years, appeared in court countless times, and I've seen and heard things that make horror movies seem tame. Through your—let's call it an ordeal—you've had all the expected emotions and reactions that a traumatic event brings, but I have to say, I've never known anyone come through the way you have. You've been remarkable and fought all the way. So, I ask myself, is it because I've gotten to know you and Matt so well? And the answer is no. I still keep in touch with some of the culprits and victims of crime from twenty years or more ago."

Deanne insisted, "Well, none of that answers my question. How can you say yes and no? Or you don't know?"

Brian said. "That's all I have; there's nothing to add. Anyway, I think Matt will be wondering why you're not back home yet." At this, Brian started to stand.

"Oh no, you don't," she said. "You're not getting off that lightly. What are you not saying?"

Brian sat down and, with a fatherly tone, said, "Deanne, I truly don't know that answer. There are times when I feel I've let you and Matt down and times when I think that good forces were preventing me from finding the guy. If I explain my reasoning, it will probably hurt you."

Deanne was calm and folded her arms. "Mm, now you have to tell me. I'll be the judge on whether you've let me down or not, OK? It's all right, Brian. I doubt you'll change my emotional state much. I may be pissed off with you, but then you'll have to buy me another dinner." With that, she leaned forward, looked into his eyes, smiled, and said, "Please, start, and don't leave anything out."

"OK. But don't say I didn't warn you." He took another sip of wine. "Victims, especially of rape or sexual assault, are mostly afraid of being blamed; this is particularly true for women. I'm talking generally, not specifically, about your situation. Do you know that 63 percent of sexual assaults are not reported? Victims are too traumatized to report the assault.

The court proceedings are archaic when it comes to this crime in particular. Why?

Because Courts are open to the public, and journalists can be there to report on the case. Plus, there's a prosecuting attorney, the defense attorney, and the jurors. So, a whole room of people listening to the victim share the most intimate details.

OK, it's against the law for anyone, including journalists, to publish your name or any details that might identify you, including on social media. But does it work 100%? No.

Apart from the victims having to go through every detail, everything that happened, for example, what clothes they wore, why they went out, what led up to the attack, and whether they tried to fight the attacker off. Basically, victims can be asked any question they think may rattle you. Every eye in the courtroom is fixed in the victim's direction as they speak. It's likely the defense attorney will show no respect, and they'll find the weak spots, which, more often than not, are humiliating questions that must be answered. The victim's character will be dragged through the mud during the trial with such questions as, *how many partners you have had? How much do you drink? Did you drink before you left home?* The defense's job is to undermine the victim. The questions are part of the unfortunate and emotionally difficult reality of what it's like for a sexual assault survivor to go through the criminal justice system. The burden is more on the victim. Remember, innocent until proven guilty. That Deanne is a brief summary of the despicable ordeal that faces any rape victim. I could go on, but I won't.

I want to catch the villain, not just because of your case, but I wonder if he has done it before and will he do it again. The odds are that he has, and he will. Every day, I hope to see a DNA match, hopefully deceased. Apart from what I've described about what would happen in court, I'm haunted with *beyond a reasonable doubt.* I've seen enough accused perpetrators smirk at their victims as they walk out of the courtroom, and that's the biggest kick in the face.

Deanne looked shocked. "What the—what more do you need, Brian? You have me, the witness, and his DNA. Plus, if you found him, a scar from where my dog bit him. These are facts, not guesses." Her voice rose, causing other diners to look in their direction. Deanne and Brian looked back at them and smiled before returning to each other.

Brian said, "I know. I know. But what would your answer be to the question, 'Did you get a good look at him? Could you pick him out in a line-up? What was he wearing?' The defense attorney would probably say something like, 'So, you don't know what he looked like, and it could be anyone. You have no description of my client at all.'"

Deanne was suppressing her anger and doing her best to be calm and speak at normal volumes. She had to sit back and begin to take all this in. More triggers were going off than from a battalion of riflemen. She poured the remainder of the wine into her glass and gulped it down. They sat quietly for a few minutes. Deanne leaned over the table closer to Brian.

"I'm OK, Brian. I'm not going to collapse or anything, but what the fuck? I'm angry, violently angry, and I feel like screaming and smashing this bottle on the table." She picked up the bottle, put it down again, and exhaled deeply. "I mean what the fuck? Sorry, sorry. Now I understand what your issue is and what my issue is. So, you catch him, we go to court, I relive my experience, get humiliated, and online, hey, and it hits the news big time. Then a pity party from all the do-gooders and rape groups, and the guy stands a reasonable chance of walking out the court and giving me the finger, or as you do in Merry Old England, the V sign. Have I summed it up?"

Brian supportively rested his hands on hers. "Yep, pretty much."

She responded, "Well, the dinner and the company were good, but you need to brush up on your after-dinner anecdotes." She was calmer; she even forced a little smile. "I will be a victor, not a victim. There is only one thing that causes a woman to be raped, a rapist, and this bastard left me for dead. Please don't mention this part of the evening to Matt. It'll bring him down, and I don't want that. Let me know if CODIS ever brings up a DNA match.

Good night, Brian, and thank you. Oh, I'm leaving you with the bill." She put her hand on his before she walked out of the restaurant.

Brian sat there for a while longer, more amazed than ever at Deanna's composure and strength. *Wonder Wife for sure,* he thought.

Deanne called Matt and said she was on her way. He asked if she had had a good night. She said the dinner was great, which it was. She did not add anything more. Reaching home, she went inside, kissed Matt, and said, "Brian's a super guy, and dinner was great." Nothing more was described beyond the content of the dinner and the nice wine.

When Matt called Brian a few days later, he asked about the evening with Deanne. He responded much as Deanne had but added, "She is an incredible woman, Matt, and yes, you're the luckiest guy I know."

Chapter Twelve

Mike Walker had no criminal record. He had accumulated traffic infractions during his thirty-three years of driving, but nothing serious. With an average height, weight, and appearance, he would not be noticed in a crowd other than the discolored skin of a faded birthmark over his right eye.

After leaving school at sixteen, Mike drifted between nondescript occupations, always for the same reason: boredom. One day, the opportunity for a stable income drew him toward general laboring for a small, local building construction company.

Initially, he would clean and prepare construction sites by removing debris, loading or unloading building materials, digging trenches, backfilling holes, and doing physical and manual work. He didn't enjoy laboring, but the money was good and enabled him to purchase a small apartment, albeit one needing decorating and modernizing. Through the next few years, he would ask, watch, listen, and learn skills from the respective tradesman, from painting to plumbing, woodwork to electric wiring, and everything in between. Mike would not classify himself as a craftsman; he was a tradesman and handyman. Through trial and error and re-dos, he modified and decorated his own abode, increased its value, sold it at a good profit, and purchased a small house, again needing decorating and modernizing. Mike repeated this action several times, ultimately affording him to start his handyman business.

Mike would drink at his local pub, The Wooden Badger, after work most nights of the week. He didn't drink excessively; it was his way of finishing up his day. This was where he met Anna. He noticed her slender figure and attractive face draped by her jet-black hair.

She noticed that he had looked over at her a few times. She picked up her glass, walked over to Mike, and asked, "May I join you?"

Mike said, "Yes, sure."

Anna sat down opposite him. Mike was not naturally a talker, especially with women, yet he found Anna easy to speak with. She told him she was born in England but had Ukrainian parents who had recently moved back to Ukraine. She worked as a waitress at a nearby hotel and lived with a female friend in an apartment. Mike shared that he was single, had a handyman business, and lived independently.

Anna remarked, "Oh, so you're not married. I thought you would have been snapped up by now."

Mike enjoyed the compliment; his normally guarded self was being exposed. This began their relationship, resulting in marriage eight months later. For the first year, married life was no more, no less, than most newly married couples enjoyed. Anna continued working at the hotel, and Mike continued to visit The Wooden Badger at the end of his working day. These two facets caused arguments between them. Mike was not comfortable with Anna being a waitress, and he would question her and become jealous at the thought of, as he would say, "all the other men ogling her."

In turn, Anna asked Mike, "Why do you have to go to the pub before you come home?"

Into the second year of marriage, Mike noticed that Anna was becoming more irritated at what he termed nothing. Their life was good. They had little debt and money in the bank. They dined out weekly, occasionally went to the movies and theater, and took four-day trips two to three times a year. Mike suggested that Anna give up her job, as they did not need her income. Maybe start a family, he suggested.

He saw a revolted look on Anna's face he had never seen before. It went as quickly as it came. Then she smiled, apologized, kissed him, and said, "Thank you, Mike. Thank you for everything. It's just me. Maybe it's early menopause or something." She joked.

After that, Anna was seemingly back to normal with no sign of irrational irritability. On a Sunday evening two weeks after their verbal exchange, Anna said, "I have an early start and late evening tomorrow. I need to step in for one of the girls who's taking time off. I should be back by eleven or so."

"You never work evenings. Can't they find someone else?"

"No. I'm doing it as a favor. I won't do it again. I promise." She smiled and kissed him on his nose.

Anna was up and dressed by six a.m. She kissed Mike on the cheek and said, "I'll see you later, sweetheart."

She parked her car at the hotel where she worked, put the keys on top of one of the tires, hailed a taxi, and went straight to Heathrow Airport to catch the 8:50 a.m. flight to Ukraine.

Mike went off to work as normal. He tried to call Anna, but it went to voice mail. This was not unusual. She would mute or switch off her phone during busy periods and call back when she had a break. He thought it odd that she had not called or texted, but he was not concerned. It was 7 p.m., so the dinner shift was well underway.

At 9 p.m., he was getting genuinely concerned, muttering, "She would have had a bathroom break and texted or called." She normally did. Mike left text and voice messages, and by 10 p.m., he was panicking. He called the restaurant host's number.

"Hi, this is Mike, Anna's husband. Do you know if Anna has left yet?"

"*Sorry. Was Anna here?*"

"Yes. She's been working the day and evening shift today."

There was silence on the line for a moment, then, "*Mike, I don't think we've met. I'm Emily. I work the evening shift. I don't know Anna well as she's usually gone by the time I arrive, though we have spoken a few times. I don't know what to say. I'd heard that Anna left a week ago from Zoey. She does the lunch-to-dinner crossover with Anna. She would know more than I do. I can see she's busy now, but she'll be finished in about an hour.*"

Mike said, "OK, I'll speak with Zoey later. Thank you, Emily." He put the phone down, feeling light-headed and bewildered, and could not take in what Emily had said. His mind was desperately seeking to make order out of disorder. *She's going to surprise me, that's it; she will tell me she's given up work, and we'll start a family. Emily must be mistaken. She said Anna stopped working a week ago. But why did Anna not tell me?*

Mike walked into their bedroom and opened Anna's closet. *All her clothes are here.* He checked the rest of the house; nothing was gone. *She'll be back. I'll pretend I don't know anything when she tells me what she's up to. I'll act totally surprised.* Deep inside, he knew something was very wrong, but he tossed out that feeling like trash.

Eleven p.m. became midnight with no sign, text, or call. Anna's phone was still turned off.

Mike was wandering from room to room for any clue, any sign. He was immersed in a feeling of dread. He sat down and started to shake; he did not know what to do. *She can't go anywhere; there's nothing missing. It's all here.* His mind suddenly went to a place he had not looked. In a panic, he ran to his closet, grabbing a stool on his way. Standing on the stool, he retrieved a small box from the top of the closet shelf. Mike opened the box, and the flood of all his fears came pouring out, along with all the crushing blows that dashed his uncertainties about Anna's abandonment. Her passport, personal papers, and £25,000 were missing. The £25,000 was the accumulation of cash they had both received since being together from Anna's tips and Mike's cash-paying jobs.

Mike felt as if all the air had been sucked out of him. His world crashed. Then he remembered Anna's friend Zoey, with whom she used to share an apartment. He did not know her well, but he remembered where they both lived. It had a blue door near a fish and chip shop. Mike jumped up, grabbed his van keys, went out the door, and took off toward Cannon Street, twelve miles away. Twenty minutes later, he was outside the door of Zoey's apartment, pressing the door buzzer.

"*Hello*," came a voice.

"Zoey, this is Mike. Can I speak with you? It's urgent. Anna's gone." The *click* of the door lock sounded, and he walked through. Zoey opened her ground-floor apartment door. Standing still in the dimly lit hallway, he saw a brighter light emerging from the second door on his right. He heard a voice.

"In here," she said.

Mike walked the short distance to where she stood holding the door open. She was dressed in a light gray cotton pajama set and black fluffy socks, her normally straight black hair now tousled as she had just risen from her bed.

"Sorry, Zoey. I had no one else to ask."

Mike scanned from right to left, seeing an open plan space containing a small kitchen and a living room with a two-seater sofa opposite an armchair separated by a rectangular black wood coffee table with white painted drawers. Pointing to the armchair, Mike asked, "Shall I sit here?"

"Yes, anywhere is fine," Zoey said as she sat opposite, curling her legs underneath her and pulling a red throw blanket off the arm of the sofa to wrap around her torso.

He felt some relief now that he had someone to ask questions of, someone who could help. "Anna's gone. She didn't take anything apart from her passport and money. I don't know what's happening. Please help."

Zoey sat opposite him, looking shocked. "Anna gave her notice and left a week ago. I was a bit surprised, as she'd not said anything about leaving, so I asked why. She just said she needed a change. It seemed odd as she'd been happy, you know, as happy as you can be when you're working." She frowned. "But something did change in her a couple of months or so ago. She seemed excited one minute, then disturbed the next. I asked her if she was taking drugs. She said no. But that's all I know."

"Did she say anything else? Do you think she was on drugs? Anything unusual you can think of?" Mike realized he was breathing hard.

Zoey shook her head. "No, I don't know. She seemed to change when…"

"What, when what?"

"It's probably nothing. We saw a lot of regulars come in, but this guy started coming in nearly every night, which is not unusual if you're staying at the hotel, which I thought he was. I used to see him around the crossover time. He was always gone when I started my shift, but I noticed that he'd been leaving about the same time as Anna lately."

"Did she say anything to you about him?"

"No, not really. She said he was a good tipper. She seemed to know him well, but that's not unusual either. You get to know regulars; knowing their name, smiling, and chatting are all part of the job. You get more tips that way." She smiled.

"I'm really sorry, Mike. It may have been nothing, but I thought you should know. Oh, he always paid cash. I remember Anna saying so. But now that I think about it, he has not been in since Anna left."

Mike sank into the armchair.

"What did he look like?"

"Not old, not young, probably forties, average looking. I think he had an accent; I can't be sure as I never spoke to him, but I walked past the table when Anna served him several times. He spoke English, but I thought it was accented."

Mike sat there, glad of the company. He shared his whole story, during which he had bouts of tears. He stood up, thanked Zoey, and left.

Mike felt numb on his drive home, thinking what he had done wrong. He felt as if he had nothing to live for. Over the next few days, he went through the motions of going to work. He didn't say anything about what had happened to the contractors he had working with him. It was obvious that something major had happened, as Mike's appearance, lack of conversation, and frequent absences from the worksite indicated as much. Over the following weeks, Mike was rarely at the work site, and eventually, work slowed down to nothing. The contractors had finished, and Mike had no follow-up work for them. They tried to lift Mike's spirits but to no avail. They knew the only spirits being lifted with Mike were in a glass; they could smell it.

Mike did receive a few calls, minor work, a plumbing leak, and a painting job. It was not much, but it was something to put money in the bank. He retrieved a voice mail for a decent-sized job with rooms to decorate, a yard to clear, easy work, and needed urgently, which would carry a price premium. This was something he could do on his own. The call had come from Matt Wallace.

When Mike returned the call, Matt provided the address. Matt arranged to meet first thing the following morning. Mike tried his best, acting as normally as possible while making notes. Matt said that he would purchase the paint or wallpaper. He emphasized that the most important aspect was that the work needed to start right away. Mike said he would negotiate a price and get back to Matt in a few hours.

As Mike began to walk to the front door, Matt told him, "I've written down what colors go in what room. I'll just go and get them." As Matt walked away, Mike approached an array of framed photographs on a side table. As he approached, he thought he saw one of Anna. When he got closer, he saw it was not, though the woman in the photograph did look similar. He picked up the 4x6" framed photo and put it in his jacket pocket.

Matt came back. Mike said, "Fine looking lady. Is she your wife?" Matt said, "Not yet." He smiled as he gave Mike the note he'd made. "I look forward to your call."

The call never came because Mike never completed a quote. He was too full of anger and envy. When he arrived home, he looked at the photograph again, then threw it into a drawer, where it remained.

As Mike had no mortgage on his house, it was easy for him to obtain a substantial loan on his property, especially as he could show a good income in his business for the prior three months. The reason given for the loan was to buy another property at an auction that he would refurbish and sell at a profit, a safe proposal for any finance institution. He set up autopay on repayments for everything he could, which left him free to do whatever he decided to do, which was nothing.

He found, then sold, Anna's car and threw away Anna's clothing, along with anything that reminded him of her. Mike did not work; he was consumed with what had happened to him. His business and cell phone were full of unanswered calls.

He played and replayed the scenario a million times. What did he miss? What did he do? Were there any signs?

There were a few signs, he thought. She had started to wear more makeup for work. She started coming home later and made abrupt "goodbyes" on the phone: exuberance one minute and irritability the next. If something was wrong, why did she not say anything or talk about it?

Whatever he thought, it resulted in one word: betrayal. He had hoped that she might return, but this also pained him. He would ask himself, "If she did, what would I do? Welcome her home? How do I know she would not betray me again? How could I look at her and not feel pain?"

The same collection of thoughts whirled around his head day after day, month after month, like the contents of a permanently shaken snow globe. Walker often spoke aloud. "Get a grip. It's just a fucking woman," was a common phrase among many others, but these increased intense emotions of fear, anger, and sadness, prolonging his symptoms. *Was it planned? Did she pick me up in that bar thinking I was an easy mark, then find out I was single, had my own house, and had good money? She never loved me anyway. She just wanted what I had. The fucking bitch.*

He was also deliberately avoiding people, places, and things that brought those emotions to the surface, but it didn't help; nothing eased, and he became a changed man. His turning point had come, and he chose a path of self-destruction. His drinking habits became severe; he also scored drugs; he would get into fights deliberately. He would troll various pubs; some many miles away, get drunk, and sleep in the car. He'd pick up women, prostitutes mostly; he'd always carry condoms. He was mindful enough to avoid catching an STD, not because of the disease itself, but of having to visit a doctor if he did, where he would be chastised due to his alcohol and drug abuse.

Going into the fourth year, Mike's world took another turn for the worse. He looked at his bank statement. He realized that he would default on the loan he had taken unless he started to do something to earn money. He needed to start working again.

The following morning, partially sober, he sat down at his kitchen table and started to write a plan of action; he wrote the header. To Do. With inner strength, he began to clear the mess in his house. At noon, he stopped, drank a few beers, and then continued until late evening. This pattern continued over the next few weeks. He'd written a plan, cut back on drinking during the day, stopped taking cocaine, and cleaned up his work van. He had deleted all messages and calls from his work and cell phone, leaving space for new ones.

His plan was a good one, but he could not keep to it. He would still drink at the pubs or at home every evening.

Mike's work efforts were shoddy. Some clients refused to pay for the work he had performed. By August of that year, the bank foreclosed on his property, forcing him into bankruptcy at the end of October. He was eligible for Jobseeker's Allowance, which enabled him to rent a small, one-bedroom apartment. He loaded the little he had into his van, took the contents to his new residence, and then returned to what was once his home to collect the last of his belongings.

As he was searching through drawers for items to pack, he found the photograph of Deanne Wallace. He recoiled in shock, as his consciousness was flooded with how Anna had betrayed him and crushed everything in his life. He began to tremble and stumble backward, his back hitting the door frame, then shouted, "I'll kill that fucking bitch! I'll get her back for everything she did!"

He clenched his fists and stomped around the bedroom, sweating, shaking, and punching at the air, ultimately punching the walls, leaving holes and cracks. Then he stopped and put his bloodied hands to his sides. He stood still, breathing hard, then clasped his hands and started walking slowly around the one-bedroom apartment, mumbling and raising his hands up and down. *No. No. She won't win this one.* He was chuckling hysterically.

He put the photo in his pocket, loaded his van with boxes, and drove to his drab apartment. The day was November 3rd.

The same evening, Mike drove past the Wallace household, parked his van at the entrance to the Woodland nearby, walked back along the road to the Wallace house, and positioned himself where he could not be seen. He stayed there for almost two hours. He watched Matt taking his dog, Smarts, for a walk.

No sign of Deanne.

Mike returned to his apartment, pacing, drinking, and talking out loud. His hate was palpable.

The following night, Mike returned to repeat his actions. This time, he saw Matt and Deanne walking Smarts. Mike almost ran out to confront them but restrained himself.

The next night, November 5th, Mike returned, and this time, Deanne was walking the dog alone. He followed her quietly, anticipating reaping his vengeance on "Anna." During the attack, his timeless thirst for vengeance was unquenchable; every sadistic blow brought him joy, ripping Deanne's clothes and raping her made him feel restored. When he looked at the crumpled body he'd formed, he smiled in satisfaction. The final blow to snuff out Deanne's life, for Walker, was the prize he sought and treasured.

Afterward, he believed he had killed her. He walked into the park area, where the fireworks display was in full swing. He saw the happy gathering, watched the spectacle for a while, and then returned to his van. On his drive back to his apartment, he laughed.

"I'm happy. I'm happy. Fuck that bitch!" He opened the window of his van and shouted, "Fuck you, Anna!" Mike felt he could rest easier now that she was dead. Once he got to his apartment, he bathed the wound he received on his arm from Smarts in vodka, wrapped his arm with a cut-up sock, and put Gaffa tape around the sock to keep it in place.

As he did not have a working TV and never read newspapers, Mike was oblivious to the fact that Deanne was still alive. The news coverage of Deanne's attack was eventually superseded by other, mostly morbid, news of the day. As he lived in a different suburb of London, he was never part of the requested DNA testing that took place after Deanne's attack.

Chapter Thirteen

The UK Division of the San Diego Economic Development Council was continuing to reap successes with companies and entrepreneurs looking to expand or start a business overseas. The US was in favor due to the deteriorating economic conditions in Great Britain combined with an improving US economy.

Wesley Snipps had joked many times that their achievement in the UK was due to his great leadership, though he would praise his whole team in their weekly meetings. His second in command, Deanne, was a major contributor. She would be as enthusiastic with an entrepreneur seeking to purchase a franchise as she would with a cutting-edge, established company. Deanne liked reciting an old English proverb, "From little acorns do mighty oaks grow."

One of Deanne's larger prospects, R-R Industries, currently providing cybersecurity to the UK and parts of Europe, was nearing making a commitment. Today, she would be visiting their office in Shepherd's Bush to deliver the finalized draft agreement. She could have sent a courier but preferred to drop it off herself; she felt the personal touch was better. She drove the short but traffic-filled distance and parked outside R-R Offices.

Deanne had been a frequent visitor in the initial stages of engagement. She had got to know many of the personnel, especially Beth Rodgers, the receptionist.

In her early twenties, attractive, petite, and always joyful, Beth was fascinated with California. She informed Deanne in many conversations, "All the stars come from California, and you're beautiful enough to be one."

Deanne walked through the door and went into the reception area.

"Hello, Deanne, I didn't expect to see you today," said Beth, with a broad smile.

"I'm just dropping this off for Mr. Rigold," replied Deanne.

"Shall I see if he's free?"

"No, that's fine. Just ask him to give me a call if he has any questions."

Deanne and Beth chatted for a while longer before she left to return to the office.

Traffic was go-stop as normal. A white van pulled up on her right side, just a foot or so in front; a movement of the driver's head turning in her direction caused her to look to her right. The driver, a man, did not look directly at her. He looked across her for a second or two, turned back, and continued to move forward. The car Deanne drove had lightly tinted windows, which was fortunate. The man she saw had his window down. Her view was not obstructed at all.

Deanne started hyperventilating and was momentarily paralyzed, oblivious to the sound of honking horns behind her. It was him, her attacker; she knew without a doubt.

The birthmark on the man's forehead appeared to resemble a leaf on her attackers' forehead on the night of the attack; it was this she remembered seeing. She felt as if her car were sinking in a circle of quicksand; everything around her seemed to stop. She shakily indicated right and pulled into a no-parking space a few feet away. Instinctively, she locked the doors, grabbed her phone, and called Matt. It went to voice mail.

She almost screamed into the phone. "Matt, call me! I'm going out of my mind; I've just seen—" She hung up, thinking of calling Brian White. Looking through her phone, she found his number and started the call. It rang twice, and then she hung up.

She was still breathing hard, her hands trembling as she tried to force herself to gather her thoughts. Deanne's feelings of hate and vengeance, mixed with fear, shock, and being thrown back into the night of the attack, had overwhelmed her rationality.

She was now catching her breath and trying to think logically. She remembered the name "Walker" on the rear of the van and 0208, the initial telephone numbers, so she knew that Brian would be able to locate him, pick him up, and throw him in jail.

Plus, he did not see me. He did not look at me. Knowing these two aspects made her feel safer.

Deanne decided to drive to a car park where she could think more clearly. She drove to the top level, where she could look over the city. Peering over the railings, she began to examine the situation she was in. In mid-thought, her phone rang.

Matt's panicked voice came over the line. *"Deanne, what is it; what did you see? I'm so sorry; my ring was off, and I didn't hear the phone. What is it? You sounded terrified."*

Deanne replied, now calmer. "Sorry, Matt, I, um, I thought I saw Julia Roberts. You know how much I like her. But it wasn't."

"What? Julia Roberts? You scared me to death. Julia Roberts?"

"I know Matt, I'm sorry. I just became starstruck."

"For God's sake, I thought it was something really serious. You sounded horrified."

Deanne reassured Matt, calming him down, apologizing again, and then mentioned she might be running a little late, assuring him she'd join him for dinner later.

She did not tell Matt whom she had seen, as she did not want to panic him. She was worried about how he would react, as she knew Matt would be merciless if he got his hands on the attacker. Also, she had no idea what she should do.

Several times, she took her phone out to call Brian White. Still, she hesitated as she remembered what he had said when they met for their private dinner a couple of months back: how the criminal justice system worked, the interrogation and humiliation of being questioned by the attacker's attorney, how she had said she had not been able to describe the attacker, how she said that she would not be able to pick him out in a lineup, and, worst of all, that the attacker might be found not guilty.

She said out loud, "I know it's him. I know it, but they will question how I recognized him when I said I didn't get a good look at his face.' Beginning to seethe, she exhaled quietly. *Reasonable doubt, Reasonable bloody doubt.*

She spent the next hour on the rooftop, walking around the rectangular perimeter, trying to decide what to do next. Her first move was to go back to the office.

Wesley greeted her as she walked in, asking, "Well, how did it go? Are they in agreement?"

Deanne smiled, "We should know tomorrow. We should be fine."

"Well, you sure have a spring in your step, so you must feel confident."

Deanne turned to say, "Yes, indeed I do, Mr. Snipps." She bowed her head in a mock gesture and went to her office.

Deanne promptly logged on to her computer and started to search "Walker Handyman London 0208."

"Bingo," she said aloud. "There you are, Mike Walker. I've got you now." There was no photograph of Walker, just a side view of his van. "OK, let's see what a background check turns up."

As a government body, the UK Division of the San Diego Economic Development Council would always vet potential clients. Only their pre-cleared personnel, namely Deanne and Wesley, had access. She went onto the United Kingdom Security Vetting website and brought up *Developed Vetting*, the single government provider of national security.

Once in, she typed in *Michael Walker* and the address she had found.

"Michael Allan Walker, let's see what you are, apart from inhuman, you bastard," she muttered. She studied Walker's photograph on his driving license record, expanded the picture, and studied his face. *His soulless eyes are empty, and his expression emotionless.*

A check of criminal records revealed traffic infractions only. A check of his credit and financial history found a full report of his drug and alcohol abuse, the government aid he had received, and details of his personal circumstances. Deanne was surprised he had no criminal record. He lived alone, had no family, and was married, though his wife had left him and gone to Ukraine.

She looked at the screen, then shut the computer, almost slamming the screen down as she found her emotions rising. Deanne sat back in her chair, fingertips together in a steeple position, remembering the words of Detective White *beyond a reasonable doubt*. Taking short, shallow breaths, she thought, *I don't have any doubt, and I'm not going to be reasonable.* She had envisioned the outline of a plan and knew the desired outcome; now, she was trying to put the pieces together as to how it could be achieved.

She was so deep in thought that she was startled when her cell phone rang. She could see it was Jane. "Hi, Jane, what's up?"

"Have you looked at the site today? You know rentals? It looks like it will be fully occupied through to after the Christmas holidays if the bookings keep up as they are. There are only a few weeks open, so if anyone from your US office is planning to come over, they best do it quick." Jane was clearly delighted.

"That's great, Jane," Deanne said. "I'll make a call to the US in the morning and check. Let's see if we can fill up those blank weeks. Oh, let Matt know I'll be leaving to come home shortly."

They said their goodbyes. Deanne shut off her computer, got up from her chair, and started walking toward the door. She stopped and mouthed, "Fuck." She sat back down and phoned Jane.

"Hello, Deanne."

Deanne spoke quickly, "Jane, I've been a dumb ass. I didn't mark the rental bookings. I completely forgot. I'm sorry. The dates are October 20th to November 9th. I was asked to book the date's weeks ago."

"Don't worry. We all forget things. That's great. That fills some of the gaps; wonderful. Who are they?"

"Oh, I have it here somewhere. I can't remember. I'll find the information and put it on the calendar tomorrow. I was just heading out the door when I remembered."

"No problem. I'll mark them in now in case someone else tries to book. See you when you get home."

Deanne closed her phone, "Shit, shit, shit, shit," she mumbled. *I'll need to sort that out pretty fast. Think, think.* She hesitated. *You need to detail your plan, Deanne, and quickly.*

She strolled to her car, and once in, she slowly began her drive home, trying to unfurl her sensations and put them in order.

She shrugged her shoulders, saying out loud, "I don't feel scared anymore, and if Walker confronted me?" Deanne paused for thought, smiled, and, in a soft voice, confidently said, "I could handle him."

Searching her emotions, she wondered if she was suffering from the shock of seeing him. The only concern she had now was explaining the details of the visitor to fill the missing booking with Jane. She decided to call Wesley's cell.

"Hi, Wes. Sorry to call you after hours."

"No problem, Deanne. What's up?"

"It just hit me that it's nearly the end of August, and this year is moving really fast. I haven't seen my family for a while, and I don't think I'll have time later this year, so I thought I'd mix business with pleasure, jump on a flight to see them, and make sure that everyone is on the same page if R-R Industries comes through tomorrow. I'll be calling Bob Rigold in the morning. Either way, I do need to get back to see the family, or I'll be in the doghouse."

"OK, Deanne. When are you thinking of going?"

"I'll see what R-R comes back with tomorrow, and if it's a go, then I'll book for the end of next week. Of course, I won't leave anything hanging here."

Wesley agreed and reminded her to use her miles for an upgrade if she were going first class. Deanne said she would and that she would not stay long in the US.

She left the office to drive home. She stopped at an electronics outlet store on the way to purchase a small electronic notepad. She took the notepad out of the box, threw the packaging in a trash can, put the notepad in her purse, got back into her car, and went home.

Jane had prepared dinner and returned to her annex apartment. Deanne walked into the house, giving Matt a tight hug and a big smile.

"Good day?" he asked.

"Yes, busy, but a good day. Oh, I may go back to see my family at the end of next week, and I have some prep work to do for a client. Is that OK with you?"

"Sure," Matt said. "It's a bit sudden, but I may be able to break off from work and come with you."

Deanne looked up, "Nice idea, but I'll be staying with my family, which will be all-consuming, and then work, especially if the company R-R signs up tomorrow. So, you may end up bored or alone with my parents while I'm working, so I don't think it's worth your while coming with me this time."

Matt agreed.

Deanne did not sleep much; her mind was too busy adding detail to her plan. She went to the office early the following day and looked online at *The San Diego Union-Tribune*. She found what she was looking for and then made the first entry in her new notepad.

"Linda Warren," Deanne muttered. "You're the one. Sorry, Linda." She closed the browser, erased the search for The Union-Tribune, and then deleted her recent history.

At 10 a.m., she called R-R to speak with Bob Rigold. There was no answer, so she left a message: "Good morning, Mr. Rigold. This is Deanne. I wanted you to know that it looks like I'll be in the US at the end of next week. It won't be for long, but if you are going to go forward with the agreement I dropped off yesterday, I could start to get things moving before I depart. Either way, let me know, please."

Rigold called Deanne just after 3:15 p.m. *"Hi, Deanne. Yes, we're going forward."*

Deanne jumped up from her chair. "Great! Thank you."

"While you're there, there's a couple of things the board would like you to look at. I'll email the list and a copy of the signed agreement. I look forward to working with you, Deanne. Thank you for all you have done to make this happen."

"Likewise, it's been a pleasure. Thank you." She hung up, then yelled, "We got R-R! It's all signed up."

Wesley, and most others, heard. Deanne came out of her office. "What a team we are," she called out. "We've pulled another one off; thank you, everyone. Even though Wesley did nothing at all to help, the rest of us pulled it together."

Everyone laughed.

Wesley came out of his office. "I heard that," he said with a fake frown.

Deanne rushed up to him and gave him a little hug. "Wes, you're the rudder that steers our ship; without you, we would crash on the rocks."

He smiled. "Yes, I know that. I know that."

More chuckles arose around the room.

The rest of the afternoon was an easy, self-congratulatory time for all.

She called Jane, which made Deanne feel uncomfortable, as she was unable to divulge all the truth, only some.

Next on the list was Jane "Hi, Jane. I'll be going back to the States next weekend for family and business. I'll only be away for a week or so. On the good news side, I have all the info regarding the rental for October 20 to November 9. Put the name Linda Warren on the calendar. Extra good news is that she's in San Diego, so I'll touch base when I'm over there."

Jane said, "You must be so excited. I'm sure you will be. It'll be good for you to get away and see them. I've already blocked out the rental dates on the calendar. Is a deposit being sent?"

"I'll pick it up when I'm there."

"OK, have a good day at work."

Deanne comforted herself by saying that she had not lied to Jane. She'd just been creative with limited truth. Later in the afternoon, she booked her flight, direct from Heathrow to San Diego, leaving at 9:30 a.m. and arriving at 3:35 p.m., local time, the departure Saturday, August 31st.

She called her parents, saying she would arrive the following Saturday afternoon, that she would be staying with them, and that she would be alone.

Deanne knew her parents were ecstatic about the news and that they were additionally ecstatic about having her all to themselves.

As she had clothing at her parents' house, she only needed a medium-sized suitcase, which had room to spare after she had packed what she needed.

Saturday came, and Matt took Deanne to Heathrow. They kissed goodbye and waved to each other as Matt pulled away from departures. Deanne loved the fast-track security that came with first-class flights, early boarding, and, best of all, the suite, where she could eat, drink when she wanted, and then stretch out, relax, watch a movie, after which she would have her seat turned into a flatbed and fall asleep.

She slept a solid six hours during the flight, something she had not accomplished for a long time.

Deanne's discovery of her attacker remained a secret, as did her plot to obtain a confession. Her plan had started the day of seeing Walker with nothing more than bullet points. The time between then and now had been spent adding details to it; this helped camouflage her mental state. To

Deanne, the specifics were an expanding storyboard, which had grown into something much more sinister and, to her, more gratifying.

After going through customs in San Diego, Deanne walked through arrivals at 4:47 p.m. local time, 12:47 a.m. in the UK. Even though it was late, she called Matt to let him know she had arrived safely, and then, seeing her parents waving frantically, quickly said to Matt, "I love you. Gotta go; my parents will take off if they flap their arms any faster."

Matt laughed, said good night, and put the phone down.

Deanne's parents, Jack and Betty, had always been demonstrably affectionate; today was no exception, with hugs, kisses, and fussing in abundance, coupled with non-stop talking as soon as Deanne was within earshot.

It remained the same on the drive to her parents' house. Once home, the roles of communication were reversed. Jack and Betty then asked Deanne to fill them in on any and all news, why she had suddenly returned to the US, why they did not get much warning, how long she was staying, how much free time she would have so they could plan a few evenings.

She answered all their questions but requested that all plans be kept minimal as she was here for work, and that is what she needed to focus on. They obviously obliged, as they were just happy to have her back.

Two hours passed, during which time Jack had taken Deanne's suitcase to her room, which had not changed from when she lived at home with her parents.

Deanne said she needed to unpack, rest for a while, have a shower, and change her clothes.

Jack and Betty said to let them know if she needed anything. Deanne went to her room, emptied her case, laid on her bed, and put her arms behind her head. She looked up at the ceiling, realizing this was the first time she had truly been alone since discovering her attacker.

She also realized that she had been non-stop in her pursuit of her plan. She had let her impulses rule her decisions and not given herself any time to reflect.

Fear started to creep in. She wondered if anyone had thought her behavior was strange over the past week. She played and replayed what she remembered. *No, I was OK. I think. But what if I'm wrong? What if it's not him? It is him. I know it's him. What, just because of a birthmark? I feel it's him. I know it is.*

Doubt had started to creep in, thinking. *Be careful what you wish for, Deanne.* Her mind then drifted to one of the reasons she had come to the US. She got up, went to her closet, opened a few boxes, and then found what she was looking for. She placed the articles into her suitcase.

Her eyes slowly started to close, and then, as if she had an electric shock, she sat bolt upright. "That's it," she whispered. "That's it, the smell. I remember the paint smell, the oil." Deanne was remembering the smell she mentioned to Charlotte when she was recounting her attack. "I knew it was familiar," she muttered. Anger, retaliation, and revenge erased any doubt.

Deanne remembered a similar odor from college when she was in the Performing Arts Program, especially as every member would build and paint scenes, which is why she recognized the smell of paint, oil, and wood on Mike Walker, the handyman.

After a shower and a change of clothes, Deanne joined Jack and Betty. "I thought you were having a nap," Betty said.

"Nope, I'm wide awake, and I'd like to take you out to dinner, on me, my treat."

During her time in the US, Deanne diligently worked in the main office, visited the two office buildings Bob of R-R had asked her to check out, covered the rest of his requirements, thoroughly discussed, and guided the US team with what to expect when Bob and his team visited.

As ever, the San Diego office was pleased with Deanne's return, commenting on how much they missed her. Matt was always her first call every morning; Deanne would be the last call Matt would make each evening.

On the Thursday afternoon of the same week, Deanne drove to visit Linda Warren; she spent about half an hour with her and then drove back to Jack and Betty's home.

Her flight back to the UK was on the next Saturday afternoon. On Saturday at 7 a.m. she was in the San Diego office for an hour, during which time she logged on to a government site and found the document she was looking for. She sent the document to print, retrieved the hard copy, and placed it in her purse.

Jack and Betty drove her to the airport. She asked them to drop her off at departures, as goodbyes were more upsetting when standing around waiting.

With tears all around, Deanne waved goodbye. The return flight to the UK was a replica of her trip to the US, comfortable and enjoyable. Matt greeted her at the airport. Both were excited to see each other. After a short kiss but a long hug, they walked to the car, and Matt drove home. Both had arranged to take the following day, Monday, off from work.

Taking advantage of not needing to rise early, they delayed their normal Sunday bedtime by over an hour and enjoyed an additional wine before retiring to their bedroom.

Matt woke up first. Lifting his head from the pillow, he sniffed the air and gave Deanne a gentle nudge. "I can smell bacon," he said. "Come on, Deanne; it's late, 8:30. Jane must be making breakfast."

Both were downstairs within fifteen minutes.

Jane hugged Deanne. "Nice to have you back," she said with a smile.

"Oh, I have something for you," Deanne said. She ran upstairs, returning with an envelope.

"This is for you, on behalf of Linda Warren." She gave the envelope to Jane, who opened it with a look of surprise to see a stack of hundred-dollar bills.

"This is the deposit and full payment for the rental period in cash," Deanne said. "Don't ask me why it's cash. I didn't ask, so I can't answer."

Jane looked at her. "This is wonderful. Did you check her out? What is she like?"

"She checked out, and as far as I could tell, she's a wonderful lady, and I know she'll be no problem at all."

"Well, if she's good enough for you, she's totally fine with me."

The rest of the day went as pleasantly as it had started.

Chapter Fourteen

eanne began to feel stronger and more decisive. She arrived at the office a little earlier, sometimes leaving a little later. Her gym routine had not changed, though some days; she also had other tasks to fulfill, arriving home later than normal.

Deanne always had ready-made excuses if Matt commented.

Now, she had formulated an objective: retribution for Mike Walker's crime. She had also given herself a self-imposed period to complete it. Though the planning consumed her, she never let it show in any aspect of her relationships, personal or professional.

She adopted routines, rules, and approaches to become more in control and emotionally compartmentalize the mission involving Walker. This enabled her to keep her focus on social and business activities.

Deanne's electronic notepad was her release and her confidant; it was not connected to the internet and was password protected. The notepad became her best friend, armed with copious notes and details. One of her listed items would be found in criminal research records. She was searching for an individual with a criminal record and some health care or pharmaceutical experience and their financial position.

Her initial search produced an overwhelming volume of drug-related crimes, over 35,000 in London and outer boroughs. Refining the search results by adding and deleting particular words, she settled on two areas, Lambeth and Southwark, the two boroughs at the top of the crime list.

Then, she refined her search to a deeper exploration of isolated criminal convictions involving the *supply and distribution of drugs*. She followed these results by limiting convictions to an individual, producing an almost manageable search list. It took several more searches to isolate fourteen potential candidates, all between the ages of twenty-five to thirty-five, and where theft of drugs had been from a hospital or pharmacy.

After another few days, she had whittled the number to four. Each one had received a light sentence of six months' probation, with leniency in judgment being due to the circumstances in which they had stolen drugs. Three had worked in a hospital, and the fourth in a pharmacy.

Armed with addresses, contact numbers, a vehicle, and license number details in her notepad, Deanne supplemented her gym nights with surveillance trips to her suspect's addresses. She did not expect this to be easy, but it took longer than she thought and included some day trips as well. She discounted one suspect after discovering he had moved back with his parents and was now on a path to a better and more stable life. The remaining three she had seen from afar: two males and one female.

Deanne's next move was to interact with each of them, as she needed to hear their voices, see their demeanor, and try to ascertain their current circumstances. Her disguise consisted of jeans, a black jacket, putting her hair up, wearing a baseball cap, and using the stage makeup she had brought from her US bedroom closet to make herself look older.

First, Deanne managed to follow the female, Debby, into a pub and sat down at a table where she could hear her conversation. After a few minutes, a man walked in, saw Debby, and sat down in the opposite chair to her.

"Hey, Debs. Sorry, I'm a bit late. I couldn't park the car."

Debby looked up and said, "Well, you best get me a drink then."

When Debby was into her third drink, she started to become loud, swearing and at one point telling her partner to "Fuck off and leave me alone." Deanne scrubbed Debby off her list and left.

The next contender was Don Foreman, a twenty-seven-year-old. She almost gave up on him as he was either sleeping or working one of two jobs as a delivery worker by day and kitchen cleaner at night. He cycled to and from the cleaning job because, as Deanne found out, his car had been repossessed for missed payments. One evening, she was lucky after she followed Don back to his flat. After thirty minutes of no activity, she decided to drive off, assuming he would be resting until his night shift began.

She pulled away, getting caught behind a garbage truck. As she looked in her rearview mirror to see if she could pull out, she was surprised to see Don exiting his door, smartly dressed and no bicycle in tow. She watched as he walked up the street to a bus stop, waited a few minutes, and boarded the arriving bus, which was now behind Deanne's car. When the road cleared, she pulled in, and the bus passed. She quickly moved behind it.

The bus was heading out of the city. Hanging back and allowing cars to get between her and the bus, Deanne followed for almost an hour before Don got off at a stop in Wimbledon. Don waved at a parked car; the car door opened and out jumped an attractive female, who got into the passenger side of her car after giving Don a kiss. They drove to The Ivy Cafe in Wimbledon Village.

An upscale and expensive place, Deanne thought.

The couple went in and got seated at a table. Deanne followed five minutes later. The day was the first Wednesday in October, which meant The Ivy Café had a jazz band playing. Deanne sat behind the couple, close enough to hear the conversation. She heard Don call her Amelia; Deanne guessed she was in her twenties.

"You managed to get your mum's car?" Don asked.

Amelia giggled. "Yes, Mum's surprisingly good like that. Dad's still pissed that I'm seeing you, you know, after what happened. He's convinced you take drugs; he reckons that if you sell them, you must be taking them too."

Don sighed. "I know. It was dumb, but I just knew that others in the hospital were getting away with it, and as you know, with my mum sick and not working, I just wanted to keep her in her own place, but the landlord is an evil bastard and wanted any excuse he had to kick her out. I didn't earn enough at the hospital to help. The doctor had already said she would not last long. With me living there with her, she at least spent her last days happy. She knew she was going. I told the shitty landlord that I'd move out as soon as Mum was gone. I knew he'd raise the rent, so I'd have to go anyway."

Amelia laid her head on his shoulder. "I know, sweetheart. But let's be happy. You should be happy. At least your Mum never had to see you dragged into court or anything, and you know she was happy when she went. I loved how she called you Donny, or her 'baby boy.' She loved you so much."

Don teared up.

Don and Amelia's conversation continued until the band began to play. Deanne finished her meal, got up, and left for home. During the drive back, she formulated a plan to intervene with Don the following night.

Once home, she made an excuse to Matt, stating that she needed to get to the office for a meeting with the San Diego team at 3 p.m., using the time difference between California and the UK to her advantage. Deanne knew Don's routine for his day and night shifts. He would leave his flat at 11 p.m., then cycle to his night job at the Kitchen Café, where he would spend four hours cleaning from midnight to 4 a.m.

At 10:30 p.m., Deanne waited in her car across the street from Don's apartment. She could see his bicycle chained to the railing in front of the three-story converted townhouse. She knew Don occupied the top one-room flat and waited for the light to go off in his room. When the window darkened, Deanne exited her car, crossed the street, put on a black ski mask, and crouched behind two trash containers. Don came through the front door, went over to his bicycle, and bent down to unlock the wheels.

Deanne walked up to him, flashing her badge, and spoke in a perfect English accent with as deep a tone as possible.

"Don Forman, I'm with MI5, the British security service. I'm not here to harm you. I'm here as we believe you may be able to help us."

"What the fuck? MI5 let me see the badge. Is this a prank or something?"

"It's no prank." Deanne held a rather good copy of an MI5 badge and put it in front of Dons' eyes." "OK?"

"OK," Don replied.

"You're not in any trouble. I want you to stand up. Don't turn around, and let's go back into your apartment." Don opened the front door. They walked up the stairs, and he unlocked his apartment door.

"Don't turn on the light. Please move that kitchen chair and face it toward the wall. I'll be right behind you."

Don started to speak, "I need to get to work. I don't want to lose my job."

"Just listen to what I need to say. Don Foreman, we're aware of the reasons you stole drugs from the hospital, and we're also aware that there is a network of people in the same hospital who have made an extra career out of selling drugs. I know you stopped stealing drugs to raise money as soon as your mother passed. Do you have any idea of the reason you were accused two months after you ceased stealing them?" Deanne continued.

"I'll tell you why. The leader of the drug ring in the hospital found out you were pocketing drugs and recruited you. When you stopped helping him, he retaliated by making an anonymous call to the police, and, of course, that's the reason you're in the crappy position you are now."

In fact, Deanne knew it was assumed the call came from Amelia's father. As far as the drug ring, Deanne based her story on the recorded data of drugs not accounted for, a common occurrence wherever pharmaceuticals were used or distributed in large quantities. Theft of drugs or prescription forms was a major problem at the hospital where Don was a hospital porter.

"Who told on me?" Don asked. "I didn't know that anyone knew. The bastard."

"This is where you come in, and this is where we need your help. In return, we'll find a job for you, and if you agree to help, you won't need to go back to your nighttime cleaning job in the kitchen, which means that you'll be able to see Amelia more frequently." Don started to turn around.

"Eyes forward."

"How do you know about Amelia?"

"We know everything about your mother, Amelia, your finances, and the raw deal you got. This should help you start to get back on your feet." Deanne took £3,000 out of her waistband and walked over to Don.

"Don't turn around." She placed the money on his lap. "Here's £3,000. That will tide you over the next couple of months, and if you're able to do what we request, we'll find you a better job, plus another £3,000."

Don raised his eyebrows, his eyes widened in surprise, and he said, "Wow. I don't really understand what's going on, but I could sure use the money. What have I got—"

Deanne interrupted. "Give me your cell phone. I'm going to place a hidden app on your phone, encrypted and coded. It'll be tracking your movement and your calls. If you say anything to anyone, including Amelia, about anything you and I discuss, you'll see the inside of a closed cell for five years. Now, you have a choice, of course. You can say no, I'll leave, and that's the end of it. But, of course, that means that I'll take the money back, and you'll be a little late getting to the kitchen tonight."

Deanne drew her breath, feeling relaxed and relieved that Don was cooperating. *At least so far,* she thought.

"We need your help in breaking the drug ring, and what you need to do is to identify the person, the one who orchestrates the theft and distribution, plus the people you said you know or suspect."

"But I don't know anyone!"

Deanne retorted, "Then why did you say to Amelia—now, what was it you said at the Ivy Café? Oh, yes! You said, 'I know some of the others in the hospital were getting away with it.' Remember?"

"How the fuck did you know where I was and what I said? This is crazy."

"As I said, we know everything about you. So, tell me what you do know or what you think you know. You won't need to testify in court. We'll use the information you provide and take it from there."

Don sat up in his chair. "Well, I don't know 100 percent, and I really don't know about any drug ring. I just know what I've seen, like when I was pushing patients or gear around the hospital. I would sometimes go into an empty room where the same three, sometimes four or five, people I recognized would be, and every time they would clam up and say dumb shit like, 'OK, we best be off,' then, 'Hi, Don,' and leave the room. On one occasion, there was a box of OxyContin in one of the empty rooms. I knew it shouldn't have been there, but I didn't really take much notice. But one of the guys came back, rushed in, and said, 'I nearly forgot this. Doctor Preston needs it,' and then he left with the box."

"I knew what he was saying was crap because a doctor would never need a fucking box full of 200 OxyContin, and the hospital pharmacy has a strict process for administering drugs. I mean, come on. The guy that came back, Tim Evans, is a pharmacy technician. I didn't really know him that well. We always said hello. He always seemed a bit jittery to me. You know, nervous. I can give you the names of the guys, but I don't want it coming back on me."

"It won't," Deanne said reassuringly.

Don provided more names.

"That's it for now, Don. Now remember, not a word."

Deanne left.

Don was confused—happy and delighted but confused. He counted the money, £3000. Though he had been scared, shocked, and bewildered, he could not have been happier. He wondered if the MI5 person would be back.

As Deanne walked back down the stairs, she took off the ski mask, left Don's flat, put the mask in her pocket, put her cap on, walked to her car, and drove home. Matt was asleep by the time she arrived, and she quietly got in beside him.

By 8 a.m., Deanne had already been into the database and found all she needed to know about Timothy Evans. Though Don had said Tim Evans was a nervous guy, the report she read indicated that he had a temper. He'd gotten into a few brawls over his thirty-eight years, nothing recent, but she made a mental note.

At lunchtime, Deanne went to her car armed with a matchstick in her purse. She removed the valve cap off the driver's side tire, pushed the match into the valve, heard the hissing air coming out, and returned to her desk. Half an hour later, she went back to her car, and the rear tire, as expected, was completely flat. She removed the matchstick from the valve, put the valve cap back on, and returned to her office. Just after 5 p.m., she said she was going home and said goodbye. Continuing her ruse, she walked to her car again and then promptly returned to the office.

"Wesley?" she called out. "I need a favor, please."

"What now, Deanne? Another trip?" he teased.

"My tire is as flat as a pancake; can I take the office Prius tonight? I'll get the tire fixed in the morning." Deanne retrieved the key from the key rack, "Thanks, Wes. You're a sweetie."

Wes mumbled, "That girl plays me like a fiddle." But he was smiling as he walked away.

Deanne knew where Tim lived. She also knew the route he would take to get home, the two miles of countryside he would drive through, and where there were no cameras. She was aware of the two sets of traffic lights on the two-mile stretch, and she prayed that one would be red when she needed it to be.

At 6:17, she had tucked the black Prius into a small lay-by, sat there, and waited. She put dark contact lenses in her eyes, put on leather gloves, flat shoes, her baseball cap with her hair tucked in, and finally, facial color tint, care of her stage makeup kit.

At 6:38, Tim's dark blue Vauxhall Corsa drove by. Deanne pulled out and started to follow, though not too closely. They approached the first set of lights; Deanne could see they were red. Tim slowed down, almost stopping. The lights turned green, and he accelerated to his prior speed. Soon, the next set of lights came into view. They were red.

Stay red, stay red, she thought.

They did. When Tim's car pulled to a stop, Deanne slowed down to *almost* a halt, deliberately and gently hitting Tim's car. He got out, slammed his door shut, and saw minor but plain damage to his rear bumper.

Deanne rolled down the window and said with an English accent, "I'm so sorry! Totally my fault. We had better move up the road to a lay-by so we don't stop the traffic."

"Yeah, right," Tim said. "Don't try and scoot off. Look at what you've done, you stupid bitch."

Deanne felt a jolt of rage at his bullying comment and tone of voice but kept control of her anger.

"I won't drive off. I'm so sorry," She responded apologetically. They drove to the lay-by about 300 feet further on and parked. Tim got out of his car again and walked back to Deanne's car.

"You're going to have to pay for this and for fucking up my evening, crazy cow. Get out. Let's see your license and insurance. Come on out. Or do I have to drag you out?" His hand was poised to open her car door.

Deanne pictured how many people, especially women, had been on the end of his verbal abuse and how he would have treated a defenseless woman in a similar situation. She thought about maintaining the façade and internally said, *no, I really don't want to. Fuck it.*

She put her hand on the door catch, then shoved the door as hard as she could, slamming into Tim and knocking him off his feet. Deanne closed the car door behind her and watched Tim get to his feet.

"You fucking bitch, I'll—" That's all he said. Deanne had side-kicked him hard in his solar plexus, knocking him back on the gravel with all the air out of his lungs. Deanne just stood there, looking at him.

"First, you apologize, then I'll tell you what you're going to do, Tim Evans," she said. Tim was up on his haunches, hands on his knees, getting air back into his lungs. Deanne knew he would try to take a swing, so she made it easier for him and turned away. She heard him begin to rise, waited a second, and then produced a back-kick into his groin. She just watched as he lay there groaning.

"As I said, first, you apologize, then I'll tell you what you're going to do, Tim Evans."

Tim looked up, "I'm sorry. All right? I'm sorry. Forget the fucking car. Who are you anyway?"

Deanne looked down at him, "Get up, you pathetic shit."

Tim got to his feet, saying, "Don't hit me again, OK? What do you want?"

"Listen carefully. Tonight was no accident. I was waiting for you, and I know all about you. I've also hacked into your home computer; the one you think is so safe. I got in remotely, so I know more about you than your wife does, including the drug ring with your partners, Frank, Jim, Riley, Ken, and others."

Deanne had not actually tried to hack into his computer, but Tim was now very scared.

"Look, I'll cut you in if that's what you want."

"I don't want in, you arsehole. You have a choice. It's simple. I need you to get me some things, a neuromuscular blocking agent. Any will do, but it must paralyze the body, a paralytic that leaves the patient unable to move or speak, one that can be injected directly into the muscle; Nuromax, doxacurium chloride, is a good one, I believe."

Tim stood there, mouth open, and he started to stutter. "I-I can't, I mean, fuck."

"You can, and you will. Now, be quiet and I'll finish. I also understand that a dose of 0.05 mg will last about thirty minutes or so. I'll need enough to last twenty-four hours by infusion pump intravenously administered. You will also bring me syringes, two plastic catheters, two I.V. bags, two infusion pumps, and extension sets. Also, a bottle of Forane. If I missed any accessories that would normally be needed to complete the package, just bring them too, including any administering instructions.

"If you ignore my request, your wife will get a copy of everything from your computer, as will the police. Or I could call your drug buddies and tell them that you are going to squeal on them. Anyway, it's up to you. Remember, I found you tonight, and I can find you anytime, any day. You have until Sunday, 7 p.m., to return here. If you don't show up with everything, your life as you know it will collapse. Now, turn around, get in your car, and go."

Tim did as he was told. Deanne got into her car, found her makeup remover, put on her normal shoes, removed her cap, and drove home, feeling pleased with herself.

Matt was used to Deanne's' occasional "outings," as he called them: the gym, Jane's rental house, early or late from her office due to a myriad of reasons, the main one being communication with the San Diego office due to the eight-hour time difference.

On Friday, October 19th, Deanne went with Jane to make sure her rental home was ready for Linda Warren's arrival the following day. As Jane's house had been vacant the prior week, only a walkthrough was required. As usual, a "Welcome" card was left for the new tenant. Deanne dropped Jane off at the Wallace household, saying she had shopping to do.

She then drove off to Camden Passage, one of the most popular markets in London, full of an eclectic mix of vintage and retro clothes, pictures, vintage luggage, interesting one-off items, collectables, and bric-a-brac. On Deanne's list was clothing, including shoes. She was looking for vintage apparel. In an hour, she had what she needed. An item that caught her interest was a *Flexible Flyer* six-foot wooden toboggan, cheap at £38.

Deanne took her purchases to her car and promptly drove to the Bermondsey Antique Market just for a look around. She already had all she wanted. She wandered up and down the market stalls, looking at the vast array of items for sale. One stall vendor caught her attention, as he was shouting, "Handcuffs from Pentonville Prison. Five pounds each, or three for ten pounds. Have fun tonight, *50 Shades of Gray*!"

Deanne walked over.

"Come on, darlin.' Buy three for ten pounds."

"Handcuffs? Why do you have so many?"

"Technology, sweetheart. Everything's technology. The cops have gone up-market. They use bloody plastic cuffs now, you know, zip ties. So, I bought a job lot, and they're going cheap. How many do you want? You can have some fun with these." He smiled.

Deanne smiled back, "I'm sure I can. I'll take three." She gave him £10, and he gave her three bags with handcuffs and keys. Deanne also picked up some spectacles for £1 a pair. With her spending done, she returned home, stopping at Jane's house to drop off her purchases.

Once home, Deanne hugged Matt as soon as she got through the door. The rest of Saturday, they enjoyed each other's company at home. Deanne did spend twenty minutes or so rifling through Matt's garage where all the yard tools, car tools, house tools, steps, ladder, and boxes of things that Matt insisted "might come in handy" were kept. Deanne found what she was looking for, put the contents into a plastic container, and put the bundle in the trunk of her car.

On Sunday morning, Deanne told Matt she wanted to pick up a newspaper and would be back in a few minutes. It was almost noon. She visited the local store, picked up a newspaper, got back in her car, and drove a couple of miles to call Tim's cell.

"We're good for 7 p.m., right?"

"It's you. "Yes, yes, let's just get it over with," he shakily replied.

Deanne put away her phone, drove home, sat with Matt, and started to read the newspaper.

At 6:15 p.m., Deanne declared, "I'm going to Jane's house. I won't be long."

Deanne did not stop at Jane's house, as, in fact, no visitor was expected. Linda Warren was a real person, but she had recently died, as Deanne had read in *The Union-Tribune*. Deanne had gone to the cemetery to visit her grave; it was there that she had introduced herself to Linda, explained her predicament, her plan, and why she needed to use her name and presence in England.

Deanne drove early to meet Tim so that she could place her car where he would not see it. After, she walked to the spot where they had their previous encounter. She hid in the foliage until she saw him drive up. After Deanne confirmed he was alone, she stepped out, told him not to turn around, to gather the supplies from his car, place them on the gravel, and then drive off without looking back.

Deanne finished their meeting by saying, "If what you have left for me is incomplete, or non-functional, or faulty in any way, you know the consequences."

"It's all there. I promise. I had a fuck of a time getting—"

Deanne cut him off. "Just go, and if you're right, you'll never hear from me or see me again." She backed into the greenery as Tim drove off. Deanne took the package to her car, put it in the trunk, and drove back home.

"All good?" asked Matt when Deanne returned.

"Yep, all's fine. I said I'd pop in again if needed." Over the next few days, Deanne deposited various articles in Jane's house, along with a few required additions to her list. On Friday, the 26th of October, Deanne finished work early and arrived home at 6 p.m.

"Nice to see you home earlier than normal on a Friday," said Jane as she was ironing the laundry.

"Oh, Linda is going to Wales. She thinks she'll be a few days, maybe a week; her grandfather was born in Wales."

Matt walked in. "Hello, darling. Who's going to Wales?"

Deanne stood and gave Matt a kiss on the cheek.

"Linda, the one who booked Jane's house. She's going to Wales, Cardiff, I think."

"The lady who paid cash?"

"That's the one. She asked if I would go out to dinner with her on Sunday. I said yes. I felt obliged. And before you ask, I did ask if I could bring you both. She asked if you were American, and I said no. She then said she'd prefer just me so that we could have a normal conversation."

"What's a normal conversation?" Matt asked.

"No idea. She's a lovely older lady, so I suspect she's stuck in her ways and feels more comfortable with a homegrown American." Deanne smiled.

"No problem," Jane said.

"Me neither." Both chuckled. "So, English not allowed?" Matt asked.

He and Jane laughed.

"You two," Jane uttered.

"I'll visit tomorrow and let her know," Deanne said.

Later, they ordered Chinese takeaway, and the three of them watched a movie together. Deanne did visit Jane's house the next day, taking her notepad from her purse. She meticulously went through the rooms, going down her list, checked everything was as it should be in the cellar, and returned home. On Sunday afternoon, she dressed in casual wear for her dinner in the evening.

"Where are you thinking of going?" Matt asked.

"Not sure yet, somewhere casual; you know us Americans!" She laughed.

"So, not the Ritz or Dorchester for you two then?"

"Nope, not tonight. Don't wait up." She kissed Matt goodbye and left the house.

Chapter Fifteen

On October 28th, a Sunday evening, Deanne drove to Jane's house, parked her car almost a hundred feet away, walked to the house, opened the front door, turned a few lights on, locked the front door behind her, unlocked the door to the cellar, and descended the stairs.

The cellar door was always locked to ensure holiday visitors did not venture there. The row of terrace houses, including Jane's, backed onto the local park. The rear door of Jane's house opened to a small rear garden; a four-foot wall on either side of the gardens separated the houses; a six-foot wall at the back of each house had a wooden door opening onto the park where a concrete perimeter path allowed for outdoor walking in all weather.

A four-foot railing enclosed the remainder of the entire park, interspersed with three pairs of large arched iron gates supported by brick-built pillars, which would be locked from dusk to dawn, except for any evening events such as visiting fairgrounds, concerts, and special occasions.

The central manmade pond, some called it a lake, was a major attraction. Ducks, swans, and other wildlife could be seen daily. Other features, children's swings, play area, sports area, as well as carefully placed trees and variously shaped flower gardens were overlooked by the original clock tower, completing the family-friendly environment.

Deanne had placed the articles she had gathered over the past few days onto metal racks in the cellar. Opening the tool kit she had assembled from the Wallace garage, she removed two screwdrivers, a crowbar, and a can of 3-in-One oil. She walked up the cellar stairs, through to the kitchen, and out the rear garden door, turning right, walking the few steps to the redundant coal- chute-cover adjacent to Jane's house.

The complete row of houses had the same covers, though some had different designs.

Deanne bent down to squeeze the 3-in-One oil on the hinges and the edges of the chute, the third time she had done so over the past week. She scraped around the joint of the cover, then placed the crowbar where she could lever it open. It took several attempts, avoiding too much initial force, as she feared she might crack the cover unless it was eased to open evenly.

She carefully rocked the cover back and forth on the hinges, eventually opening it completely and laying it flat on the concrete. Deanne carefully closed the cover, gathered the tools, and returned to the cellar. She pulled the notepad from her purse, sat down on a wooden chair, and started to go over her list of intended actions and articles.

Next, she walked back up the cellar stairs and went outside, returning to the coal chute. She looked at her watch, put the timer on, and began walking, almost jogging along the concrete path until she stopped at her destination.

She looked around the unlit park, looked at her watch, and muttered, "Seven minutes. I best add another seven, so, let's say twenty-eight minutes, including getting back to Jane's house."

She walked back past Jane's home and further on until she reached the end of the row of houses, turned around, and walked back.

She looked at her watch; it was 7 p.m., time to make the call on the prepaid pay-as-you-go phone she had purchased at the market, no contract required.

Deanne called Mike Walker's work phone number. It went to voice mail, the message saying, *"If this is an emergency, call my cell."* Deanne called the number Walker gave; this too, went to voice mail.

Deanne spoke in the manner of an elderly British woman. "Mr. Walker? I got your number from your van. I have an emergency. My boiler's not working, and I can't get anyone to come out. Please call me back. I'm happy to pay extra if I need to."

Deanne left her new phone number and waited. She waited for ten minutes and was about to call again when her phone rang. For the first time since her initial sighting of Mike Walker, Deanne was anxious.

"Hello, this is Linda."

"You called me. What's the problem?" Walker said in a weary tone.

"It's my boiler in the cellar. It's not working, and I don't know why. I'm sorry to call, but I'm—"

"It's probably the pilot light. Just go down the cellar, and you'll see if there's a light or something."

"I can't get down the stairs to the cellar. I'm too old, and my knees are bad."

Walker sighed. *"Just ask a next-door neighbor. It's Saturday night, and I'm not coming out for that."*

"I called next door, but they are away until Monday. I've already called several other plumbers, but no one will come out now."

Walker huffed, *"If I come out, and it's just the pilot light, I'm still charging £150. Where are you anyway? What's your address?"*

Deanne gave him the address.

There was hesitation in his response. *"Yeah, uh, I think I know where it is. Look, find someone else; it will take me almost an hour to get there anyway."*

"Please, I'm OK with paying for your time. I just don't want to freeze to death. I'll pay cash," Deanne said.

"OK, £250 cash, and I'll include an hour's labor if it's not the pilot light. But remember, if it is, it's still £250. OK? I'll be there in one hour." Mike remembered the area, though bizarrely, his thoughts were self-comforting memories of what he had done there before and to whom.

Deanne rushed to the cellar, took two pre-packed bags from the shelf, and went upstairs to the bedroom. She took her outer clothes off, then pulled her hair back and started to apply the stage makeup she had brought from her bedroom.

After twenty-five minutes, her makeup applied; she put on one of the dresses she purchased from the market, placed and pinned a wig on her head, slipped on a loose cardigan, and added a pair of conventional gloves in one of the pockets. She went to another bag, removing the contents she needed for the evening.

With a syringe in one hand, Forane in her pocket, and her market shoes in the other hand, Deanne returned downstairs into the cellar. She placed the syringe carefully on a shelf and then returned to the kitchen. After putting on a pair of thin latex gloves, she retrieved a small plastic bowl from the cupboard and poured the Isoflurane - a clear, colorless liquid - into the bowl along with a small cloth. Deanne noticed the pungent, musty odor. She put the doused cloth in a Ziploc bag. After sealing the bag, she washed her gloved hands along with the bag, using lavender-smelling soap; she dried and then placed the Ziploc bag into her pocket.

Deanne did not have to wait long before she heard Walker knocking at the door. Deanne opened the door.

"Thank you, Mr. Walker," she said, stepping to one side to let him in.

Mike saw a semi-stooped old lady with partially gray hair and glasses. Her mobility was aided by a walking stick. He could smell a musty odor and thought it to be what he would call "old people smell."

She opened the cellar door.

"The light switch is on the right side of the wall, too high for me to reach." As Walker's right arm was feeling the wall, she took the Forane-laden cloth from the Ziploc bag. Standing behind him, she thrust the cloth over Walker's mouth and nose with her right hand while punching his left kidney with her fisted left hand, forcing Walker to take a deep, involuntary breath. The struggle lasted a few seconds; he collapsed, tumbling down the stairs.

Deanne followed him down the staircase and pulled the jacket off Walker's crumpled torso, under which he was wearing a sweater and T-shirt. She noticed he was twitching, which meant he would be coming around soon. Deanne swiftly went to the shelf to seize the ready syringe, located a vein in his arm and injected the paralytic-blocking agent.

"Are you fucking crazy? I'll kill you, your stupid old fucker," Mike mumbled.

Deanne knew that twenty seconds was all she needed before the contents of the syringe took full effect. Walker was trying to move, but as each second ticked by, he became more helpless. Mumbling a few more words then lay in a contorted shape at the bottom of the stairs. His wide-open eyes showed intense fear. Deanne had immediately recognized his odor when she opened the door, the smell of paint and oil leaving no doubt as to the identification of her attacker.

Deanne removed her cardigan, put on a new pair of gloves she retrieved from the shelf, and then grabbed Walker's feet, dragging him to the center of the cellar. While rolling him over, she saw him looking directly at her, showing indescribable panic in his eyes. Deanne, not uttering a word, took off his shoes, socks, pants, and underpants. Grabbing under his arms, she propped him up in a sitting position against one of the cellars supports, where she proceeded to take off the rest of his clothes. Deanne went through his jacket, retrieving his van keys, wallet, and phone.

After placing his clothing on the shelf, she took Gaffe tape and handcuffs over to where she had sat Walker. Standing behind him, she pulled both his arms back so she could join the two handcuffs behind the support he was leaning against. As a final touch, Deanne took incontinence underwear from the collection of articles she had placed on the shelving.

She had purchased side-fitting incontinence pants, as these were easier to fit and remove. These were necessary, as Deanne did not want the cellar permeated with the stink of Walker's bodily evacuations. Once fitted, Deanne pulled up a chair to face him. She sat looking at him for any signs of movement.

After thirty minutes, she saw a small twitch around his right eye. She looked at her watch, looked at him, got up, and walked to the shelf, returning with a night vision camera and a dose of paralytic in a syringe. She placed both on the chair, turned on the camera, checked that her phone was receiving the image, and then turned to Walker, who looked horrified as she injected him again.

After placing tape over his mouth and eyes, she took off her glasses, grabbed the man's jacket, keys, and shoes, and went up the stairs and through the front door to Walker's van. She had replaced her dress with a pair of jeans, his jacket, shoes, a black baseball cap, and gloves of her own, placing his phone and wallet in the jacket pocket. She knew the location of Walker's second-rate apartment block and that his apartment on the second floor was near the left-hand corner of the building. She pulled away, driving at normal speeds to the location.

On arrival, she saw overfilled trash cans and strewn litter, people loitering outside the entrances and others walking in and out. Pulling up to the entrance to Walker's apartment complex, she saw there were no predefined parking spaces.

She pulled into an area close to where she assumed Walker would park his van, turned off the engine and lights and retrieved her phone to check on Walker via the video camera she had placed. Seeing no change, she put Walker's phone and wallet in the driver's side door pocket.

Turning the interior light on, Deanne looked over the cab of the vehicle. Feeling comfortable that she had not left any evidence of her presence, she got out of the van, leaving the doors unlocked and pulling her cap low, walking casually toward the entrance, doing her best to walk in a manly fashion. As Deanne was draped in Walker's jacket and had already removed her makeup, her femininity was not apparent.

She felt confident that she had not left any suggestion that she had driven Walker's van and was convinced that the clumsy way she was sauntering in Walker's shoes was like some of the other inhabitants who had been drinking or drugging. So, she was not out of place.

Deanne walked through the entrance to the other side of the building, exiting into another part of the apartment complex. Deanne's next aim was to find one of the electric taxis with rear-facing seats, but she knew she would have to walk out of the area to a hotel where taxis were more plentiful.

Half an hour later, she had reached a Hilton Hotel, waited until the right taxi dropped off a guest, opened the rear door, sat with her back to the driver, gave him directions, a pub almost a mile away from Jane's house, then sat with her head down until they arrived. She passed cash to the driver and got out.

By the time Deanne reached her destination, her feet were aching, and she could not wait to get out of her clothes. She stank of Walker. She grabbed a plastic bag from the kitchen, rushed upstairs to the bathroom, stripped off, put all clothing she had worn into the bag, turned on the shower, and immersed herself under the spray of hot water until she felt rid of any facet of her captive's scent. After dressing in her own clothes, and with the addition of a clean pair of jeans she had brought with her, she was ready to go home.

She grabbed a few blankets from a cupboard and went down to the cellar to see Walker squirming, trying to stand up. He heard a noise and was making sounds from his taped mouth. Deanne said nothing. She threw two blankets at him and left. She arrived home a little before midnight, snuggling up to Matt a few minutes after midnight.

He mumbled, "Hello, darling," and went right back to sleep.

In the morning, Matt asked, "Did you have a nice time with Linda last night?"

"Yes, it was a good night; I like her. She has quirks, though. She bought a couple of security cameras, you know, the ones where you can see what's going on from your phone. She has one inside facing the front door and another at the back. She's American. What can I say?" Deanne chuckled.

Jane was wandering in and out of the kitchen and heard the conversation.

"Well, at least I know my stuff is safe."

"Jane, Linda did ask me if I'd pop in now and again while she's in Wales. I said I would. She said that she'd prefer that only I went in as she feels she knows me. I said it would not be a problem."

"Fine by me," said Jane. "When is she due back?"

Deanne stood up to leave for the office, "I'm not sure. She said she'd call. Anyway, I'm off. I've got a couple of hard weeks ahead of me." She said goodbye to Jane, kissed Matt on his cheek, and headed out the front door. Once Deanne arrived at her office, she checked Walker via her cell phone. He looked the same as she left him but had a few marks around his wrists that she could see. "He'll do until later," she said to herself.

Deanne left the office around 4 p.m. and stopped at West12 Shopping Centre in Shephed's Bush to purchase some clothing. She was in and out within thirty minutes, arriving at Jane's house in another fifty minutes.

Her destination was the small storage unit just outside the kitchen door. She opened the lid, removed the fifty-foot expanding hose, closed the lid, and then made her way to the cellar.

She turned off the light and could see him writhing manically like a snake, fierce and overloaded with anger. Once again, she doused a cloth with Forane, went to the side of him, and put the cloth over his nose. Walker savagely moved his head from side to side. Deanne followed his head movements with the cloth. Soon, he was unconscious.

Deanne's next step was to inject him with paralytic, enough to last thirty minutes. She waited until his body was completely limp, about one minute. She removed the blankets with which Walker had tried to cover himself. While removing the incontinent pants, she spoke in her old lady voice.

"Oh, now, that's a shitty mess. We're going to have to clean you up." She unlocked the handcuffs from the pillar, grabbed his hands again, and dragged him close to a drain hole in the floor. She placed the adult diaper into a large Ziploc bag.

With Walker lying motionless on his back, Deanne fastened the hose to the water spigot above the old cast iron sink unit, mixed the flow of hot and cold water until it was warm, and began to spray-hose Walker, rotating him over on his stomach and back until she thought he was clean enough.

Draping him in a clean blanket, she dragged him back to the center pillar and dressed him in a fresh diaper, T-shirt, sweater, windcheater, woolly socks, and an extra-large pair of pants, all from West12. Deanne plugged two electric oil-filled radiators into an extension cord, placed them on each side of the pillar, and sat Walker in a sitting position, finishing by wrapping the chain she obtained from her home garage around Walker's chest, just under his armpits, secured with a lock.

She put one handcuff on his right arm at a right angle behind the pillar, the other part of the handcuff attached to the chain, leaving a little movement. She used the remaining two handcuffs for his ankles. Walker started to move around. Deanne turned off the light, placed herself behind the pillar, and reached forward; she took the tape from his eyes and mouth and waited.

"Are you with us, Mike?" she asked. "Here, has this water." She placed three open bottles within reach of his left arm. He said something, but it was incoherent. He slowly picked up one of the bottles, seeming to need all his strength to do so.

Moving his head from side to side, he said, "Where are you? What the fuck is this? Where am I? Who are you? Are you there?" He picked up another bottle of water, more swiftly this time, and drank it all. He could feel his senses coming back and tried to access his position.

"I'm here," Deanne said.

"You old bitch! When I get out of here, I'll kill you. What the fuck are you doing?" He started to yell, "Help! Help! Get me out of here! Someone help!" Deanne anticipated the outburst. Within seconds, she had her right hand over his mouth with a Forane-laced cloth. Walker grabbed Deanne's arm, but the effect was already rendering him comatose. This was swiftly followed with an injection of the neuromuscular blocking agent.

After taping his mouth and eyes, she took the handcuffs from his ankles, replaced them with tape, cuffed his left arm, put it behind him, and attached the cuffs to the chain. Knowing he was secure, she stood up, looked around the cellar, picked up anything she needed to dispose of in a trash bag, including the diaper, and then walked up the stairs.

She dropped the bag by the front door and continued up to the bedroom to change into her normal attire. Checking the bedroom, then returning to the front door, she picked up the trash bag to put in the trunk of her car, drove to the nearest park gate, deposited her trash into a large waste container outside, and drove the short distance home.

For the following two days, Deanne's activities with Walker were much the same. On the third day, Friday, Deanne drove to Jane's house, went upstairs, and changed her apparel to clothes resembling the night of her attack. Looking at herself in the mirror, the horror of that night returned. She took a deep breath and regained her composure before going to visit Walker in the cellar.

"Hey Mike, do you remember my voice?" she asked, tearing the tape off his mouth.

Walker held his head up, asking, "Can you get me out of here? Get me away from that maniacal old bitch?"

Deanne reverted to her aged English accent. "Do you mean me, Mike?"

"Both you bitches will spend a long time in prison for this. That's if I don't kill you first." Deanne went over to him and peeled the tape from his eyes.

He looked up, startled. "Anna? I thought you were . . ."

"What? Dead?"

Walker thrust forward as much as he could, his eyes full of hate and obsession. He looked more like a rabid dog. His confusion was palpable.

"It's got to be the fucking drugs," he muttered. "This isn't right."

Deanne looked at him. "Mike, dear, bewildered Mike. It's not the drugs, you ferocious bastard. The 'old lady' you saw was me. Good make-up and a good accent, I thought. What do you think?"

Walker replied with more profanity. Deanne went over and put tape over his mouth, not easily as he kept moving his head, but Deanne won.

"I'll leave you to it for tonight. Let's see if you're able to recall tomorrow, shall we?" Deanne went up the stairs, changed into the clothes she wore to the office, and went home.

Walker tried to piece together what had happened. He was still reeling from his first impression that the woman was Anna, bringing his loathing to the forefront of his mind. To him, killing that woman after raping her had given him enough satisfaction to move on.

He had still not recognized that Deanne was the woman he attacked. *After all*, he assured himself, *she was dead.*

He was also convinced that he was in no real danger. *If that woman wanted me dead, she could have done it anytime, so she's going to let me go at some time. She's making sure I don't freeze to death by putting heaters near me.*

Chapter Sixteen

The following day, Saturday, Deanne drove to the park with Loppy to see the preparations for Monday's festivities, Guy Fawkes Night, the 5th of November.

As in past years, local council trucks delivered timber for the bonfire. In the following days, a team of council workers came armed with tools to complete the annual project. The most-used tools were nail guns, the sound of which could be heard a mile or so away.

The annual Guy Fawkes spectacle had grown each year, becoming more of a competition throughout the London districts, all fighting for airtime on TV. The largest firework displays in South London, such as Battersea, Dulwich, Morden, and Wimbledon, found it hard to compete against for national TV. Nevertheless, airtime for local TV, even for ten or twenty seconds, was valuable for the local parks, as the video would be displayed on their website for the following year.

Even at a local level, computers were used in providing complex firework displays. A slow buildup in quantity, color, and size became standard practice, saving the best for last, some using as many as 1,500 computer cues for a ten-minute finale. A single cue might start more than one device simultaneously or in sequence with single devices firing multiple times.

Timing between these events was crucial and required an understanding of pyrotechnic chemistry. A professional company provided this expertise, placement, sequencing, and control.

The lattice wood frame for the bonfire started with a twenty-foot square of 12x2" timber. The next size would be a little smaller with a 2x4" frame nailed to the one beneath. This would be built twenty feet or more in height on the first day, leaving an area open at the top for offcuts from overhanging tree limbs near the streets the council had collected through tree trimming. Once it was filled, the team would return to complete the pyramid; each layer would be used as a step to lay the next length of timber. The top would have a five-foot flat square with four holes drilled in it to let the legs of a high-backed wooden chair be firmly positioned where the dummy of Guy Fawkes would be sat in and secured. The dummy was generally made from discarded clothing, using wood for framing the body appendages with paper stuffed around the wood inside the pants and shirt, shaping a more human-like form; shoes were placed at the bottom of the pants for authenticity. A black cloak would be draped over the dummy, including the back of the chair. A tall, broad-rimmed black hat was fixed to a lifelike head made of plaster of Paris. For the final touch, glued collar-length fake hair, beard, and wide mustache would be added.

When the structure was complete, a lightweight tarp was draped over the top, and a temporary fence was erected around the bonfire to prevent onlookers from getting too close.

The electronics would arrive on Guy Fawkes Day. This consisted of four strategically placed flat-bed trucks for the display, plus a fully equipped computer center. Wi-Fi repeater extenders would be placed for the firework firing system to control the synchronized music.

On the Eve of November 5th, Guy Fawkes dummy would be strapped in the chair atop the bonfire and the tarp covering replaced, leaving everything ready for the following evening.

Food and beverage vendors, security, and the fire brigade would be ready hours before the bonfire would be ignited.

Deanne walked the path, passed the row of terrace houses, including Jane's, then continued to the base of the bonfire, which was already being set in its usual spot at one end of the park, backing onto the adjoining woods, and leaving a distance of about 300 feet between the bonfire and the woods. This would be where the obligatory fire engine would be stationed, more or less out of sight during the festivities but ready should the bonfire get out of control.

After she had surveyed the area, she took a slow walk back home. Matt was engrossed in the football match on TV. Jane was in the kitchen preparing the evening meal. "Can we make it around eight o'clock instead of seven tonight, Jane? I have some errands to run and things to pick up?" She called back to the TV room, "Is that good with you, Matt?"

"Sure, anytime is good for me."

Jane smiled and said, "Let me know if I can help you with anything, dear."

"Thanks. You're a sweetie. I'll let you know."

At around 5:30 p.m., Deanne announced that she would return in a few hours, left, and drove to Jane's house. She opened the front door and went upstairs to the bedroom. To her shock, the doorbell chimed. Deanne rushed downstairs and saw it was Jane. Deanne opened the door. "Is she here?" Jane whispered.

Deanne gathered herself, "No, she's not." She smiled. Jane started to walk through the door.

"No, don't; there's a camera, remember?"

"Oh, shit."

Jane wrinkled her face, "Damn, I forgot about the cameras. You're right. OK, I'll leave you it. See you at home later.

Deanne waved, then closed the door. *Shit, that was close. I need to park my car elsewhere.*

It was almost six o'clock. The park gates would be closed.

Deanne returned upstairs to dress herself in her old lady costume. She walked downstairs, into the cellar, turned the lights on, went over to Walker, and took the tape off his mouth.

"Is that you bitch?" mumbled Walker, his tone pretty much the same as the prior two nights, but not with the same venom. "When is this going to stop? Can I have some water and something to eat? Listen, lady, I don't know you; I don't know what you want."

Deanne walked behind him and said, "I have a few questions."

She ripped the tape from his eyes, which forced a yelp from him.

"Now, let's get your eyes used to the light," Deanne said as Walker turned his head from side to side, trying to see her. "How much do you weigh, Michael?"

"What. Why?"

"Just interested,"

Walker said nothing.

"Would you like some water? If so, tell me how much you weigh."

"About eleven fucking stone."

Still standing behind him, Deanne put a bottle of water in his mouth, which he guzzled down fast.

"So, eleven stone is about 150 pounds or so, but you've lost weight, of course, so I guess 140 pounds."

Deanne walked in front of Walker and stood there.

"Do you remember me, Michael?"

"What's with all this Michael shit?" He looked her up and down, then squinted.

"Well, I know you're not Anna. So no, I don't know who the fuck you are."

Deanne walked closer, saying, "It's been a while, a couple of years or so, and around this time of year."

Walker looked Deanne in the eyes; his squinted expression turned to shock, his eyes widened, and his jaw dropped; he gulped and became noticeably breathless. "You're, you're . . ." He stopped and tried to get control of himself. "You're no one I recognize."

"Really? So, you don't remember me. You don't remember raping me, beating me, sticking a branch in me, and leaving me for dead, and I guess you don't remember killing my dog or the dog who bit you?"

Deanne's voice got louder as *the attack* came to the forefront of her mind. She clenched her fists and jaw while pacing in every direction. With her heart racing and sweat oozing from her pores, she bent down and put her face near Walkers, shouting, "You don't fucking remember? I do. I do. I fucking do. You worthless, disgusting remnant of humanity."

She grabbed his cheeks and twisted them in her hands hard until Walker yelped and screamed. She got within one inch of his ear and screamed at the top of her voice, slowly annunciating, "You. Don't. Fucking. Remember?"

Slowly elevating herself, she started to take deep breaths. She strolled around in a circle and faced him, clenched her fists, her face distorted with rage and her eyes as wide as she could open them, glaring at him. She lifted a clenched fist sharply, lunging as if to hit him, and saw him flinch back in fear. She pulled her punch, stood up, and stepped back a few paces.

One more deep breath, and straining to regain composure, she said in a softer but sarcastic voice, "That scar you have on your left wrist looks like teeth marks where a dog bit you. My dog. Why did you kill my dog?"

She turned around and walked up the stairs, closed the door behind her, and collapsed, silent tears streaking down her face. She sat on the floor with her back against the cellar door, her chest heaving. Ten minutes went by before she recovered from her anguish and began to reverse the toxic condition she had been in. As she stood up, she decided, *I need him to confess; I want to know from his lips what he did.* She had conceived a risky plan.

Deanne went to the bedroom and changed from her dress into the jeans and top she had arrived in.

She returned to the cellar, asking, "More suitable clothing, don't you think?"

Walker's senses had returned to full capacity. He was no longer hungry, thirsty, or in pain; his entire focus was on her.

"Lady, I don't know you. I don't live near here, and whoever you think I am, I'm not that guy. So, why don't you just let me go? I won't report you to the police, and we can both continue with our lives. What you think are teeth marks from a dog came from a bow saw years ago."

"So, Mr. Walker, as it's an honest mistake, you would let me go free and not tell the police. Is that right?"

Walker just nodded. "Yes, that's the sort of guy I am."

Deanne put her finger to her lips and pondered for a while, seeing Walker looking at her with a smile, doing his best to look sincere.

"Well, if I can trust you, then I guess it would be OK. I'm sorry. I mistook you for someone else. I'll go and get the keys to the handcuffs."

Walker smiled again, inwardly saying, *Stupid bitch.*

Deanne walked behind him. "The keys were here all the time," she said in a cheery voice.

She was apprehensive and aware he would probably lash out at her as soon as he was free.

She carefully released his legs. Walker didn't kick out; he just flexed and wiggled them to get circulation back. She freed his left arm, then his right. Nothing, he just shook them and stretched his arms back and forth.

"Do you need help getting up?" Deanne asked.

"No, I should be fine. I just need to steady myself."

After a couple of attempts, Walker was on his feet, and then he walked around the chair he'd been sitting in. He picked up a bottle of water and drank it down, then picked up another and took a couple of mouthfuls. He walked back to where he'd been sitting, Deanne in front of him by the chair she normally sat in.

"Do you have my keys, wallet, and clothes?"

Walker sounded congenial, for which she was not prepared. This changed her focus for a few seconds, enough time for Walker to leap forward with all the force he could muster, which was considerable. Spurred on by a mixture of hate and adrenaline, he slammed both hands into her chest, pushing her backward over the chair and onto the floor, knocking the wind out of her.

He kicked her in the side, straddled her, and, with both hands around her neck, shook her head. "You stupid women are all the same, dumb as shit and weak as babies. Of course, it was me that fucked you, and boy, what a lousy lay you are. How come you're still alive, eh? Answer me that?" He let her head go, and Deanne just lay there.

"I'm going to chain you up and let you rot, though I may keep shagging you while you're still breathing. You useless shit. Keeping me handcuffed no fucking food, and drugging me day after day after day.

"I've never fathomed women out. You're good for one thing only. The others I fucked whimpered to, just like you." He mimicked a female voice, "I'm sorry. I mistook you for someone else.

"No mistake. They all said, 'Please, don't hurt me.' I just fucked them. You were different, you were like Anna, she took everything from me. You and that dick of a husband had it all, and it should have been my fucking life with Anna. I thought leaving the branch up you were a nice touch, artistic in fact." He sneered. "They must have taken photos. Have you got any? Eh, have you got any?"

He smacked her across her face, making her lip bleed.

"Please don't hurt me, Mike, please," she whimpered.

He screamed, "Hurt you! Hurt you!" He broke out into an old Carpenters' song. "'We've only just begun, la, la, la, we've only just begun.' Now, let's get you up, shall we, and lock you up in the fucking chair. Get your clothes off and have some fun, shall we?"

"Don't hurt me, please."

Walker laughed, got behind her, and put his arms underneath her armpits, and dragged her upright.

"That's it, walk this way," he said as he pushed her nearer the chair. "Just another couple of steps."

Deanne got to where she could put her hands on the chair arms.

Walker instructed her to turn around. As he took his hands off her shoulders, she gripped the chair arms and kicked backward, right into his solar plexus, knocking him back across the room.

Deanne stood up and faced him. "Get up, Mike. This is where we'll have some fun."

Walker looked up, got up, and readied himself.

"Surely you don't think you can take me down?" He knew he had expelled most of his aggression in the fight but thought; *I have enough left for this.*

Deanne strode purposefully up in his direction. He swung a punch. She deflected it with her left arm and punched him square in the mouth with her right. He staggered back, wiped his mouth, and Deanne saw the blood, rage, and evil in his eyes. But he had nothing to back them up.

He grabbed the chair and threw it at Deanne. It hit her, but not hard. Walker started to scramble up the stairs and reached the fifth stair before

Deanne grabbed his ankles and dragged him down. She used both her fists to punch both his kidneys. He collapsed and was soon back in the position he had been in less than an hour before. Deanne had one more task to complete before she went home.

Using Forane and the neuromuscular blocking agent again, she rendered Walker helpless. Undoing his restraints, she lay Walker face-down on the floor. The next move she had not made for over a decade, in a college play. She had needed to lift another actor playing a drunk boyfriend from the floor and carry him out of the side of the stage.

She bent to put her arms under Walker's armpits and around his back. "Up you come." She placed her right leg between his legs, right hand over her shoulder, head under his armpit, arm around his right knee, and up. "There, not so bad. Oh, did I say thank you for the confession?" She distributed his body weight equally on each side and walked around the room. After walking up the cellar stairs and down again, she placed Walker back in the chair, shackled and taped. She cleaned her face of blood, left, and went home.

"Hi, all! I'm back," she announced. "I'm smelly and dirty and need a quick shower. Won't be long." She ran upstairs, showered, changed, and returned to the living room by 7:40.

"What did you do to your lip? It's bruised," Matt said.

"Mishap at Jane's, no big deal. It's the penance of a handywoman. Anyways, I'm famished, let's have dinner." They were enjoying their dinner in the dining room at twenty minutes past eight.

Chapter Seventeen

On Sunday, as on most weekends, Matt enjoyed walking through their garden to take care of anything that needed to be done, which was not much at this time of year. If the weather was above freezing, he would clean the cars, though this too was not often, as they returned to being as grubby as they had been within twenty-four hours.

His main project for this winter was to organize the Wallace garage, beginning with installing three cupboards. He had assembled one of them the weekend before. Today, he was determined to assemble the other two, anchor them to the wall, and strap them side-by-side with a metal strap.

Weekends for Jane were like weekdays, though the three of them would venture out together for an occasional Sunday Brunch. Jane was never obtrusive but always on hand when needed. When she was not on duty, she would spend her time in her apartment and have her own friends or family visit. She was also an avid reader, never without a book nearby.

She comfortably and perfectly maintained the house while also being a sounding board and confidante to Matt and Deanne and was an expert at avoiding giving advice. When asked, she would listen, let either Matt or Deanne ramble on, and reply, "Sounds like you already have the answer," or, "I think you've solved that one yourself." Her other short, non-answers always elicited a "Thank you, Jane."

The three of them would also have a movie night together, either at the movies or on TV.

To Matt and Jane, Deanne had seemed preoccupied over the past few weeks, either with work, working out, shopping, or preparing what she said were "papers for the next day."

Neither noticed that Deanne had been taking Loppy for walks more frequently or that she turned right when exiting the house. She had always turned left before that, avoiding the area where she was attacked.

Deanne spent most of the day in the house this Sunday, though she made a short afternoon trip. She checked on Don Foreman's whereabouts and found he was still living in the same apartment. She drove to his address, parked a few houses down, put on a baseball cap, walked up to the house's front door, and placed an envelope in his mailbox.

Returning to her car, she called Don's number from her new phone. He picked it up.

"Hello?"

"Don, Donny, there's an envelope in your mailbox as promised. There's also a number you should call for an employment opportunity." She hung up.

Seeing the call was finished. He frowned, walked downstairs, and retrieved the envelope. It felt thick. He opened a corner, then swiftly tore off the top.

"Fuck me," he whispered, then ran back upstairs.

Deanne returned home, announcing, "I need to be up crazy early tomorrow. I'll be careful not to wake you."

"Poor you," Matt said. "They are working you too hard."

"It'll ease down next week, I promise," she said and gave him a quick kiss on the lips.

"Oh, do you have any glue? I need to stick a piece of carpet down at Jane's house."

"Yep, near the pile of carpet off-cuts in the garage."

Deanne went into the garage, picked up the glue and a piece of carpet, put them in the trunk of her car, and drove to Jane's house. She took the glue and carpet piece to the cellar, grabbed the toboggan, turned it upside down, and pasted glue across the entire base. She turned it over and placed the sticky side directly onto the bottom of the carpet, placed a couple of heavy objects on top, and left, not even looking at Walker. Returning home, she went into the garage to grab a box cutter, put it in her car, and went inside the house.

On Monday morning, Deanne woke up really early before the alarm; it was just after two a.m. To avoid disturbing Matt, she had her clothes ready.

She took them, grabbed her toothbrush, hairbrush, and makeup bag, and quietly went downstairs to use the half-bath to get ready.

By 2:30, she was in the cellar at Jane's house, looking into Walker's eyes. "Well, the good news is you'll be out of here this morning, and I'm sure you're happy to hear that."

Walker was wriggling and making a noise through his taped-up mouth.

"Be patient. I have to check a couple of things out. I'll only be gone half an hour or so."

Before she left, she used the box cutter to remove the excess carpet from the Toboggan, then she went upstairs and picked up three empty trash bags as she walked through the kitchen, out the back door, and through the back gate to the park.

She walked along the path in the direction of the bonfire frame. The moonlight was enough to make out the wooden pyramid, now complete with Guy Fawkes' Dummy, covered over by the temporary tarpaulin.

Deanne stopped at the rear of the bonfire, the side opposite the woods. She untied the rope, securing the bottom of the tarpaulin on the rear and on the side to her right. She could feel the adrenalin pumping as she started to roll the cover-up.

It was not heavy, just cumbersome, though the step lattice form made it easy to move from one side to the other. Once at the top, she carefully pulled the cover over the high-backed chair, its top about six inches higher than the hat placed on Guy Fawkes' head. When she saw the mask, it gave her a jolt. It looked scary in the moonlight; in fact, the whole effigy looked scary.

"Come on, Deanne. Get a grip," she muttered.

Taking the box cutter out of her pocket, she cut the ties and tape used to secure the dummy in the chair. Once freed, she lifted the thirty-pound effigy from the chair, put it over her shoulder, and walked backward, one step at a time, down to the ground.

She removed the head, mask, and hat and placed them in one of the bags. She did the same with the cloak and shoes. Dismantling the dummy template was easy. She dispersed the wood torso and paper into the pyramid to join the other deposits of combustible debris—the clothing she placed into the third plastic bag. After lowering the tarpaulin and lightly securing it in place, she returned to the cellar to join Walker.

"Hi, Mike!" she called out. "Michael, how are we doing?' She smiled and placed the three bags on the floor. It was now 3:47 a.m. Deanne looked at Walker, pointing at the bags and answering an unasked question. "These bags? Basically, you, Michael.

"I want you to know that I've really enjoyed every minute of getting to know you. It's like a, well, it's a cleansing for me, I guess. And, of course, after you spilled your guts about the other women and what you did to me, I feel I've done a service. You prevented me from giving life, a gift God gave me. 'Vengeance is mine,' said the Lord, an eye for an eye, a life for a life. Now, I'm not saying I'm doing God's work or being righteous, but He gave me a gift of giving birth, and you stole it and butchered it from me, so I think He's probably going to be more on my side than yours."

As Deanne talked, she used Forane to render Walker unconscious, injected him with the neuromuscular blocking agent, and placed a cannula inside one of his veins to provide venous access and I.V drip, secured by Gaffa tape. She liberated Walker from the restraints, laid him on the floor, and pulled the tape from his eyes and mouth.

"Can you see me, Mike? Are you there? Now the real work begins; I need to get you to the concrete chute so I can get you out of here." She pulled a small table to the pillar supporting the chute, picked Walker up in a fireman's carry, laid him on the table, his head toward the chute, bound his wrists together with rope, and left him there. Deanne gathered the items she needed to attach to the Guy Fawkes chair, I.V. tubing, bag, roller clamp, back check valve, drip chamber, and Luer lock.

As she fingered through the items, Deanne said, "Yep, all here."

Deanne had the paralysis solution ready and calculated the drops per minute for the infusion over fourteen hours. She inserted the liquid into the plastic bag. Carrying the bag in one hand and the remaining bagged items in the other, she returned to the lattice framework, partially removed the tarpaulin as before, climbed the structure, and deftly put the medical ensemble together, Gaffa taping everything securely.

After draping the tarpaulin back into position, she returned to Jane's house. It was now 4:38 a.m. Entering the cellar; she saw Walker's eyes dancing back and forth in trepidation. Deanne grabbed the toboggan and attached a rope to the front. She took another rope and tied a nose-style knot, tying Walker's hands together.

Picking up the toboggan and a crowbar, she went upstairs and outside the rear garden gate. She was startled by a sudden glare of light from a bathroom window from the house next door. Deanne waited for the illumination to disappear, which it did after two minutes. As she reached down to retrieve the crowbar from the path, her shoulder knocked the toboggan to the floor, making a thudding sound as it landed. The light came on again, and she saw a face as the curtain was pulled back. A head moved from left to right, then the curtain closed, and the light was turned off.

Deanne hesitantly picked up the crowbar and toboggan, her eyes focused on the bathroom window for any movement as she eased back through the gate, into the kitchen. She placed the toboggan and crowbar on the floor whilst she steadied herself on a stool in order to gain composure. Though calm through the incident, the reality of almost being observed had rattled her nerves. She put her hands in front of her to see if they were shaking; they were not. "That was a near one. Don't blow it now, girly. What to do now?'

She knew time was not on her side and that giving up now was not an option. Picking up the toboggan, she went back, placed it outside the gate and returned to the cellar. She raised Walker to his feet and, with a fireman's carry style, proceeded towards the stairs. Slowly but surely, step by step, she carried him up through the kitchen and outside the gate, where she laid him on the toboggan. Placing Walker squarely on the sleigh and with a focus on every window, she began pulling him along the path, near the wall, and out of sight. The carpet piece she had glued to the bottom made the journey easier and virtually silent.

After reaching the rear of the bonfire pyramid, she again raised the tarpaulin. The most difficult task now was to carry Walker up the lattice frame and place him in the chair.

Deanne's' heart was racing, and with adrenaline pumping, she was able to resume the fireman's carry and climb the 45-degree angled wooden frame, using her free hand to steady and secure him each step of the way.

When she reached the top, she sat Walker in the chair, taped his arm, legs, and torso to the chair, connected the tubing, cannula, and clamp together, and started the paralytic flow. She had rehearsed the assembly many times, but she still checked three more times to be totally sure. It was now 5:42 a.m. I have time; the gates won't open until 7 a.m.

She descended the frame to retrieve the bag she had secured on Walker's torso containing the finishing touches. After taping around Walker's forehead and chin, she placed the cloak over him and the back of the chair. Next, she layered glue inside the mask, placed it on Walker's face, and finally secured the hair-and-hat combination.

"Hey Mike, we've made it to the top, great view too. "Oh, I'm sorry, you can't see anything yet," she said cynically as she ripped the tape from Walker's eyes. "Can you see me, Mike? I can see the moonlight reflecting in your dark, wide-open eyes. How romantic," said Deanne with a resolute glare, moving closer to his face. Then, slowly tilting her head from one side to the other, she said, "Enjoy the fireworks, you sick bastard."

Then she carefully pulled the tarpaulin over his frame and chair and started to unfold the remaining cover down the lattice frame, tied one end, and went to tie the other.

She saw vehicle headlights at the front gates. She looked at her watch; it was just after 6 a.m.

What the? Of course, they came early to get a head start. She finished tying the cover as the gates opened, and the vehicle came in, swiftly followed by another, larger van aimed in her direction. She could not move, or she would be seen.

As she waited, other vehicles entered the gates, vendors taking their spots, a flatbed truck with portable toilets, and firework display company flatbeds. Listening to the hubbub of vehicles and vendors greeting familiar faces, likewise the council workers, Deanne waited and timed her exit. Close by, she heard,

"Hi, Jack." The voice came in her direction from one of the council trucks that had pulled up.

"Hi, Fred. I see you're on shit duty with Portaloos then." Jack laughed.

"Yes, same old shit."

Everyone laughed even more.

"We've only got to erect the barrier around the bonfire. It'll be about an hour. I guess you'll be about the same time after you've dropped the Dr.

Who boxes around. We'll meet you by the front gates and have a cup of tea when you've finished."

"OK, see you later." The vehicle drove off.

Deanne slipped away, walked across the grass as if she had a purpose, then geared herself toward the path, successfully entering the backyard gate to Jane's house without any suspecting eyes noticing her. The time was almost 7 a.m. She quickly showered, changed, brushed her hair, and arrived at the office by 7:55 a.m. She called Matt to say good morning and told him she would finish earlier today. She said it was a good idea for them to go and see the fireworks display.

Matt said it was a great idea and was looking forward to it, though he *thought it was surprising, as she had never mentioned the park or the fireworks display since her attack. That's still a great leap forward.*

Wesley, as usual, popped his head into Deanne's office and said, "You're later than usual. Are you OK? You look worn out. Are you sick?"

Deanne looked up and smiled. "No, not sick. I went for a run this morning and lost track of time, so I had to get ready quicker to get here. My boss is tough, and I didn't want to be fired."

"Yes, right." He snorted.

"Oh, Wes, is it OK if I leave early this afternoon? I'm going to the fireworks with Matt tonight, and I need to pick up a couple of things beforehand."

"No problem at all."

Deanne left in the early afternoon, drove to the park, and saw that some vendors were already open for business. Portaloos, clearly visible by their color, and flat-bed trucks held various positions.

The drivable vertical mast lift would enable the placement of cables, receptors, and lights on trees or poles. The firework display trucks were in place, most containing pre-programmed displays.

Parked nearby was a small van from the same company, equipped with a control computer to regulate and direct the displays. This area was the most active, with people going in various directions, shouting commands while reading from their worksheets, then pointing their fingers to specific locations to the labor crews. Commands were also being made via radio to distant positions.

She walked out of the park and drove the short distance to Jane's house, immediately going to the cellar to gather up everything she had brought there and loaded it into the trunk of her car. Returning to the cellar, Deanne collected and bagged all she wanted to dispose of, including the clothes and items she had purchased at the market.

She made sure the bedroom, bathroom, and kitchen were cleaned, and lastly, she hosed the cellar down. The last function she performed was to move the camera from the cellar and place it at the top of the stairs, plugged into the wall, facing down to the front of the house.

Deanne went home and drove her car into the garage. With Matt's tools and boxes returned, she went into the house, leaving the trash in her trunk to deposit in one of the containers outside her office building the next day.

Going through the front door, Deanne announced, "I'm home. I'm treating us all to dinner tonight; I'll pay for everything!" she bellowed. "Jane, are you here?"

"Yes, sweetie. What did you say about dinner?" Jane walked in. Evidently, Matt was not home yet.

"Hi, Jane. I called Matt and said we should go to the fireworks display tonight, so dinner's on me. You have so many choices with all the food and beverage vendors there." The women laughed.

"I like eating junk food, so, yes. Let's go. What time are you thinking?"

"Six-ish will be good. I think Matt said he would be home shortly. Oh, I have news about Linda. She won't be back. She's going to fly to London and from there to San Diego. She asked me to mail what little she had left behind. I stopped by and gathered anything I could see that didn't belong to the house. I'll send it from my office tomorrow."

Jane said, "Oh, that's a shame. She spent more time out of the house than in. Did she ask for a refund?"

"No, she didn't. As far as I know, she was very happy where she was. I'll visit her when I return to the US to say hello."

Matt walked through the door and kissed Deanne on her cheek.

"So, fireworks it is, ladies."

Deanne recited what she had relayed to Jane. At 6:14 p.m., they left the house and walked to the park, which was already busy with families with young children. Music played across the park, and the aromas from the food trucks permeated most of the area. The bonfire was not due to be lit until about 7 p.m.

An announcement came over the speaker system, informing everyone that the fireworks would begin at 8 p.m. and forewarning that some fireworks would initially be set off to "set the mood" when the bonfire was ignited.

The trio bought wine and hotdogs from one of the vendors and strolled towards the unlit bonfire. As they got closer, Deanne could see that the tarpaulin was being taken off, exposing the effigy of Guy Fawkes. Oohs and ahhs rose from the gathering, especially from the children, as they looked up at the black-cloaked figure sitting in the chair. All could see the menacing mask, a depiction of Guy Fawkes.

Anyone within ten feet of the barrier surrounding the bonfire needed to tilt their head backward to see the effigy at the top. It looked eerie against the moonlight, more so as the view was intermittently veiled by passing clouds. Many voices stated how real it looked. Deanne remained expressionless, looking up and wondering if Walker could see her.

He could see the crowd and hear the voices, the music, and the announcement.

"In a few minutes, we will have Councilor Jorden and his lovely wife Audrey light the bonfire." In fact, igniting the fire was controlled externally. The liquid and solid combustible material would be kindled with a lit taper via a tube on either side of the structure. A grandiose gesture was performed, and a simultaneous *whoosh* accompanied the fire inside.

Cameras had been rolling from different angles, covering the bonfire and the crowd. When the fire took hold, fireworks went off in various directions for about three minutes, just enough to provide a sample of what was coming.

Deanne had placed herself where she thought Walker might see her during the burst of light produced by the display.

"Deanne? Deanne?" Matt asked. "I asked you if you wanted another drink twice. You looked mesmerized."

"Sorry, Matt. Yes, please."

"Are you coming with me?"

"Must I? I'm toasty here."

Jane said, "I'll go with you, Matt. I want to get another hotdog anyway."

"I'll get a burger this time. Anything to eat, daydreamer?" Matt asked.

"No, I'm good, just wine. I'll watch the bonfire and fireworks." Her eyes were transfixed on the open eyeholes of the mask.

Walker could smell the smoke. He thought this surreal, unimaginable horror could not happen, would not happen, not when all the people could see him. Inside, he was screaming in terror, begging, and pleading, descending into hysterical, disjointed phrases, *"I'll never do it again, I promise. Just see me, someone see me. She deserved to die; I don't. I'll repair your house for free, you fuckers, just get me out."*

The heat followed soon after, increasing every second. The direction of the wind was blowing the smoke away from him at an angle, preventing his release by a rapid death of suffocation.

He was terrified, still wanting to deny what was happening. His thoughts went in every direction; would someone see him and rescue him? Surely, they could see his eyes.

As Walker started to feel the heat, sheer panic and total fear set in.

Please, no, no. I beg you, no.

As the flames grew higher, his feet started to burn in excruciating pain, lasting for several minutes before the flame burnt the nerves dead. His mind became almost blank as the fire reached his upper body, face, and hair. Eventually, his heart would beat no more, and his throat would become so swollen and blistered from the hot air that he would be prevented from taking in any more oxygen.

Matt and Jane had returned, munching on their selected choice from the vendor stall. The three of them stood with the crowd, watching the fire consume the effigy of Guy Fawkes. Some alarm and an intake of breath murmured through the crowd as the heat from the fire increased and blew the black cloak upward.

It looked as if Guy Fawkes was getting ready to stand up. Soon, it and the rest of the bonfire structure were a mass of flames and smoke. Hidden beneath the mass was the wood base on which the chair had been fixed atop the pyramid. The wood base, less robust than the 2x4," had collapsed through the frame, along with Walker's charred body. As his semi-skeletal remains descended, his skull hit the frame, separating from his torso and cascading down the remains of the structure among the ashes and other debris. The plastic mask melted and molded to the bone.

The main spectacle started shortly after. The ensemble looked on in amazement as the four flatbed trucks, not seen yet by most onlookers, shot display after display, with occasional fifteen-second gaps of dark skies; the last gap, twenty-five seconds, indicated that the display was over. Loud cheers started, soon to be overshadowed by the finale, after which applause and shouts thundered through the sky.

Smiling happy faces were everywhere, except for that of the person at the pinnacle of the bonfire, who, now deceased, had experienced excruciating pain as the heat and flames attacked his nerves and the skin over his entire body bubbled for several minutes before death removed all sensation.

By midnight, the trucks, vans, cars, and occupants had departed. The last vehicle was the fire engine after the firemen had ensured the embers, ashes, and remains were doused, contained, and without risk of re-igniting.

Chapter Eighteen

At 6 a.m., the clean-up trucks would arrive to remove trash, spent fireworks casings, temporary fences, and cables. The remnants of the bonfire would be taken in a separate truck; the ashes, unburnt wood, and remains would be incinerated, some of which would be used by the council for mulch around the base of trees and on paths and walkways when it snowed.

Matt asked his companions, "Shall we head home?"

Jane agreed. Deanne slowly nodded and said, "OK."

Deanne was not OK. She was suddenly overwhelmed with a suffocation of dread. For her to carry out her mission, her reasons had been twofold: vengeance and neutralizing her perceived mortal threat of Walker. The focus on planning and executing her mission had consumed her. What had she done? The questions and realizations came cascading into her head from every direction. She lost control over her body, collapsing and passing out.

She slowly recovered and found herself sitting up with the aid of Matt and Jane. She could hear Matt saying, "Deanne. Deanne."

She opened her eyes, then started to sob, mumbling apologies. Matt and Jane exchanged quizzical looks.

"You don't look too good; shall we call for an ambulance?"

Deanne shook her head and started to get up. Matt and Jane quickly helped her to the car.

It was a quiet ride home. Matt and Jane verbally fussed over Deanne. But they received no acknowledgment; she just gazed forward.

Deanne's obsessive mission had given her a powerful sense of direction and order, which had affected her overall sense of connection and purpose, pushing her motivation for revenge in anticipation of the emotional release that would help her feel better and gain closure.

But so far, it hadn't worked out as she planned. Now she had accomplished her retribution she was trying to put order to the barrage of somersaults in her head. In addition, she felt she no longer had a goal or a sense of purpose. Now, there was a void inside her, coupled with guilt, uncertainty, and fear.

Arriving home, Deanne was helped through the front door and to the sofa.

Matt said, "You're shaking. Lie down, and I'll get a pillow and blanket. Just rest there a while. Can I get you anything, anything at all?"

Trying to smile, as she said, "No."

Jane had already run upstairs for pillows and blankets, "There you are, dear," she said, placing the pillow under Deanne's head and covering her with the blankets. "Try to get some sleep. If you need anything, we're here." Jane patted the blanket and started to walk to the kitchen. "I'll make a nice pot of tea, just in case." She looked at Matt and tilted her head slightly back, indicating he should follow her. Matt took the hint.

Once the kitchen door was closed, Jane said, "We should not have gone to the bonfire. It was a bad idea. I know she wanted to go, but look at what happened. It's brought everything back."

Deanne heard Jane's comment, which she knew she would use as the reason for the dramatic change in her demeanor. Her mental turbulence had eased as she tried to regain her logic and take her emotions to a more manageable level. Revenge had provided extraordinary bursts of mental determination and energy to achieve her goal, and now it was over. She was satisfied, not regretful.

Looking back now, it all seemed unbelievable, as though it had not been her, and for some reason it had happened a long time ago.

Jane came in from the kitchen carrying tea—Matt behind her. Deanne was in the same resting position. She opened her eyes to see both Jane and Matt peering down at her. Deanne produced a small smile, saying, "I'm sorry."

This was immediately repeated back to her. "No, we're sorry; we should not have gone. It was a bad idea, stupid idea—"

Deanne sat up, "It's OK; it's not your fault. It was I who suggested it. I'm OK. I just need to take it all in and get back to a good place inside. I just need to unscramble my head."

"Can I do anything?" asked Matt.

"Yes, both of you can stop mothering me. I'm only tired. Overall, it was a good, fun night, but it was long. The vendor's food and drink didn't do me any favors, and I think it's time for bed."

Seeing Deanne smiling and standing up, Jane responded, "That's a good idea."

The tea was left untouched. Jane departed for her quarters, and Deanne and Matt walked up the stairs to their bedroom. Ablutions were completed, and they got into bed. A couple of minutes after saying their goodnights and I love you's, Matt said, "I'm really proud of you. I mean, really proud."

Deanne snuggled closer to him, confirming her appreciation. Within ten minutes, the only sound to be heard was the wind passing through the foliage outside. All three occupants enjoyed a fitful sleep.

Chapter Nineteen

The park extravaganza of November 5th was partially relived via the local TV news stations. The park, however, was swiftly returned to normal usage. Minds were now in preparation for the Christmas festivities.

For the London boroughs, the lead-up to Christmas was their busiest time of the year with decorations, trees, lights, and large crowds. A less festive high priority was the proactive preparation for potential winter snowfall and icy roads that could disrupt traffic. Rail and road networks needed to remain open even in severe weather.

The spreading of salt, sand, and ash, stored in large containers, was made readily available at key locations across the capital for disbursement where and when required.

Ashes from the park near Matt's house were on the collection sites and remained on two trucks until Wednesday, November 7th. Lining up at the depository, the two trucks deposited their load onto a sieve segregator, separating ash from bigger material, larger remains being transported to a conveyor belt for sorting into various sized fractions.

The employees overseeing the process had ceased to be surprised by any object passing through. Still, today would be different, and it would be the first in a series of tales that would be often recited from this day forth, more so during the month of November.

"Fuck me!" shrieked Tommy Erbank, the first person at the head of the conveyor. His yell was swiftly overridden by the louder sound of a pulsed alarm resounding across the entire building, put into action by Tommy's pushing a large red emergency button that stopped the machinery. Tommy jogged to join his coworkers, repeating the words, "Fuck me. Fuck me." Tommy had not been an advocate of exercise and needed to get his breath back after his short jog.

The small group exited the building through one of the side doors where they could speak and be heard. Again, "Fuck me," were the only words being spoken. Tommy's colleagues were silent and staring.

Impatiently, someone demanded, "What the fuck, Tommy?"

As Tommy started to answer, his colleagues became quiet and pensive. "I saw this white thing on the belt. It looked like a dog's bone but longer. Then another came by, and right after, this big ball came by with bits on, so I picked it up. It was heavy, and as I turned it around. I could see it was a head. A human head with, like, well, like, melted skin on it. So, I dropped it, pushed the button, and came out here. Scared me to death."

Two of the group lit a cigarette in anticipation of a long discussion.

This was thwarted as the side door flew open, and the floor manager appeared. "Tommy, you come with me. The rest of you go home for the day. You'll be told when you should come back to work."

The grumbling and inquisitive gathering departed. Tommy was led off to meet an awaiting police officer, where he would provide every detail of what had happened. After an hour, Tommy was ushered past the yellow tape the police officers used to secure the core area and then allowed to go home.

As Tommy left the building, he saw several police cars and two crime scene investigation vehicles, one identified as Forensic Services Crime Scene Investigation. The building became a hive of activity under the direction of the crime scene officer.

By 6 a.m. the following morning, after collecting, processing, and preserving forensic and photographic evidence, the vehicles departed. The skeletal remains were delivered to the offices of the forensic anthropologist, who would determine age, gender, ethnicity, and cause of death.

The news of the remains of a corpse within the debris of the bonfire hit the media the next day. This created shock and more concern for Matt, more so as the media made the most of the gruesome event. Like everyone else, Deanne shared concern and intrigue over the who, the why, and how. That morning, Charlotte Morgan, Deanne's therapist, called Matt to tell him she would call Deanne and propose a follow-up visit.

"You've seen the news, Matt. How is Deanne taking it; how is she?"

"She went to the office yesterday and the day before. She seemed subdued but definitely an improvement, though not herself. She saw the news this morning as she was about to leave for work. She didn't make a comment. She just looked at me in an odd way, kissed me on the cheek, and said she would not be late as she drove off. I hope she does not break down like she did—Charlotte, I don't know what to do, and I don't want to call and bring the events up."

Matt waited for an answer for about fifteen seconds, then said, "Charlotte?"

"Sorry, I was thinking. Leave it with me. I'll call you later. Let me know if you hear anything or if she comes home before I've contacted her. Bye for now." The phone went silent.

Deanne's determination had put her demeanor in a better place. Though she was still in shock, it was not apparent to people who did not know her well. Those close to Deanne, her family and coworkers had continuing reservations about her decision to go to the park to watch the November 5th festivities.

Only Matt and Jane knew of her collapse. Others were interested to see her reaction. No one had brought the subject up on the 6th or 7th, but today, the 8th, it was a different matter. After all, a human being found at the base of the bonfire was national news.

When Deanne left the house, she was breathing hard and thought her heart would come out of her chest. She knew that when she arrived at work, it would be buzzing with the news.

On her way to the office, she told herself to take deep breaths and channel her thinking in a more encouraging direction. Her mental and emotional focus was morphing into survival mode, and she was fearful of being caught. *Of course, I collapsed. I'm the victim. I'm bound to be in shock after I've revisited the scene of the crime. Who wouldn't be scared shitless, all the memories flooding back? And it's me; it's me who can't have children, so fuck you all. He deserved it, and I'm glad I did it. If I'm not in shock, they would wonder why the hell not.*

Her phone rang.

"Deanne, this is Charlotte. I know it's been a while. Matt called, and he told me what happened on firework night, and now, coupled with the news this morning, I think it would do you good to come and visit today, preferably. It's not wise for you to be consumed with your thoughts and unable to share your emotions properly."

Charlotte's tone was friendly and inviting.

"I was going to call you to see about coming in," Deanne said. "I was all over the place, then started to get it together, and, bang, it's all over the TV. I can't get away from it."

"Could you come to my office now? I'll clear the decks; you can take all the time you need."

Deanne said she would be at Charlotte's office within the hour. She called Wesley and needed no explanation for why she wanted the day off.

"Deanne, take your time; I understand

Within the hour, Deanne was sitting in Charlotte's office, truthfully conveying what had happened, though omitting she knew the identification of the discovered corpse and or talking about the actions she had taken.

"Charlotte, I've been trying to improve, to reach a place where I would restart the rest of my life and I guess, exorcise the ghosts, the past. This November 5th was my coming out, my proof to me and those near to me that I was getting past it, or at least, it was now behind me. I worked hard in every direction, physically and mentally. I regained my confidence.

"On bonfire night, I felt exhilarated, not angry, no self-pity, and really looking forward to the future, then out of nowhere, what I'd been through, what had been done to me, wiped me out; so, you see, it was everything. Now, after the news of the body, I feel that it will be back to avoiding topics and a repeat of pity and superfluous conversation. So, today is not a good day, and it feels like my progress t on what I personally term my achievement has been cancelled."

Charlotte listened intently, giving what support she could in a double session that lasted two hours. They continued to see each other over the coming weeks.

The rampant news of the November incident became less of a feature and was replaced by other sordid news events. Deanne's acquaintances were proud of her progress. As the days turned into weeks, everyone, except Deanne herself, believed she had returned to her prior self before the awful aftermath she had endured.

To Charlotte, the sincerity of Deanne's emotions was clear and real: fear and dread. Deanne would say, "I feel so scared. It's like a lump in my throat and weight in my chest."

Charlotte asked the appropriate questions and provided responses she felt would help alleviate her fear.

Deanne did benefit from the visits, though she benefitted more from the elapsed time and the diminished news of the November corpse.

Chapter Twenty

It took time for the forensics team to assemble the fragments of bones from the burnt skeleton. Some out of the 206 individual bones in a human skeleton were missing, but more than enough were recovered to determine the manner of death was not due to violence.

The report was sent to the police criminal investigation unit and placed in a priority inbox along with other reports. It was two days before the report was opened and read.

Evidence that could determine the victim's identity was sent to the relevant DNA laboratory for analysis: hard tissues, bones, and teeth. The DNA extracted from burnt bone fragments was highly degraded, making amplification of genetic markers difficult. In addition, the heavily burnt bones were prone to contamination with external DNA.

News of the discovery soon leaked, and coverage rapidly expanded to national news. Recorded footage from many sources was collected, collated, and categorized into a montage of gruesome streaming videos. It was coupled with a content warning of "viewer discretion advised," thus securing more viewers and their full attention.

The locality, especially the park, had become an attraction for tourists and locals, delighting the nearby vendors and stores.

The news coverage remained intent with questions, "Who was the victim? Was it murder? What are the police doing? Why do they not have any answers?"

On the sympathetic side, some newscasters feigned an expression of concern by voice and mannerism: "Let's not forget that the victim may be a father, husband, or have a family?"

Detective White was keeping abreast of activities. His suspicions were different from most of his counterparts, who thought the dead body could be a vagrant, and maybe youths found the corpse and thought it would be a good prank to place the body on the bonfire.

Brian felt the perpetrator was on a mission, making a statement, and it was too elaborate, too well planned to be a prank. Plus, with his decades on the force, he felt sure he would have heard something, some whisper.

Within seventy-two hours, the DNA laboratory sent in their findings, which were inconclusive. X-rays from teeth were included to identify the individual, which would be used to compare with dental records, but tracking those records could be challenging. A random piece of tissue cut from flesh close to a bone fragment provided enough for a partial profile, which was sent for comparison to the national DNA database.

Throughout the November 5th case, which was now two years old, Brian had been wondering about various pieces of the puzzle, but he had other cases demanding his attention. He was hoping a missing person's report would come in and make his job easier.

After a few days, his assistant detective, Peter Miller, received the results from the DNA report. His eyes widened as he read there was a match. He almost tripped over his feet, trying to get up from his seat and take the news to Brian.

Peter rushed into Brian's office: no knock, no hello. "You're not going to believe this. We got a DNA match on the bonfire victim. It's the same person that attacked the Wallace woman." Seeing the lack of reaction from him, Peter said, "Really, I mean really. That's crazy. Right?"

There was silence. Brian lifted his head, looked into middle distance, and said, "Interesting."

"Interesting? My God, this is huge news! Shall I—"

Brian got up from his chair, raising his hand, stemming Peter's vocal flow.

"You do nothing. You say nothing. The last thing we need is for anyone to be alerted. Does anyone else know?"

Peter, looking forlorn, replied, "No, I just came in to see you as soon as I got it."

Brian put his hand on Peter's shoulder. "Good, let's keep it that way. If this gets out, it'll be a circus, and we need to get a handle on this before we can think about answering any questions. We need to get a better picture before we start alerting anyone, especially the Wallace's."

Peter nodded.

"As soon as we have anything, we can work out when you can announce it, OK? Until then, there's work to do and a lot more we need to find out."

Peter agreed and left Brian's office.

Brian spent the rest of the day looking at the evidence of Deanne Wallace's case and the November 5th victim. It was late in the afternoon when he called Miller back into his office. Peter appeared quickly, knocking politely while opening the door swiftly, smiling in anticipation of an update.

His expression changed when Brian said, "Sit down and take that smile off your face. Unless we find out who this guy is, we have nothing. The questions we have are why he was there, was he taken there, where he came from, and all the things we don't know. We'll never know unless we know who he was. He could not have been there by coincidence, and our only connection is the Wallace case. So, does that mean that he was a local? Was he indeed a local vagrant, which may be why he did not move out of his comfort zone? Forensics stated natural causes of death, no broken bones, and no indication of violence, suggesting that a dead body was hoisted up to the top of the bonfire. Why?"

"Any ideas?"

"We've covered missing persons, checked with down-and-outs to see if there's someone they haven't seen in a while, and none of the tips that came in via news networks have panned out. The guy had to be local, so contact the local news networks. Ask them to tell people to contact us if they have not seen their neighbors since the beginning of November or other people they would normally expect to see, and preferably the name of who they think could be missing."

Peter opened his eyes wide, "You know we'll be inundated?"

"Yep, but I can't think of anything else."

Peter organized a team, mainly made up of temporary labor, to take and filter the calls before passing them through for investigation. Hundreds of calls were followed.

The reason people go missing varies widely; someone with Alzheimer's may accidentally go missing, or a teenager runaway, or a partner leave because of a relationship breakdown. Peter's team narrowed their inquiries to male individuals missing from their residences.

In early January, a call was received from an irate manager of an apartment block. The caller blurted out, *"I've just opened the door to one of the apartments as I couldn't get an answer. He hasn't paid his rent, and I haven't been able to get an answer for the past month. I wasn't too worried as his van is still here, and normally his rent is paid automatically from his bank, but nothing came through, so I checked his mailbox, and it's full, and I can see letters from a bank."*

One of the temporary employees who had been assigned to Peter's team, MaryAnn Frost, picked up the call. She followed protocol and took his contact information and the name and apartment number of the tenant. As the call matched the criteria, she immediately took the information to Peter.

"Mr. Miller, I've just received a call fitting the benchmarks we're working with."

Peter smiled, looked up, and said thank you. There had been several "fittings" that met most of the requirements. They were checked out, and resulted in nothing. Peter read the transcript and then listened to the recorded call; his interest became more earnest. He spent the next thirty minutes online, checking both names in the databases. He also called the tenant's bank to ask a non-invasive question. When he received the answer, he immediately went to see Brian White.

"Would you like to accompany me? I think we may have something, and I'm going to check it out. We can be there in twenty minutes."

"No, thank you; you said the same thing about two of the others."

Peter relayed the information he had, closing with, "What is interesting is the tenant hasn't had any transaction at his bank since the end of October: nothing going in, nothing coming out, not a penny. His background is rough; drugs, his wife left him, and he is a troublemaker. Are you coming?"

"OK, let's see what we have. What are the names again?"

"Dennis Sheppard is the apartment manager, and Michael Walker is the missing tenant."

Chapter Twenty-One

Deanne's emotional collapse on the night of November 5th led to continued internal dialog and distress, none of which she could share. To obtain release from her emotional solitude, there were times when she felt compelled to confess every detail to Matt or Charlotte or just go to Brian White and confess what she had done. When she was absorbed in conversations or occupied in other mental diversions, she felt less anxious.

Prior to November 5th, her sole drive had been planning, subterfuge, and revenge. Now, there was no mission other than self-preservation and the burden of potentially being incarcerated for murder.

She used inner strength and determination to direct her vacillating thoughts and fears. She felt like running away and hiding.

Talking to herself, she self-discussed her attack and how retribution had been served and future victims saved. She hoped that repeating her thoughts would form a mental habit, including the way she acted at home, where she increasingly put effort into appearing her normal self. Her attempt at doing so backfired on occasions, resulting in Matt's commenting that she seemed a little hyper at times.

"You seem excited. What are you up to? Are you planning something?"

Matt was sitting at the breakfast bar eating a mid-morning sandwich. Deanne walked over to him, hugged him from behind, and then sat next to him.

"Yes, you're right on both counts. I'm jubilant because I'm up to scratch with my workload. I've completed an important contract and delegated some duties. As I'm much less preoccupied, I'm putting focus on home, you, and our next Christmas."

"Christmas?"

"Yes, I was thinking that we should spend Christmas with my parents in the US and New Year here at home. I can combine a tiny piece of work into the trip, so my ticket will be paid for. What do you think?" she asked with a broad smile.

Matt smiled back, "Does that mean I won't need to put up the lights and decorations?"

"Just the Christmas tree. We must have the tree to come back to, or it will look drab."

"Fine, you've got a deal. Book the flights, and we'll go."

Being with her family at Christmas was not the core reason to be in the US. Deanne felt driven to visit the grave of Linda Warren to pay her respects and say, "Thank You," as she felt she could not have completed her mission without her. She sensed that she had had inspiration from Linda that kept her going through the darkest of times.

Deanne knew the way to El Camino Memorial Park, where Linda had been laid to rest. Driving the distance slowly, she recalled the content of the *Union-Tribune* obituary and that Linda had been married for sixty-four years and was a sister, mother, grandmother, and great-grandmother who died peacefully in her sleep due to complications of being ninety-three years old. It was Linda's picture that warmed Deanne the most. She thought it radiated kindness, sweetness, and the hazel in her eyes seemed to sparkle.

She visited a flower shop close to the cemetery, startling her when an old-fashioned bell rang as she opened the door.

"Hello. How can I help you?" asked a bespectacled, short, and slender, mid-thirties woman. "Excuse my hair. The nozzle of the water spray was twisted the wrong way," she added while patting down her short, black, wet hair.

"It's fine," Deanne said. "I'm looking for flowers and a vase to take to my—a dear friend that I've known from afar. Just to say thank you for being there for me."

"I think something pink or light carnation or rose. They represent appreciation, friendship, and gratitude." She raised her eyebrows questioningly at Deanne.

"Yes. Yes. That sounds good. Just make an arrangement of what you think is enough, please, in a vase."

Twenty minutes later, Deanne had the beautiful arrangement in her car as she drove cautiously into the cemetery, her right hand making sure the display did not topple over.

She parked her car close to Linda Warren's grave, retrieved the intact flowers, and walked to where she lay. Pleased to see the gravesite was cared for, Deanne placed the flowers in front of the headstone, stood up, bowed her head, and softly said, *"Thank you. I only know what I read about you, condolences, and memories from family and friends. You meant so much to so many. To me, you were, still are, my rock. My only friend at times and the only one I could talk to, I mean, really talk to."* Deanne's eyes became misty. She looked up at the clear blue sky, contemplating, then looking at the endless seam of rectangles across hundreds of acres before looking back to Linda.

Tears gradually form. "I'm sorry for me, and I'm sorry for you too. You're alone, and I'm alone, and nothing will ever change that. The only difference between us is that you've moved on, and I'm stuck here, alive. You've been the strength that kept me from joining you. When I wanted to end my life, it was as if I could hear you whispering, 'No, no, don't give in. Don't give your life away.' So, dear, wonderful, beautiful Linda. You can see why I love you and thank you, and I'll never forget you. I hope God is taking care of you, as you, my guardian angel, take care of me." Deanne burst into tears, ran back to her car, and drove back to her parents' house.

The peace of the cemetery reminded her that the same peace would come to her one day and to learn to accept that the negatives of her trauma would lessen with time. Triggers would still force recollections of her ordeal, but as new, better memories filled space, her persecution eased, though a chest-pounding fear would emerge at times, the fear of being caught for Walker's demise, or as she phrased it at times, his murder!

Chapter Twenty-Two

Leading up to and during the time Deanne and Matt were in California, Brian and Peter followed up on the Walker lead they had received and went to visit the apartment manager.

On the way to visit Dennis Sheppard, both were trying to piece together the facts they had so far. They also agreed to keep information regarding Michael Walker and the attack on Deanne private until they had all the details. They met Sheppard at the apartment block. After the introduction, Brian told Sheppard they would need to see Walker's apartment and his vehicle and that nothing should be touched until they gave him the go-ahead.

"How long will that be? I need to clear Walker's stuff out if he's not coming back, and I need to get it rented."

Brian said calmly, "Mr. Sheppard, it's going to take the time that it takes, and the sooner we can get into the apartment, the sooner we can start working."

"This way," said Sheppard, not sounding happy at all.

Peter asked, "What was Walker like? Did you know him?"

"He was shit, grumpy, miserable, and drunk most of the time. He wouldn't say fuck all, even when I said, "Hello," he'd just grunt. He would get into fights at the local pubs too. He was banned from most of them; even the Dog and Duck wouldn't let him back in, and he'd been going there for years."

Brian interrupted, "Is Sy still there and running the place?"

"You know him?"

"Yes, I knew him thirty years ago, and he was as tough as they come, a real cockney and a bit of a villain in those days. I haven't seen him for some time. I'll pay him a visit."

In fact, Brian was also a villain back in those days, though less so. As Sy would say, he had joined the other side. They remained friends, though they didn't meet often. As Brian put it, "They were in two different trades, and they didn't mix well."

When they did meet, they would reminisce and exchange confidences, knowing that neither would betray the other. Nevertheless, due to the different trades, they never put the other into an awkward position of revealing too much detail; hints were enough.

Peter and Brian entered Walker's apartment, leaving Sheppard outside and closing the door behind them. It didn't look abandoned; it was dirty, unkempt, and stank, but it had no sign that Walker had decided to leave permanently.

Also, there was no sign of an intruder or a struggle from a forced departure. The men went in opposite directions in search of anything that might provide a clue as to his disappearance and, ultimately, his death. Brian went into the bedroom, looking in cupboards and opening drawers, fingering through clothes, books, papers, and other objects. He stopped in shock at the sight of one article. He heard Peter walking in his direction. Quickly, he put the item in his pocket.

Peter said, "Nothing I can see is relevant."

"Ditto here. Let's look at Walker's vehicle."

They left the apartment. Sheppard was nearby. "Well?" he asked.

Peter ignored the question and asked where Walker's vehicle was parked. He also threatened Sheppard with imprisonment if he entered the apartment and told him to wait until the crime scene investigators had visited. They would inform him when he could go in. The men then walked away, seemingly deaf to Sheppard's protests.

Walker's van was easy to spot. They walked around outside, donning gloves. They looked under the vehicle and scrutinized the surrounding ground for anything that may be of interest. Brian tried the vehicle door. To his surprise, it opened.

"Our lucky day, Peter."

"I'm surprised it wasn't stolen or ransacked?'

"It's a van and a wreck. Who's going to steal that? And what's to ransack? It looks like a trashcan inside."

Peter tried the other door; it, too, was unlocked. Both collected and bagged items from the front of the vehicle, then in turn went to the rear. Under dirty painters' sheets, drop clothes and used rags, they saw paints and other materials typically used by a general handyman.

"We'll let processing take care of the rest of the vehicle. We probably have the most important pieces, especially Walker's wallet, keys, and what I assume to be his phone."

Brian paused. "Nothing adds up. He left his apartment as if he were coming back, presumably got in his van, left his keys, phone, and wallet, then ended up in the park on top of a bonfire, miles away."

They got inside their car and headed back to the police station.

Peter said, "Maybe he pissed someone off, and he was waiting for Walker to come out, hijacked him, killed him, and then tried to cover it up by putting his body on the bonfire. Crazy, I know, but that's all I've got."

"On a bonfire? If you're going to those lengths to get rid of a body, why display it on a bonfire? Whoever did this was smart, resourceful, strong, and no amateur, so why not use acid or burn the body in a furnace? Bury it in concrete? Chop it into bits? It would have taken the same, even less effort. No, this was a statement; it was to make a point.

"Just drop me off at the station. I'll get my car and pay a few visits. The first one is Sy at the Dog and Duck. See what you can get from the phone. Get prints for DNA from the van and see what the process teams come up with too. Call me if you get anything to share, and I'll get back to you later."

Brian called Sy, and they agreed to meet at his pub. Brian opened the door to see the burly figure of Sy walking toward him with a huge smile on his face.

As a greeting, Sy boomed, "Fuck me, Brian. You've aged. Come here, you fucker, and give this poor old soul a hug." Sy embraced him.

"I'm surprised to see you still alive and upright. I thought you'd be dead by now."

"Come on, let's sit somewhere private, have a drink, catch up, and then you can grill me. I know you're only visiting to arrest me or ask for my help."

They both chuckled as Sy led the way. Sitting down at a table in the bar, drinks in hand, they reminisced for a solid thirty minutes or more. Bursts of loud laughter could be heard through the door of the nook they had seated themselves in.

Back in the day, Sy had had many fingers in many businesses, though he gave up other enterprises over ten years ago to focus on the Dog and Duck. Sy had always been well-liked and respected among the old villains. "What can I do for you now? Are you on official police business, or is this a friendly visit?"

"Just a friendly visit with a few questions." As he said this, he slid a photo of Walker across the table.

"Do you know this guy? I heard you banned him from your pub?"

Sy looked at the picture. "I remember him. He used to be a regular, miserable bastard. Used to like to sit in the corner near the window. If anyone tried to sit near him, he'd say he was waiting for someone. No one ever showed; he just didn't want company. He'd drink a lot but handled it well most of the time. I couldn't stand him, to be honest, neither could the staff, but I said to leave him as I guessed he had a reason to drink like he did, and who am I to judge?

"But I saw another side of him a while back; he was in his usual spot. Hang on, let me call Nancy. She was working behind the bar that night and knows better than I do." Sy turned his head and shouted, "Nancy! Come on in here, darling."

Nancy promptly came through the door; she was fifty-nine years old, just over five feet tall, average build and mousey black-and-gray hair. "Another round?" she asked, pointing at the glasses.

"No, not yet. Would you tell Brian that ruckus we had with thrush a while back?"

Nancy raised her eyes, knowing exactly who Sy meant.

"Sy, you're terrible." She shook her head. "His name is Mike. I referred to him as M&M, 'Miserable Mike.' Yea, odd night, that. This woman came in; I had never seen her before. She sat at the bar and said she was waiting for someone. She was attractive, nicely dressed, with a nice figure and black hair, not from around here. I'd guess she was maybe thirty. As she walked up to the bar, I could see Mike in his usual spot. He was looking at her, and I could see he was trying to get a look at her face, so I thought, is she waiting for him? Anyway, Mike gets up from his seat and sits next to her. She looked startled. Mike said, 'I'll buy your drink; what are you having?' She looked at him and said, "No, thank you. I'm waiting for someone,' then turned away from him. He started to turn her chair round to face him and said, 'You're just a fucking whore; my money is just as good as anyone else's.' She got up and started to walk for the door. He got up and started to follow; that's when I called Sy. He went out the door, and Sy knew the rest. Mike looked crazy when he walked out. It's as if he knew her. He can tell you the rest," she said, pointing at Sy.

"Thanks. I'll give you a shout when we want refills." She smiled and left. Sy raised his bushy eyebrows. "Yep, fucking crazy. When I went out, he'd got the woman against the wall, and she was screaming. I pulled him off, and she ran off, got into her car, and drove. I never saw her again. Mike came charging at me and took a swing. I hit him hard, and he went down. I told him never to come back, and that was it. Lord knows what got into him. I know he used to go off with some of the women, you know, the local slags. Most of them had seen better days and would hang around outside, hoping to earn some money with a quick favor. The Walker incident got around, and rumors started that he'd attacked women before, but no one ever had any other added information, you know, no details, so I figured they were just rumors. It didn't happen to any of the women that would hang around here; otherwise, I would have known. We have a reputation to keep." He chuckled; so did Brian.

"Sy, I'm going to share something with you. I'm asking as an old friend. Whatever we say to each other must be kept between you and me. OK?"

Sy looked curious. "You have my word. I'm all ears."

Brian sat back and said, "Mike is the guy who was on top of the bonfire in the park on November 5th."

Sy was taking a sip of his beer when Brian announced this. Sy burst into laughter, spitting some of his drink over Brian. It was a belly laugh and brought tears to Sy's eyes.

He managed to say, "Now, that's a gem."

Brian laughed.

Nancy walked in. "What's going on with you two?"

Brian said, "Oh, nothing, just something I said."

Sy and Brian laugh even more.

Nancy walked out, mumbling, "You're like two kids."

It was a full fifteen minutes before any meaningful conversation could be regained, as when the laughter did begin to subside, one or the other would make a comment that would start the hysterics again, such as Brian asking, "So, I guess your reaction means that this is the first you heard of it."

"Fuck me, yes. It's a classic. I've never heard anything like it. This is a new one to me."

When they did settle, the laughter died when Brian continued the story, adding that Deanne Wallace had been the victim of the brutal attack that got so much attention over two years ago and on November 5th.

Sy had heard nothing and wondered if it were a turf war among the rival villains, but there was nothing, not even a whisper, on the streets, and he felt sure he would have heard something.

"Maybe the husband, wife, or family member?" asked Sy.

"No, the only people who know are me, you, and my partner, and we've only just found out."

"So maybe someone found out. Walker may have bragged to someone. He seems like the type that would. Or what if he threatened a woman with the same fate, and she told her boyfriend or pimp about it?"

"Then why not just kill him? Why make a spectacle of it? The theory back at the shop is that he could have been found dead, and some youngsters were high or drunk and found him and did it as a prank or a dare. Though that seems a stretch, too."

"Leave it be. The fucker's dead, so good riddance."

Brian stood up and nodded. "Good to see you again, Sy. It's an odd one for sure, and maybe it is just a coincidence."

Sy stood up, and they hugged, "Come back soon, old fella. Neither of us can last forever."

Brian took a detour on his way back to the police station to visit the park. He left his car at the entrance, walked along the path, passing the townhouses on his right, and up to the site where the bonfire had been. He stood there, surveying the area, and then walked back along the path to his car and drove back to the police station.

On arrival, Brian sat in his car for five minutes, trying to make connections with the information he had. He concluded that nothing was connecting yet. He said, "Bollocks," got out of his car, and aimed for his office. On the way, he saw Peter.

"Hi, Peter. I got nothing. Did you?"

"The phone didn't reveal much. It looks like the last call he made was a few days prior to November 5th to a pay-as-you-go phone. It was anonymous, and no other calls had been made to or from it, so it's a dead end. What's next?"

"I don't know. We'll still keep this quiet for now, at least until I have a handle on as many facts as I can, something at least to present to the commissioner."

Brian left the office, went home, poured himself a whisky, sat in his favorite chair, steepled his fingers, and pondered. He decided to make a call.

"Hi, Matt. This is Brian White. It's been a while, and I know this is out of the blue, but could you spare ten minutes or so to meet me for a quick drink? I need your help. Don't tell Deanne you're meeting me; I don't want to alarm her."

"Hi, Brian. Are you OK?"

"I'm fine. It's work stuff."

"*OK, sure. I can meet you in about an hour if that works. It sounds mysterious.*"

Brian chuckled. "Thanks, Matt. Let's meet, usual place, say in an hour."

Matt made excuses to Deanne, saying he'd be back in a couple of hours. He arrived five minutes before Brian. "Hey, how are you? What's all the mystery?"

"Thanks for coming. I have a picture of a guy, and I wondered if you would take a look to see if his face is familiar or if you've seen him. Apparently, he may have been wandering around the area and up to no good."

"Sure."

The inspector pulled Walker's photo out of his pocket and slid it across the table, looking directly at Matt's face.

"Have you seen this guy before?"

Matt picked it up and held it toward the light so he could see; he frowned a little, "I'm not sure, maybe, but no, I don't know him, but I think I've seen him before."

Brian saw genuine curiosity and interest, with no signs of hostility, suspicious behavior, or lying. "Are you sure? You said he looks familiar?"

Matt looked at the photo again and then made eye contact. "No, nothing. Do you have a name?"

"Mike, Michael Walker."

Matt smiled enthusiastically. "Yes, of course. He's a builder; he came to the house years ago before Deanne came over from the States. I was having the house spruced up before she arrived. He was one of the contractors that came over to quote. Odd guy, I remember I gave him the dimensions of the rooms I wanted quoted, you know, painting and papering. He said he would get back to me but never did, so obviously, he didn't want the job. I never heard from him again, not that it mattered. I got what I wanted done. How can I help?"

Brian was relieved at Matt's obvious naiveté. "You already have. It's a guy from another neighborhood. I don't want the name to get about, not to Jane or Deanne, no one. Just keep it quiet, please. Just between me and you."

"Sure, no problem."

As Brian's suspicions regarding Matt eased, so did the conversation. General topics and their respective Christmas and New Year activities were exchanged. Matt went into detail about the trip to California to visit Deanne's family for Christmas and how they spent the New Year at home with friends in England. He finished off by saying how Deanne enjoyed herself and how she's improved over the past few months, her work less frenzied and spending more time at home.

She had even brought up the subject of adoption while in California, and he shared how great it was to see that Deanne was returning to her old self. Brian listened intently.

Matt looked at his watch. "Well, I best get back. I know Deanne will be waiting, which is a nice change. Normally, I'd be waiting for her. Let me know if you need anything, and let's get together again soon. I'm sure Deanne would like to see you too."

Matt left, leaving Brian in a fog of impossible notions.

The following day, Brian asked Peter to bring him the phone report, wallet, and what processing and forensics had found from the contents of Walker's van.

Peter brought back a box containing everything he had. "Did you find anything else, Peter, anything of interest?"

"Only what I let you know yesterday. Most of the papers were receipts, bills, and a few nondescript notes, but nothing unusual."

Brian went through the contents of the box, scrutinizing phone contacts, texts, fast food receipts, and the various notes Walker had written, most related to supplies from hardware stores and customer requests.

One scribbled note caused him to halt. On a small sheet of paper was the name "Linda Warren" and an address near the park, but there was no phone number. Brian looked the address up on his computer, and the county records showed Jane Tilling to be the owner. He typed in *Jane Tilling* and the address; his stomach churned when he saw *London Short-Term Holiday Rentals* on the screen.

"Fuck." He put everything back in the box and called Peter in. "You can take it away now."

"Did you find anything?"

Brian hesitated, "No, nothing I can pinpoint. You carry on. I've got an errand to run."

Peter took the box away.

Brian left the office; his destination was the street where Jane Tilling and the Wallace homes resided. He drove past the homes, made a mental note of the location of Jane Tilling's house, and then returned to the park. He walked the path until he reached the rear of Jane's house. He stood there, looked up to the second-floor window and started to walk back.

As he did so, he noticed the path had ornamental coal hatches for each house. He turned around again, stopped at Jane's house, and looked down, noticing the hatch had been opened recently, not too worthy of note as other coal hatches had also been used lately. Brian looked back at Jane's house. He wanted to look inside but was unclear as to how he could do so. One word came into his head: subterfuge.

Returning to his car, he drove round to the front of the house, parked, and knocked on the door of one of the houses next door to Jane's. He saw a curtain covering the door frame glass move and an older man peering through, his head at a right angle and frowning.

"Hello, can I help you?" he asked through the glass.

The man squinted, taking a look at the photo and police credentials, then at Brian, then back at the photo.

Brian heard a door chain unlatching, followed by a partial opening of the door.

"There's been a few break-ins about two miles up the road, and I'm checking a few houses here to see if there's been anything missing or if you've seen anything suspicious?"

"No, not that I know of. Should I be worried?"

"No, we've caught the kid that did it. I just wanted to make sure he hadn't come this far, so there's nothing to worry about."

Brian repeated the same charade at other houses in the row, all with the same expected result. Brian left Jane's house until the last; he knocked, and Jane came to the door, her hair tied back and wearing pink rubber gloves.

"Hello, ma'am, sorry to bother you." He repeated the same story, then added as he handed her his card, "Would you mind if I come in and check your windows and doors, just to make sure you're safe? You don't have to let me in. It's just a courtesy."

"No, come on in. That's fine. You're lucky to catch me here. I rent my house out, and I'm adding the final touch before the next batch comes in."

She took her gloves off and took the card Brian had offered her. She looked at it, paused, then looked at Brian,

"You're the one who helped Deanne through her ordeal, aren't you?"

Brian smiled. "Yes, I am. But I don't know if I helped much."

"While you're checking around the rooms, I'll make you a nice cup of tea. I insist."

Brian did exactly that. His final stop was the locked cellar.

"Can you open the cellar door, or is it permanently locked?"

"I can open it; it's just used for storage. It's always locked when guests are coming. We don't want them falling down the stairs."

She smiled and unlocked the door, and Brian descended the steps. He could see where the coal hatch had been opened and looked around for anything out of place or unusual.

He heard, "Tea's ready!"

He went upstairs and sat down. Jane brought tea, milk, and sugar.

"Am I safe?" Jane asked.

Brian's reply was consistent with what he had said to Jane's neighbors.

Jane wanted to ask questions regarding Deanne but felt that Brian's short response indicated that it was the end of any discussion on that topic. As such, she found neutral territory for a conversation. "I have cleaners come in after guests leave, but I like to titivate on the eve of the next occupants with flowers and a welcome card, that sort of thing, you know?"

"So, you own the house?"

"Yes, I've lived here most of my adult life, but as I started to spend more and more time working with the Wallaces, it made sense for me to move in with them, especially when they offered live-in accommodation. Deanne has visitors from her office who would come in for a few days a week or so, paying top dollar and the holiday renting took off from there. She helped me an awful lot. Most visitors are from the US. They have more money, I guess."

Brian conjured interest, saying, "As I'm retiring soon, I was thinking of selling my house and getting a smaller place. Maybe I should consider renting mine out as opposed to selling it. Mind you, I wouldn't know where to start, and I don't know if I'd want to spend all my time chasing around for tenants."

Jane was very helpful, relaying that she didn't have any idea either when she started or how Deanne had helped her. She offered to show Brian her website. Brian, now an enthusiastic student, was keen to know more. Jane got up to fetch her laptop.

"Look, this is the website for vacation rental properties. It's the best one for me as I just pay an annual fee, no commission. Here's my place with images, video tour, description of the property, rates, and calendar availability, and that's it, all done."

"Looks great. They pay online, I assume?"

"Yes, like this." Jane went into her rental calendar. "You can see the bookings, the security deposit, how many people, and you can see how many bookings I have so far for this year."

Brian quizzed again, "Is it profitable? Do you have a lot of bookings every year?"

Jane changed the calendar to the prior year, stating, "I do know that I get repeat visitors. You can see on the calendar that out of fifty-two weeks, I had forty-four weeks booked, including eighteen weeks from Deanne's office, her family, and friends." Jane expanded and changed the view to show more detail of October, November, and December.

"The last three months were almost full. This shows you the time they are arriving, their full information, confirmation, and when they paid in full."

Brian looked at the dates in October and November, making a mental note that Linda Warren from San Diego had booked from October 20 to November 9, 17743 Roberts Landing Drive, San Diego.

"I'll make a note of the website and have a think about it. I may be back for help." He smiled and added, "Well, I've taken enough of your time; thank you for showing me the ropes."

Jane saw him to the door.

Sitting in his car, Brian rewrote his scribbled information into a more readable form. Once done, he drove to his office, where he went online to look up Linda Warren of 17743 Roberts Landing Drive, San Diego.

Linda Warren had lived at that address until she died a while ago. She and her husband owned the house for forty years. Alex Warren, her husband, had been dead for six years. Their son, Cameron, had moved to New York, where he went to college and now worked. None of the Warren family had been to England, and 17743 Roberts Landing Drive had been recently sold to Mary and Max Merrigan.

Brian got up from his chair to retrieve an item from his jacket pocket, a frame containing a photograph of Deanne, the one he had hidden when he and Peter were going through Walker's apartment.

He looked at her picture, returned it to his pocket, and returned to his chair. On the secure server, he typed *ANPR*, put in his password, entered the license plate of Walker's van, added a date range, sat back, and watched the Automatic Number Plate Recognition do its work, filtering through countless images that had been captured. Infrared lighting allowed the camera to take pictures at any time of day or night, including the driver.

Brian's eyes did not leave the screen, stopping on occasions to expand images. After fifteen minutes, he'd seen all he needed to see. The facial images, though less clear, showed Walker as the driver. One of his destinations was out of his normal radius, where cameras were far less frequent. No other data were found.

He decided to run one more sequence of Walker's travels, this time limiting the video to daylight, as the content would be clearer. Again, he halted at images. One of them caught his attention, a car alongside Walker's van. He expanded the view, but the clarity was poor. He entered the license plate number to check ownership, and he was jolted when he read *San Diego Economic Development Council London.*

Though incredible to him, Deanne's involvement in Walker's death was becoming more probable. He brought up the images of the car alongside Walker's van again and studied the driver with more scrutiny, concluding, though blurry, that there was a resemblance to Deanne. But if it were, this was months before Walker's death.

Clearing the current data from his computer, Brian did a background check on Deanne Wallace, formally Deanne Jackson, characterized as an independent, type-A personality. At school and college, she excelled at sports, lacrosse being her highlight. She was academically sound, enthusiastic, and successful in performing arts, though she did not achieve her ambition to become an actor.

She also joined charitable and tutoring groups. He sat back in his chair, trying to assess Deanne's potential involvement in Walker's death. With his years on the force, he worked on the principle that everyone is capable of murder, mostly impulsively, far less are premeditated. He resigned himself to the fact that Deanne could have killed Walker.

He had far too many questions and too few answers.

After logging out of his computer, Brian called Nick Adkins, the police commissioner, to request a meeting.

Chapter Twenty-Three

Brian and Nick had been in the police force for about the same amount of time, worked together, and knew each other well. Nick had kept his eyes on elevating his position since day one, whereas when Brian made detective chief inspector, he was content to remain in that position. As hoped, the commissioner could give him some time right away.

Brian got up from his seat and walked to the elevator a few feet away. He pushed the button for the fourth floor, went up, and then exited, turning left in the direction of the only office on the floor with double doors. He saw one of the doors opening and Nick Adkins waiting to greet him with a broad smile. His frame, almost six feet tall, was dressed impeccably in a tailored dark gray suit, white shirt, and red tie. He was clean-shaven with short but shaggy hair, which gave him a carefree look.

He put his arm across Brian's shoulders and hugged him through the door, saying, "You could have had this, you know. Shit, you could have ended up on the only floor above me." Both laughed.

"Look at this place," Brian said. "An outside view? More like a flashy apartment with your huge, damned oak desk and leather chairs. Plus, *another* new carpet since I visited last,"

Brian walked around the office, wiping his fingers on the edge of a television and then the two large monitors on the oversized desk.

"Come and sit down on one of the comfy leather chairs and tell me about life on the street, and tell me how you manage to work in that tiny office you laze in."

Brian poured a cup of coffee and sat opposite Nick.

"Thanks for seeing me so quickly, Nick. I appreciate it."

"Of course. You don't see me often enough, so I presumed it must be important,"

"Nick, it's about the Guy Fawkes death. I've been tracking down a possible lead, just me, as what I'd found took me on a path I hoped would be a dead end and a coincidence. Now, I'm in a quandary as to what to do."

Nick could see Brian was pensive. "You, in a quandary? This is a first. How can I help?"

"Peter and I found out who he was. It was the attacker of Deanne Wallace, you remember?"

Nick stared at Brian with a stunned expression. "And?"

"Forensics conclusion is that he was dead before being incinerated, seemingly natural causes, and the general theory a drugged-up group of youths came across a dead body and put it on the bonfire as a prank, but I don't think so."

Nick nodded.

"What we know of Walker, a drunk, drug taker, abuser of women and violent, makes me think that he found his way in the area again with an idea to find another victim on that night but dropped dead before he could do so. He had no family and no friends. Moreover, no one I have spoken to have any time for him. So, what do we do? If we announce the connection, it will be pandemonium; the media will have a field day. Deanne Wallace and her attack will be center stage again. We will be questioned as to why we had not caught him as he was in our backyard. My opinion is that we just let it be. Or I would let it be.

Nick looked up. "There's a 'but' coming. Spit it out, Brian."

Brian raised his eyebrows, looked at Nick, and said, "I think Deanne put Walker on the bonfire. Shit, she may have killed him beforehand. I don't know how she could have done it alone, but I think she did."

Nick was visibly shaken; he picked up the internal phone to his secretary and said, "No calls, no interruptions, please, Kate."

"OK, fill me in," he said.

Brian relayed his discovery and the evidence he had accumulated, closing with the comment, "There's no smoking gun. There's good circumstantial evidence, but what would be the crime? We can't prove murder, though the unlicensed cremation of a dead body is an offense under common law. I looked it up, and it's seldom charged, but it could go to trial on indictment, and she could receive a maximum sentence of life imprisonment. But given the circumstances, she'd probably end up with a slap on the wrist if she were found guilty. So, what do we do?"

Brian looked into the middle distance and said, "The poor woman was the victim of a brutal rape and attempted murder. She'll never get over it, and if she did plan it and kill the fucker, well?"

Nick had remained quiet throughout Brian's report, but frequent facial and physical gestures expressed his disbelief.

"How do you know she did it alone? How the hell could she?"

"I don't know 100 percent, but I haven't found any potential link to anyone. I do know from her husband that she was into heavy-duty exercising at the local gym. I spoke to her trainer. She was into weights, did a hundred pushups every day, and was an expert in kickboxing. Heck, he said that she kicked his arse and, quote, 'was like a machine.'"

Nick drew a deep breath, looked at Brian, and simply said, "Fucked if I know, Brian. We can't take this on our own back. We'll need to inform the Crown Prosecution Service and speak to Shawn O'Hara, the director of public prosecutions. We both know him."

"You know him better than I do," said Brian. "He's too sullen, and his office must be the same as in the 1800s. I've only been there a couple of times. I always expect Marley's ghost to come in. Old books stacked in every corner, and the furnishings look ancient too."

"Yep, and he gets paid over £2 million a year. The King's Council he may be, and a king's ransom he's paid, but I wouldn't want his position for £10 million. He's never off the clock."

"Let's just lay it at his feet. He'll have to decide whether to prosecute, and you know as well as I do he can be a stickler and leaves all sentiment behind when he goes through a case. He just looks at the facts, and he'll preach. He'll recite the damned official text word for word, but he'll be logical and fair. You'll need to leave it with me. I need to gather my thoughts before I take any action. Write everything up, compile the evidence, including the initial attack by Walker, and for heaven's sake, don't leave anything out because he'll be picking at every detail. Have it on my desk first thing tomorrow. You and I will review it, and then we'll go to Shawn. Don't forget the short summary. You know he likes to have bullet points on a page or two so he can get a mental picture before he goes through the details."

Brian nodded and walked out of the office. Nick sat and shook his head.

Brian worked solidly until the early hours of the next day, gathering, collating, and itemizing facts, conclusions, and opinions. The resulting paperwork needed a box, which was placed on Nick's desk at 7:20 a.m., ready for him to delve through when he came in half an hour later.

Nick spent two days going through the contents. He called Brian to his office on the morning of the third day.

As he walked into Nick's office, Brian asked," What do you think?"

"I've been through it time and time again; the facts are plain to see regarding Walker's guilt. With Deanne Wallace, there are a lot of questions and implausibility as to a conclusion, and I can't begin to think what O'Hara will come up with."

Nick made the call to Shawn, saying he would send the details of the case over to his office that afternoon. Two weeks went by before any communication came from the DPP's office; the request came for both Nick and Brian to visit O'Hara the following day at 2 p.m. Nick called Brian to share the news. Dutifully, both arrived at the DPP's office at 1:48 p.m. the following day.

Shawn was unintentionally intimidating, and both men felt awkward when he welcomed them with, "Sit yourselves down." Brian gave Nick a knowing, wry smile, trying to indicate that the office was as he had described.

They did as requested while glancing side-to-side at the office, which gave off the opposite vibe from Nick's. The shelves were still crammed with books and files, some open on the floor with yellow sticky notes attached. Orderly piles of papers lay on either side of O'Hara, twinned by two brass desk lamps with blue glass tops, giving a bright light on the desk but a blue hue above the desk, delivering an austere feel to the meeting.

"The Wallace and Walker case remarkably interesting, in fact, scintillating. I just have a few questions. Brian, did you interview Deanne Wallace?"

Brian was startled. "Yes, Sir, I did the initial interview after she was attacked and follow—"

Shawn abruptly stopped him. He looked at Brian while grasping his own hands.

"No, I read those. I mean after. Did you interview or speak to her after the death of Walker?"

"No, sir."

Shawn said with a brow raised, joined by a faint noise from several index finger taps on his desk, "Of course, if you had interviewed her, and she had pleaded guilty of either murder or burning a corpse, we would have saved a lot of time and had answers to questions we are not privy to at the moment. A confession, a truthful confession, un-coerced, is always preferable.

"The facts are that Walker committed a heinous attack with intention to kill Mrs. Wallace. As for Mrs. Wallace, murder is not excusable in any form. This is why we have a justice system, and if there is evidence of Mrs. Wallace, especially with premeditation of her committing this crime, she will be prosecuted. A jury will decide the outcome."

Shawn glanced at Brian and Nick in turn. Seeing their faces expressionless, he continued.

"However, with the evidence, or lack of evidence, it will be difficult to prove beyond a reasonable doubt that she committed the crime. These are the facts as I see them.

"My supposition, nonfactual, gives me leave to say the jury could be sympathetic due to the savageness of the attack and seeming intent to murder Mrs. Wallace, even if they think she did it. Some may feel the task of her carrying a body onto a bonfire without being seen difficult to believe, and, of course, some may conclude she did not commit murder and Walker was already dead. So, it wouldn't be a major crime.

"Did Wallace see her therapist after the attack, a psychiatric therapist?"

Brian answered, "Yes, sir. Charlotte Morgan.

There was silence while Shawn was obviously thinking, looking down and tapping his nose with his forefinger.

"This would mean that Mr. Wallace, her client, did not pose an imminent danger to herself or others, as a therapist has to break confidentiality to resolve the danger if violence is a serious possibility and warning signs are witnessed. That indicates that Wallace did not pose such a risk."

"Should I interview Deanne Wallace, sir?"

"No, don't interview her until you've spoken with me first." He looked up at them. "OK, that's it for now; thank you, gentlemen."

Brian and Nick walked out the door, out of the building, and did not say a word until they were outside.

"Well?" Nick asked.

"It was better than I expected. He got to the point, and basically, he's just looking at justifying a prosecution or not. I don't think he has any feelings either way. His comment regarding Dr. Morgan hadn't occurred to me, and he's right. Of course, she would have to take action if she thought Deanne would be a danger."

"So, you're changing your mind and thinking she's innocent?"

Brian let out a sigh, "No, I'm conflicted. We just need to wait for a decision."

Two weeks went by before Brian and Nick were called back into O'Hara's office.

They sat dutifully and waited, impassively, for Shawn to lift his head and speak.

"OK. I sent the report and evidence to the Crown Prosecution Service, specifically CPS Chief Executive Lauren Copper, who is running the organization. As DPP, I was the one who appointed her. We have had several discussions.

"This is a serious and complex case for the prosecutors to decide whether Deanne Wallace should be charged with a criminal offense, and if so, what that offense should be.

"Is there enough evidence against the defendant? Can it be used in court? Is it reliable and credible? Is there other material that might affect the sufficiency of evidence? And is there enough evidence to provide a realistic prospect of conviction?"

Shawn looked up at Brian and Nick sitting steadfast in the chairs.

"In addition, a prosecution will take place unless the prosecutor is sure that the public interest factors tending against prosecution outweigh those tending in favor. Is it in the public interest to bring this case to court?"

Hearing, "a prosecution will take place," both Brian and Nick concluded a prosecution would take place and were speechless. There was silence while Shawn shuffled through the papers in front of him as if looking for something specific.

After clearing his throat, then looking in turn to Brian, then Nick, he continued, "As I mentioned, this is a complex case. However, after reviewing the evidence and concluding that the public interest would not be served, prosecutors decided that the case should not proceed further. Thank you both. Any questions?"

"No, sir," came in unison from Brian and Nick.

"OK. Off you go."

Brian and Nick looked at each other and rose from their chairs.

"Thank you, sir."

Once through the door, both smiled at each other.

"He did that on purpose," Brian grumbled.

"What?"

"The hesitation, pretending to read something, and cleverly working in the phrase 'a prosecution will take place.' Come on, he knew what he was doing."

"Yep, for sure. I'm relieved, to be honest. It's a shitty case and would have gone on for years. I'm fine that the decision was not ours. You may not have seen it, though, unless you had suspended your retirement date."

"Now, it's nice and quiet, and given that I am retiring soon, I could really do without the department's being embedded in a big case before I go."

Nick nodded. "The spotlight would have been on us and Wallace, so I'm relieved. The ramifications of putting prosecution info out there would have been a nightmare. Officially, this is still an open case, so there are considerations. Deanne Wallace, according to you, could have committed the crime, and if she didn't, she'll believe her attacker is still out there, and she deserves to know. Do we, you, tell Wallace she was under suspicion?

Brian said, "I've been thinking the same. Yes, she does need to know about Walker, but I don't feel the need to tell her she was under suspicion."

Nick nodded. "Take care of it for me and get a basic press release out re the body. You know, what the conclusion is, and then comment about possible macabre activities of teens, a vagrant, already dead, and we're following leads etc."

"Will do."

Brian informed Peter of the decision of the director of public prosecution.

"Thank heavens for that. Let's get it closed and move on. I was thinking about the ramifications of putting the info out there. It would be a nightmare," Peter said, wiping mock sweat off his forehead.

"OK, I'm off. See you tomorrow," Brian responded.

Once Brian was enclosed in his car, he called Deanne.

Deanne knew Brian had visited Matt and Jane; she remembered almost passing out seeing Jane's smiling face and saying the words, "That detective came by," and, "He was really interested in letting his home," and how she felt as if lighting had gone through her body.

Then she did her best to look at Jane's face and equate what she was saying to the reality that the police could walk in at any moment and arrest her. It didn't make sense. It was only when she heard the words, "He was just checking as some houses had been burgled or vandalized," that some reprieve came. She pushed the anxiety away, trying to convince herself there was nothing to it.

She thought too of when Matt had told her about Brian. Though internally jolted again, she felt her feelings of fear and dread ease when he told her it was nothing really, just a chat. She told herself she needed time to work out what had gone on and why and that *if she had been in danger, she would have been arrested by now. I just need time, that's all.*

Deanne's phone rang and seeing the caller ID started to make her panic. Though not as overwhelmed as she was with Jane, she was now reconciled within herself that it may be all over and that she would be going to prison. She cocked her head and, in an accepting voice at her potential fate, answered the call.

Breathe and be normal, she repeated to herself.

Picking up the phone, she responded, "Hello, stranger. How are you?"

"Caller ID, where would we be without it?"

"Matt and Jane said they saw you."

"Yes, nothing really, just catching up on a possible burglary, kids' stuff. If you're free, Deanne, I need to discuss something more serious with you, though not over the phone. Are you free now?"

"Sure, it sounds official." Instantly regretting her words, she mustered a chuckle. "Though Matt's not home yet. He'll probably be about an hour or so."

"That's fine; I'm about ten minutes away. Is that OK?"

"Yes, no problem."

She hung up and tried to quell her anxiety by going to the windows at the rear of the house. Her eyes followed the trees gently swaying, watching the grays and greens of the branches mix with hints of blue in the sky. She felt her eyes filling up with tears and sniffed as they drained into her nostrils.

Deanne started to rhythmically imitate the shift of the trees with her body, slowly, gently.

"It's not so bad," she said out loud, not really understanding why she said it. She felt her unease drifting further away and didn't understand that either. She broke out of her trance by the sound of tires reorganizing the gravel drive. Whimsically, she recalled a closing line she had read in her early teens. While walking to the door, she said, "I surrender Sydney, though not so valiantly."

Brian knocked, and the door opened to show Deanne smiling. She hugged him.

"Come on in. Can I get you anything?"

"No, not yet. I wanted to share some private news with you before Matt gets home."

Deanne looked directly at him as he sat down opposite her. He began. "This will be a shock to you, I'm sure. We discovered a DNA match to your attacker from a corpse, though no identity as to who the person is. He's not in any database. We just have a match between the DNA samples, which means, of course, he's gone and can never harm you or anyone again."

Deanne started to shake. Slumping forward, burying her head in her hands, crying uncontrollably, and audibly screaming in gulps, "Oh, my God! Oh, my God!" Her expectation of hopelessness and a ruined life resulting from Brian's visit turned into pent-up emotional relief. She stayed in the same position, letting her breathing pace reduce and asking herself how she should react to the news while trying to keep the almost overwhelming liberation and joy that she was not being arrested or under suspicion. Getting up quickly, she said, "Excuse me, I just need to . . ."

"Yes, of course." Brian watched as she walked upstairs to her bedroom. He stood up, interlocking his fingers and circling his thumbs. Not being aware of Deanna's real trepidations, he said to himself, *Shit, she'd be a hell of an actress.* He heard a squeak as the bedroom door opened and watched as Deanne walked down the stairs.

Deanne said. "I'm sorry. It's been such a long time, and I wasn't expecting any news like that. It's such a relief to know he's off the streets for good."

"No. I'm sorry. I should have been more tactful in sharing the news," replied Brian. He thought, *"That was good but lacked sincerity.*

He continued to explain the outcome, how the case was officially closed, and, as he had discussed with Nick, that they felt the impact of the discovery would create unbearable and unnecessary stress for Deanne if the news became public at this time. He explained they would release the information in the future when it became old news.

"So, Deanne, it's better for all our sakes that you, that we, keep this to ourselves."

Deanne nodded. "Of course, it's such a relief."

"Any questions?"

"No. Thank you for letting me know. I don't know what to say."

Brian stood up. "It's been a long day, so I won't wait for Matt. Do you have a bottle of water I could take, please, Deanne?"

"Sure," she replied, turning to walk back to the refrigerator.

When her back was turned, Brian took the frame containing the photograph and put it where other family photographs were placed.

"Here you go." She passed him the water. "Thank you for coming over. I'll sleep better now."

Brian smiled a caring smile, "Good, I'm sure you will."

Deanne almost collapsed after he closed the door. Her fears were washed away; she thanked God repeatedly,

An hour later, Matt came through the door and gave Deanne a kiss and a hug,

"Good day, sweetheart?"

"Yes, just about the best day ever."

Matt took off his coat, hanging it in the hallway closet. "Any reason?" He asked.

"No. Every day is the best day ever."

Matt spotted the photograph on the sideboard, "Where did you find that? I lost it a long time ago. That's one of my favorites. It went missing when I had the contractors in before you came to stay. I'm sure I told you about it."

"He knew," Deanne said.

"He knew what?"

"I said, it's not new. I must have found it and put it there."

Life in the Wallace household remained blissfully happy. Deanne had triggers, but not every day, not anymore. When she did, she dismissed the negative as swiftly as possible; nudging the demons away with happy, positive memories coupled with hopes and dreams of the future.

****

Shock too far outside the parallel lines of human expectancy tends to leave memories hanging like a curse.

The End